THE CORPSE
FLOWER

Also available by Anne Mette Hancock

The Collector

THE
CORPSE
FLOWER

A KALDAN & SCHÄFER MYSTERY

ANNE METTE HANCOCK

CROOKED
LANE

NEW YORK

This is a work of fiction. All of the names, characters, organizations, places and events portrayed in this novel are either products of the author's imagination or are used fictitiously. Any resemblance to real or actual events, locales, or persons, living or dead, is entirely coincidental.

Copyright © 2022 by Anne Mette Hancock

All rights reserved.

Published in the United States by Crooked Lane Books, an imprint of The Quick Brown Fox & Company LLC.

Crooked Lane Books and its logo are trademarks of The Quick Brown Fox & Company LLC.

Library of Congress Catalog-in-Publication data available upon request.

ISBN (hardcover): 978-1-64385-828-9
ISBN (paperback): 978-1-63910-114-6
ISBN (ebook): 978-1-64385-829-6

Cover design by Kara Klontz

Printed in the United States.

www.crookedlanebooks.com

Crooked Lane Books
34 West 27th St., 10th Floor
New York, NY 10001

First Edition: October 2021
Trade Paperback Edition: September 2022

10 9 8 7 6 5 4 3 2 1

To my parents

CHAPTER

1

A NNA REGULARLY DREAMED about killing him. About creeping up on him and swiftly running the blade across his throat. That was why, on this particular morning, she didn't sit up in bed with a jolt but calmly blinked as she woke from yet another dream that left a kaleidoscope of violent images on the inside of her eyelids and filled her with excitement.

Is it over?

She lay still in the darkness as reality sunk in.

She checked the clock on the tiled floor next to her bed: 5:37 AM. It was the longest she had slept since renting the house.

A dog's barking echoed through the cloisters of the old monastery on the neighboring street. Two barks followed by a short, suppressed howl, then total silence. Anna raised herself up on her elbows and listened. She was about to lie down again when she heard a spluttering car approaching slowly.

She got out of bed and quickly made her way to one of the bedroom's two windows. A wave of unease washed over her. She opened one of the faded green shutters slightly, sending a ray of morning sun through the room in a narrow beam, and looked down into the street two floors below her.

Apart from a cat waving its tail languidly on the wall of the overgrown courtyard garden of the building opposite, Rue des Trois Chapons lay deserted.

Anna scanned the houses.

Her gaze stopped at the ground-floor window of the building across the road. It was wide open. Normally, all the windows in that house were covered with shutters. This was the first time she had seen any sign of life in the run-down property. The dark hole in the wall seemed to zoom in on her like a probing eye.

Her fingers started tingling, and she felt her pulse throb in her ears.

Is it him? Have they found me?

She stayed hidden behind the shutters until she'd gotten her breathing back under control. Then she nodded in an effort to reassure herself. There was no one down there. No one was hiding in the shadows.

In fact, very few people frequented Rue des Trois Chapons. The small street ran from the church on the square to the town's high street and was winding and narrow. You could touch the cobblestone houses on both sides by simply extending your arms. At street level, a sweet stench revealed that stray cats sought refuge there at night. They'd lurch and squeal pitifully in their search for company. But Anna rarely saw any people here. Not in this alleyway.

She closed the window and walked naked up the uneven stone steps. On the rooftop terrace she turned on the water hose, and it started wriggling on the tiles. She picked it up and washed herself in the spray. The cold water hurt, her body still warm from sleep, but she didn't flinch.

She brushed off the water and raked her fingers through her wet hair. She let her fingertips sink into her hollow cheeks and studied her reflection in the window of the terrace door. She had lost weight. Not much, no more than maybe three or four pounds, but her breasts were smaller, her arms lean and her face gaunt. She couldn't decide what she looked like more: an overgrown child or an old woman. Both made her stomach turn.

She put on a jersey dress and a pair of espadrilles and walked downstairs to the kitchen, where she found a lump of baguette and a jar of fig jam. She ate by the open window and listened to the clatter of stalls being assembled on the market square.

Yesterday, she had sent the letter.

She had made the three-hour drive to Cannes, where she'd first picked up the FedEx package at La Poste on Rue de Mimont. Back in the car, she had ripped it open and made sure the money was inside. Then she'd popped the letter into the post box outside the post office and driven back to Rue des Trois Chapons.

In a few days, she would send another letter. And then another.

In the meantime, all she could do was wait. And pray.

She swallowed the last mouthful of baguette and put on a cap, grabbed her backpack and left the house. She walked down the high street to the market in the square, where she stopped between the stalls and shoppers to savor the atmosphere.

A group of children had gathered around a small, rickety table. On the table was a cardboard box, and inside it, a kid goat was being fondled by the children's eager hands. A sturdy man in dirty dungarees pushed his way between a pair of twin boys and stuffed a bottle into the goat's mouth. With the other hand, he held out a plastic basket to the parents who were watching and smiling at their children's excitement. Reluctantly they fished out some coins from their pockets and tossed them into the basket. The man thanked them mechanically and immediately yanked the bottle from the mouth of the hungry goat, milk spraying all over.

Anna watched the man repeat the performance. She was about to angrily snatch the bottle from his hand when she noticed an elderly couple sitting under a flourishing wisteria at the café across the street.

The man was bald and wearing a bright-yellow polo shirt. His attention was fixed on a croissant. His shirt was what had caught Anna's eye, but it was the small, apple-cheeked woman in the chair next to him that made her stop dead in her tracks.

She didn't have time to register what the woman was wearing or eating. All she saw was the camera she was holding up and the look of disbelief on her face as she stared directly at Anna.

Anna turned and walked with measured steps to the nearest street corner and turned around it.

Then she started to run.

2

"IT'S NOT THE same thing. It's not even *close* to being the same thing."

Detective Sergeant Erik Schäfer looked perplexedly at his colleague across the desk.

He and Lisa Augustin had shared an office for almost a year, and not a day had gone by without them having an amicable but heated discussion of some sort. Today was no exception.

"Sure it is," she said. "You're just from an older generation, so you have a different mind-set. Society has brainwashed all of us into believing that one thing is completely normal and socially acceptable while the other is morally up there with fraud and manslaughter. Ultimately there's no difference between the two, but for reasons unknown to us, we've decided to *think* there is." Augustin emphasized her point by waving with the half-finished turkey sandwich in her hand.

"Right, explain it to me again, then," Erik Schäfer said. "You're telling me there is no difference between having sex and getting a massage? Same ball game?"

"I'm telling you that they're both physically satisfying at a very intimate level. Imagine that you and Connie have both booked a full-body massage—"

Schäfer found the prospect highly unlikely.

"—and your massage therapist is a woman, hers a man. You're both shown into a small, dimly lit room with some sort of bed-like device. You undress, and then you let a total stranger rub their oily hands up and down your naked body. You can smell the rose oil, meditative seductive feel-good music is playing, while you lie on your separate beds thinking, 'Oh, that's great, please don't stop, yes, right there, oh, that feels so good.' "

"You've got mustard on your chin." Schäfer looked at her matter-of-factly and pointed to the yellow stain.

She found a crumpled napkin in the Subway sandwich bag in front of her and wiped the mustard off while she continued to build her case.

"Afterwards, you and Connie meet up, pay the check, and tell each other how wonderful it was. You've never felt better, and no one seems upset by the fact that the other person has just been physically satisfied by a stranger. Quite the contrary, in fact. You actually agree that you really ought to do this more often." She turned up the palms of her hands and shrugged wildly, implying that you had to be exceptionally stupid not to see the logic of her argument.

Schäfer blinked a couple of times. "So, you're saying that getting a massage should be as forbidden as having sex with someone other than your partner?"

"No, dummy. I'm saying that both ought to be equally legit."

Erik Schäfer's eyes widened.

"It's a scientific fact," she continued. "Marital bliss increases with fewer restrictions in a relationship; couples would be far less likely to split up if especially the wife was allowed to hook up with someone other than her husband."

"You're full of shit!"

Augustin laughed out loud.

"This is all just because you think like a man," Schäfer went on, referring to the fact that in her twenty-eight years,

Lisa Augustin had scored more women than he had in nearly twice that amount of time.

"You don't believe me?" She turned 180 degrees in her chair and was starting to pound the keyboard on her computer to find the evidence for her claim when Schäfer's phone rang.

"Saved by the bell," he laughed, and answered the call. "Hello?"

"Hi, there's a woman down here who wants to talk to you." The voice on the other end belonged to a receptionist on the ground floor of police headquarters.

"What's her name?"

"She won't say."

"She won't say?" Schäfer echoed. "Why the hell not?"

Augustin stopped typing and looked up at him with a frown.

"She'll only say that she has something important to show you. Apparently it's about one of your murder investigations from three years ago."

Schäfer regularly received emails and phone calls from members of the public who thought they had valuable information to contribute. It was rare, however, for someone to turn up in person, and even rarer for them to have information about a case that old.

"All right, get an officer to take her up to the second floor and put her in interview room one."

He hung up and stood.

"Who was that?" Augustin asked, nodding to draw his attention to the button on his trousers, which he had discreetly opened under his desk to make room for his stomach while he ate his lunch.

"That was my wife," Schäfer replied. He pulled in his stomach and buttoned his pants. "She's just had sex with the gardener, so she thought I deserved an Indian head massage. The massage therapist is making her way up the stairs as we speak."

CHAPTER

3

FINE, ALMOST SILENT September rain descended upon Copenhagen for the fifth day in a row. The summer, which was long over, had been grayer than usual, and it was starting to feel like the four seasons had been replaced by one long, muddy autumn.

Heloise Kaldan was closing her kitchen window, where water was dripping onto the windowsill, when her cell phone started buzzing.

It had been ringing off the hook all weekend. This time she didn't recognize the number. She rejected the call and popped a dark-green capsule in the Nespresso machine, and immediately it started spluttering out a pitch-black *lungo*.

From her living room she had a view of the huge, verdigris dome of the Marble Church. The old attic apartment on the corner of Olfert Fischers Gade had been neither spacious nor appealing when she had bought it. It hadn't even had a real bathroom, and the old kitchen, which was now Heloise's favorite room, had been downright disgusting. But from the small living room balcony, she had a clear view of the Marble Church, and that was one of the few criteria she had insisted on from the estate agent: she'd have to be able to see the dome from at least one window in the apartment.

As a child, she had seen her father every other weekend, and the dome had been their special place. Every other Saturday they had first gone to get hot chocolate and cream cakes at Conditori La Glace, where he had charmed all the waitresses, and then strolled down Bredgade toward the church, where they had made their way up the winding stairs with familiar ease and crossed the squeaky floorboards in the loft under the roof before sitting down on one of the benches in the cupola at the top.

Snuggled up, they had savored their view of Copenhagen. At times the city had been covered in snow, at other times bathed in sunshine, but mostly it had just been gray and windswept. Her father had pointed out historical buildings and told her long, spellbinding tales about the country's old kings and queens. She had sat there listening, gazing at him with an expression that revealed that in her eyes, he was the nicest and wisest man in the whole wide world.

On every visit, he had taught her three new words she was to practice before their next meeting.

"Right, let me see," he had said as he moistened the tip of his finger and pretended to be leafing through an invisible dictionary.

"Aha! Today's words are *braggart, baroque,* and . . . *opulent.*"

Then he had explained their meaning and given examples of amusing contexts they could be used in, and Heloise had lapped it all up. She had loved the times the two of them spent together at the top of the church, and it was there, cuddled up safely against his big belly, that her love of storytelling had been born.

In the first apartment she had moved into as an adult, she'd had an unobstructed view of the dome from her bedroom window, and over time it had become her lucky mascot: a memento of a safe and meaningful childhood. Whenever she traveled, she missed the dome more than anything.

It was, however, rare for her to be standing as she was now, looking toward the church on an early Monday afternoon. Normally she would be at an editorial meeting at the newspaper where she worked, discussing this week's main issues and planning her research.

But not today.

Today's papers lay spread out in front of her on the kitchen table. The Skriver story was on the front page of every single one of them.

She opened page two of *Demokratisk Dagblad*, her workplace for the past five years, and read the editorial. The editor in chief was apologizing for a story published a few days earlier about the fashion mogul Jan Skriver's investment in an environmental disaster of a textile factory in Bangalore that used child labor. The paper had "acted naïvely in its search for the truth," he wrote. The piece was filled with pathos and well-choreographed hand-wringing, and its sole purpose was to make the paper appear honest, neutral, and—this was the crucial bit—to dodge any management responsibility.

Fair enough. It wasn't the editor in chief's fault. It was hers. She had written the story, she had trusted her source, and she had allowed something resembling trust to trump due diligence.

How the hell could she have been so stupid? Why hadn't she checked and double-checked her facts? Why had she trusted him?

Her cell phone started vibrating again. This time it was a number she couldn't dismiss. She let it ring three times before she answered in a weary voice.

"Kaldan speaking."

"Hi, it's me. Were you asleep?" Her editor, Karen Aagaard, sounded tense.

"No, why?"

"Your voice sounds a little rusty, that's all."

"I'm up."

Heloise had been up most of last night and had finished off the bottle of white wine she and Gerda had opened yesterday. She had mulled over the story and examined it from all angles, reviewed every single detail in the course of events in an attempt to get to grips with it, but no matter how hard she'd tried, it had remained blurred, fuzzy. Or perhaps she just didn't like what she was seeing? She was a journalist—a damn good one, too—and it just wasn't like her to be so horribly wrong. She was furious with herself—and with *him*.

"I know I told you to take today off," Karen Aagaard said, "but The Shovel wants to see you."

Carl-Johan Scowl, aka The Shovel, was a greasy garden gnome of a man who worked as readers' editor at *Demokratisk Dagblad*, taking his lead from the guidelines for good press ethics. He dealt with readers' complaints about errors in the newspaper's stories, and whenever he knocked on your door, you knew it would be a long day, maybe a long week, and possibly the end of your career.

"Again?" Heloise closed her eyes and let her head fall backward. She felt emotionally drained at the prospect of yet another exhausting review of the sequence of events. They had been over it three times already.

"Yes, you need to come in so that we can finish it off. There are still a few things he wants to go over before we can move on. Surely you'd like that too?"

"I'll be there in fifteen minutes," Heloise said, and hung up.

She grabbed her black leather jacket, kicked aside a pile of junk mail on the doormat, and slammed the door behind her.

* * *

Demokratisk Dagblad's offices were in a listed building in Store Strandstræde whose antiquated, regal expression and decor matched the paper's conservative views. The vaulted ceilings were high, the walls decorated with handmade wallpaper, and the glass in the old casement windows was so thin that Heloise always froze her butt off during the winter months.

She parked her bicycle in front of the building and nodded to a couple of guys from the paper's sales department who were smoking, sheltered from the rain on a café bench across the street. A black awning stretched out above them, filled to bursting with water, and drops of rain trickled down the big metal posts that held it up. Heloise watched the canvas, half expecting it to split above their heads.

One of the men returned her greeting with a cheerful, "Hey, Kaldan, what's up?"

His buddy leaned toward him without taking his eyes off Heloise and whispered something that made them both smirk.

She turned away and swiped her card through the electronic lock to the right of the entrance. She entered her personal code, and the door made a buzzing, mechanical sound before it opened.

Heloise climbed the stairs to the news desk on the third floor and jogged up, taking two steps at a time.

Karen Aagaard was waiting for her on the landing. They had always been on good terms, and Heloise liked and respected her, but they had never been close. Heloise knew that Aagaard lived in ritzy Hellerup, that she was married and that her son was in the military, but apart from that she had no notion of her editor's private life—or vice versa. It was a level of intimacy that suited Heloise just fine, especially today.

"Let me guess: you don't believe in umbrellas, is that it?" Aagaard studied Heloise's soaked clothing quizzically.

Heloise smiled and shook off some of the raindrops. "Yeah, I'm just not *that* grown up yet."

"I assume that you've read today's editorial?"

"Yes."

"And?"

Heloise gave a light shrug. "What else could Mikkelsen write?"

"I suppose you're right, but he was seriously pissed off when I spoke with him this morning. If you hadn't produced so many of the paper's scoops this year, I really think he'd kick you out on your ass. I'm still not a hundred percent sure you're in the clear."

"Thanks. That's exactly the pep talk I was hoping for." Heloise opened the door to the open plan office. "After you, boss."

"There's nothing more to the story than what you've already told us, is there? Something The Shovel might dig up that I should know about?"

"Such as?"

"I don't know. *Anything* that might make you appear worse than you already do? And a spontaneous *no* would have been much more reassuring, let me tell you." Karen Aagaard looked at her over the rim of her tortoiseshell glasses.

Blurred images of naked bodies, sweat, and salty kisses appeared like a runaway slideshow in Heloise's mind. She wanted to be helpful, because she didn't enjoy having her name on a story that didn't hold up to scrutiny, but she also didn't want to share details of her private life. Not just because it was none of her boss's business. She was also too proud to admit to having trusted Martin.

"No," she said, placing a reassuring hand on her editor's shoulder. "There's nothing more to the story. Let's just get it over with, shall we? Where's The Shovel?"

"He should be here by now."

Karen Aagaard stuck her head inside the conference room halfway down the editorial corridor. There was no one there.

"He was still in his car when he called me, so perhaps he hasn't arrived yet. Grab yourself a coffee, but stay on this floor. I'll let you know when he gets here."

On her way to the kitchenette, Heloise passed the pigeonholes. It was rare for her to receive actual mail these days. Today, however, a big pile of letters was waiting for her.

She carried the letters and a cup of instant coffee to the investigative section, swung both feet up on her desk, and opened the first envelope. It was a heavy thing, nine pages of densely written outrage about the use of child labor in India. The same theme recurred in letters two and three, while the fourth contained a small, yellow Post-it, bearing a single word: *Slut!*

"Wow, that's original," she said, holding up the Post-it note to her colleague, Mogens Bøttger, who was sitting on the other side of the double desk.

He looked up from his notepad with an unimpressed raising of an eyebrow.

Heloise scrunched up the note along with the envelope and threw the paper ball toward the wastebasket at the far end of the room. It landed on the uneven herringbone parquet floor well clear of its target.

"Swish!" Bøttger said in mock admiration. "The NBA will surely be waiting to scoop you up if Mikkelsen kicks you out."

"He won't."

"I wouldn't be so sure, if I were you."

"He won't fire me," Heloise stated.

She picked up the next envelope and started opening it.

"He fired the one with the warts," Bøttger declared in a singsong voice, referring to a fellow reporter who had just been canned for having invented a source. The firing had echoed throughout the building and left chief editor Mikkelsen with a burst blood vessel in one eye. He had been incandescent with rage.

"She damn well deserved it," Heloise said, "but my case is completely different. I acted in good faith. I'm not saying that I wouldn't do things differently if I could turn back time—the bright light of hindsight and all that—but Mikkelsen and I, we . . ." Heloise shook her head dismissively. "He's not gonna fire me."

She unfolded the next letter and started reading. Bøttger went on talking, but the sound of his voice faded away as a cold, uncomfortable tingling spread inside her.

The letter was short.

It contained only a few sentences written in a neat hand, but the words made her mouth go dry and a cold, bubbly sensation fill her chest.

Bøttger's voice cut through just as Heloise realized she had stopped breathing. "But you really shouldn't let anyone tell you—"

"Mogens," she interrupted him. "Didn't you cover a story a few years ago about a lawyer who was murdered?"

"Huh?" He looked blankly at her across the desks and straightened up slowly in his chair when he saw her expression. "Who are we talking about?"

"That lawyer who was murdered. Was it in Kokkedal or Hørsholm or somewhere up north? What was his name?"

"His name was Mossing. And he lived in Taarbæk. What about him?"

"Did you cover that story?"

In the investigative section, Mogens Bøttger specialized in crime and social affairs, while Heloise was responsible for business and consumer issues and only rarely dealt with violent crimes.

"No, I was still on the news desk back then. It must have been Ulrich. Why are you asking?"

"What was her name? The woman they think did it?"

"Anna Kiel. And it's not something they just think. They *know*. She was caught leaving the scene on a security camera in Mossing's driveway. And when I say *caught*, I mean she stood staring directly into the lens for several minutes before leaving the crime scene without trying to remove or damage the camera. Covered in blood from head to toe, frozen like a statue. She just stood there gazing at the camera without moving a muscle. A total psycho."

"Where is she now?"

"I don't know. She was never found. Why?"

Heloise went over to Bøttger and placed the letter in front of him. She leaned over him while they both read it.

Dear Heloise.
Have you ever seen someone bleed to death?

It's a unique experience. Or at least it was for me, but then again, I had been looking forward to it for a long time.

I know they say I have committed a crime.
That I must be found, tamed and punished.

I haven't.
I won't be.
I can't be.
I already have been.

. . . And I'm not done yet.

I wish I could tell you more, but I have promised not to.

While I am denied your presence, Heloise, give me at least through your words some sweet semblance of yourself.

Anna Kiel

Bøttger looked up at her, stunned. "Where the hell did you get this?"

"It was in the mail."

"Do you know her?"

"No. I remember bits and pieces of the story, but apart from that, nothing. Never met her."

"Christ . . ." He scratched his head so hard his big, dark-brown curls waved from side to side. "Do you think it's legit?"

Heloise shrugged.

"It might be a hoax," Bøttger said. "I get the craziest emails from readers all the time. There are weirdos everywhere, Heloise; you know that. This letter could easily have come from one of them. Now that you're in the public eye with the whole Skriver scandal, your in-box automatically turns into Freak Central."

Heloise went back to her desk and examined the envelope in which the letter had arrived. It was medium sized and pale blue, and it was postmarked in Cannes eleven days earlier, a week before the whole Skriver thing had exploded. So, whoever sent it, they hadn't acted in response to the media circus.

"It makes no sense," she said, looking across to Bøttger. "Why write to me rather than to Ulrich if he was the one who covered the story? Do you know where he's working now?"

"I don't think he is. Working, I mean." Bøttger picked up his cell phone and started swiping.

"What do you mean?"

"He was doing these sleazy tabloid stories for *Ekspressen* for a while, but I think he has been battling depression or something, and he hasn't been back to work for a while. He's covered so many violent crimes over the years, and maybe it all just caught up with him. I think that I have his . . . yeah, I have his private number here. You want it?"

"Yes, please."

Heloise reread the letter. Then she turned on her computer and Googled *Anna Kiel*. Two hundred and thirty-eight search results appeared on her screen. She clicked on the first one—an article from her own newspaper, which was indeed written by Ulrich Andersson and dated April 24, 2016.

Murder Suspect Named

The identity of the woman who is wanted in connection with a murder in the small town of Taarbæk has now been established, according to a Copenhagen police press release to Ritzau today.

The suspect is 31-year-old Anna Kiel, a Danish native who is considered armed and dangerous. She is wanted in connection with the fatal stabbing of lawyer Christoffer Mossing, 37, on the night of Sunday 21 April.

The victim was attacked in his home. Police believe that no one else was present at the time of the murder, and no other residents are registered at the address.

"There's nothing to suggest that the victim and the suspect knew each other, but we do know that the woman in question has a history of mental illness. We therefore ask anyone who might come into contact with her to keep their distance and to contact the police," says Detective Sergeant Erik Schäfer, who is heading the investigation.

Anna Kiel is of Scandinavian appearance, 5 foot 7 tall, and of medium build, and at the time of the incident she had long, medium-blonde hair. Anyone with information about her whereabouts or who can assist the police with their inquiries in any other way, please contact Copenhagen Police at telephone number 114.

UA, *Demokratisk Dagblad*

"Kaldan . . ."

Heloise looked up from her computer.

Karen Aagaard was standing at the end of the corridor, gesturing for Heloise to join her. "You're on."

4

DETECTIVE SERGEANT ERIK Schäfer pushed open the door to the interview room with a filthy Ecco shoe the size of a brick. A plump, old woman was sitting with her handbag on her lap at the large laminate table. She nodded respectfully as he entered the room.

"Hello," she said. "Are you Erik Schäfer?"

"I am." He stuck out a callused hand to the woman, who shook it politely. "But I didn't catch your name, Ms. . . . ?"

"Do I have to tell you?"

Schäfer shrugged. "It might make things easier if I know who you are and what you're doing here."

"It's my husband, you see," she said. "He doesn't want us to get involved. He's a very private person, and he doesn't want us getting mixed up in anything nasty. I haven't told him that I'm here, and I don't want him to know."

"All right. Then let me start by asking what brought you here." Schäfer took a seat opposite her.

"It's that lawyer."

"A lawyer?"

"Yes, that nice man who was murdered. Just north of Copenhagen."

"Christoffer Mossing?"

"Yes, that's the one. That was your case, wasn't it?"

"Still is," Schäfer said. "It's been a few years, but the case is still open."

"It was that spring my sister and brother-in-law visited us," the woman began. "I remember we had been to Tisvildeleje Beach, and on the way back, the men wanted to buy pipe tobacco from that little shop next to the tourist office. We waited outside, my sister and I. The tabloids outside the shop were plastered with gory details of the murder. It must have been in the days immediately after." Her gaze grew distant, and she appeared to have lost her train of thought.

"Yes, I'm afraid that his death was rather macabre, poor old Mossing," Schäfer conceded. "But I'm failing to see where you're going with this. Are you here to tell me something about him?"

"I remember the girl," she said. "The one everyone said had done it. There was a big picture of her on the cover of one of the newspapers. It was used over and over in the weeks that followed, also on the TV news. It was a kind of holiday picture where she was standing in front of a scenic landscape. The Grand Canyon, I think it might have been. Do you remember it?"

Schäfer nodded.

The picture was in his case file one floor below where they were sitting, along with other pictures from the crime scene: one of Mossing's waxy head, which after the attack had been barely attached to his body; photographs of the murder weapon; photos of all the blood.

An unbelievable amount of blood . . .

"I remember thinking that she looked very sad," the woman continued. "She was standing in the sun, smiling at the photographer, but there was something about her eyes. It was as if they were . . . extinguished. Perhaps it was all in my mind, but she certainly made a lasting impression on me." She picked nervously at the handle of her handbag.

Schäfer cleared his throat and was about to ask her to get to the point when she looked up again.

"I think I've seen her." She clasped her hand over her mouth as if her own words had shocked her.

Schäfer said nothing for several seconds as he watched her.

"You think you've *seen* her?" He could feel his heart beginning to race. "What do you mean?"

"I saw her," she replied, with greater conviction in her voice. "She looked different. Her hair was much shorter. Darker. But it was the same face, the same eyes. It was her. I'm sure of it."

"And where did you see her?" Schäfer took out his pad and pen from his inside pocket and started taking notes.

"We always spend August and September in our holiday cottage—"

"By Tisvildeleje Beach?"

"No, in Provence, France. We have a farmhouse just outside Saint-Rémy, which we bought when Vilhelm retired." The woman jumped in her seat when she realized she had given away her husband's name.

She looked at Schäfer with startled eyes.

"I didn't hear that," he assured her with a wink and asked her to continue.

"Well, so my husband and I have this house in the South of France. We've been going there for twelve, maybe thirteen years now. For the first few years we only explored the area close to where we lived. It takes a while to get to know a new town, although it's really quite small. But in the last few summers we have made trips to various other towns in neighboring departments. To explore."

"And you think you saw her on one of those trips?"

"Vilh . . . my *husband* didn't see her, but I did. We had gone to a small village an hour's drive north of Saint-Rémy and we were people-watching in an outdoor café when I spotted this woman. I think I noticed her because she was standing apart from everyone else, and she looked angry. Or maybe *angry* isn't the right word, but certainly not happy.

And as I sat there watching her, it occurred to me. It was her. The woman you've been looking for."

"Did you speak to her?"

"No, she walked on immediately afterwards, and I'm afraid I didn't see her again."

Schäfer's initial hopes were shattered. An old lady catching a glimpse of a someone who sort of looked like Anna Kiel in a village in the middle of nowhere wasn't exactly what he would call a solid lead.

"It all happened so fast," she said, as though she could read his mind. "So, I understand why you might find it hard to believe. But I think this might help."

She opened the clasp of her small, bulging handbag, fished something out of it, and handed it to him.

Schäfer got up from his chair to take it as a warm, tingling feeling spread across his upper body.

In his hand, he held a photograph. Red digits in the bottom corner revealed it had been taken a week and a half earlier. The picture showed a group of children and a tall, brusque-looking man gathered around a small table. They were looking at something and Schäfer couldn't see what it was, but everyone's eyes were on a cardboard box at the center of the table. Everyone with the exception of one person. A woman who was standing a short distance behind the gathering.

She was looking straight at the camera, and Schäfer instantly knew.

It was her.

It was Anna Kiel.

5

Readers' editor Carl-Johan "The Shovel" Scowl was sitting at the big, moss-green conference table, flicking through a fat case file, when Heloise entered the room.

At the end of the table, Mikkelsen, the editor in chief, was picking restlessly at his reddish-brown beard. He got up briefly to greet her and waved her eagerly toward the table.

"Come on in," he said. "Let's get this show on the road so that we can all move on with our lives, dear friends. After all, we have a paper to publish, and I think we've spent quite enough time going over this sorry tale."

Mikkelsen's tone was mild, bordering on cheerful, and Karen Aagaard, who was standing next to Heloise, looked at him rather taken aback. Then she turned her attention to The Shovel, who didn't seem to have registered the peculiar jolliness coming from the end of the table.

"Yes, do sit down, Heloise." He mispronounced her name, and she suspected him of doing it on purpose.

"The *H* is silent," she said. "It's pronounced É-louise."

The Shovel looked up. "Whatever. I'm glad that you were able to come at such short notice."

"Not a problem. Though I have to admit, I'm surprised that we're back here again." Heloise looked around the room.

"We've gone over the story several times now, and I've nothing new to add."

"And you're sure about that? You haven't overlooked some detail? Information that could influence my decision?" The Shovel's voice was surprisingly dark and guttural, ill suiting his slight, almost girly appearance.

"I am. I've already told you everything relevant to the case."

"Right. Then let me briefly summarize events as you've described them, so we can be absolutely sure I've understood you correctly before I finish writing my report."

Heloise crossed her legs and waited.

The Shovel turned a couple of pages in his file and cleared his throat. "According to your statement, you were made aware of Jan Skriver's investment in Cotton Corp, one of the biggest textile factories in Bangalore in India, in June of this year."

"Yes, that's correct."

"In an article on August second, you write that at the same time Skriver made that investment, he ended his agreement with Glæsel Textiles in Vejle, thus moving the majority of his clothing production out of Denmark. His decision resulted in the loss of eight hundred and fifty Danish jobs and was politically, let's say, an 'unpopular' one."

"That's one way of putting it. It was highly unpopular with the government, and it was an unmitigated disaster for the local town."

"On August third, you were contacted by an—and I quote—'anonymous source' who asked you to investigate the move, more specifically Cotton Corp's use of child labor and the factory's use of a hormone-interfering substance called nonylphenol ethoxylate, better known as NPE. Have I understood that correctly?"

"Yes."

"And it is the case that the EU has banned the import of clothing produced using NPE?" The Shovel looked up for the first time.

"Yes."

"Who was your source?"

"I don't know. I just got a telephone call. There was a voice on the other end—a man. He mentioned several things, which he encouraged me to investigate more closely, but he didn't give me his name."

"But you have some idea of his identity?"

"An idea, yes. But no proof. As you yourself pointed out, politically there was much dismay at Skriver's decision to move production out of Denmark, so my hunch is that a politician tipped me off. But your guess is as good as mine."

"Hmm . . ." The Shovel held Heloise's gaze for several seconds before he continued. "While undertaking your research, you came into possession of what appeared to be internal, confidential documents from Skriver's organization, including an extract from his contract with Cotton Corp. Documents that confirmed the allegation that the factory did indeed use child labor and illegal chemical substances."

"Correct."

"Documents on which you chose to base your recent article."

"Yes."

"Who gave you those documents?"

"I'm afraid I can't tell you that. My source wishes to be anonymous, and I have to respect that."

"But you know the identity of your source?"

"Yes."

"And to the best of your knowledge, the information was genuine?"

Heloise felt her mouth go dry.

"At the time in question, I had no reason to think otherwise. I've used this source on many other occasions over a number of years, and the information has always proved reliable. The documents seemed real, and I trusted them."

"And that turned out to be a rather reckless decision," The Shovel observed. "Did you practice due diligence?"

"With the benefit of hindsight, no."

"And if you ever find yourself in a similar situation, would you then base a story on such one-sided, amateurish research, or would you back up your conclusions with facts?" He held his palms up to illustrate the two options he was presenting her with.

Heloise wanted to reach across the table and strangle him with his slim, curry-colored tie. Instead, she licked her lips calmly.

"Obviously, I'll strive to practice due diligence in the future. No one wants a repeat of this meeting any less than I do." She flashed what was supposed to be a smile across the table.

"Right. Well, that's *that*, then!" The editor in chief signaled from the end of the table with a contented clap of his hands that he had heard what he needed to hear.

In contrast to Karen Aagaard, Heloise wasn't surprised at Mikkelsen's uncharacteristic leniency. A few months earlier, after a long day at work, she had been strolling along the harbor front, wanting to cross Palace Square and pass the Marble Church on her way home. It had been one of the first light, warm evenings of the summer, and she had been halfway through the Amalie Garden when she noticed them.

In the darkest corner of the garden, half-hidden behind a big cherry tree, the editor in chief had been sitting on a bench in a passionate embrace with a dark-haired woman who was young and quite pretty—and definitely not his wife.

The sound of Heloise's footsteps had made him look up and their eyes had met briefly, before Heloise looked away and left the garden. But she knew what she had seen, and he knew that she knew.

If her job was in jeopardy, Mikkelsen would tip the scales in her favor.

"Yes, I don't have any further questions either," The Shovel said, slamming his file shut. "Oh, wait, by the way.

I do have one more thing. The source who gave you the documents—that wouldn't happen to have been Martin Duvall, head of communications at the Ministry of Commerce, would it?"

Heloise sat very still in her chair.

A hint of a smile began to form at the corner of The Shovel's mouth.

"Like I said, I can't reveal my source," Heloise said. "I'm sure that you, as the upholder of good press ethics, can understand that better than anyone."

"In that case, let me ask you this." He took off his reading glasses, folded the temples carefully, and placed the spectacles on the table in front of him. "What is your *personal* relationship with Mr. Duvall?"

Heloise opened her mouth, but no sound came out. She turned her head and looked at Mikkelsen, and before she'd had time to answer, he stood up. His eyes were suddenly black with anger, and a blood vessel bulged on his forehead.

"Thank you, Scowl, that's quite enough!" He practically spat out the words. "Miss Kaldan's personal life has nothing to do with this."

* * *

Karen Aagaard closed the door to her office and turned to Heloise.

"What. On earth. Was *that*?"

"Are you referring to that odd staccato way you're speaking?" Heloise produced a packet of chewing gum from her pocket. "I don't know, but perhaps you should get it checked out. It sounds serious."

Aagaard flopped down in the leather armchair in the corner. She threw up her hands in resignation. "Oh, you think this is funny, do you?" Her tone was astounded rather than angry.

"Not in the least," Heloise said, taking a seat opposite her editor. "But what do you want me to say? I screwed up, I've admitted it, and it won't happen again. So now you have to decide whether to give me a new assignment or to send me home."

She popped two pieces of chewing gum into her mouth and held out the packet to Aagaard, who took it tentatively.

"Hmm. It just feels like there's something going on between you and Mikkelsen that I should know about?"

"There isn't."

"Is there something going on between you and Mikkelsen that I *shouldn't* know about?"

". . . No."

"Kaldan!"

"Nothing is going on!" Heloise held up her hands to shut her up.

"Okay. I'll pretend to believe that." Karen Aagaard drummed her fingers on the coffee table in front of her while she looked pensively at Heloise, trying to decide what to do with her.

Heloise beamed a smile at her, which Aagaard waved away in halfhearted irritation.

"Stop it! I know exactly what you're doing," she said. "Okay, well, do you have something you can get started on right away, or do we have to summon the troops for an editorial meeting?"

Heloise instinctively moved her hand to the inside pocket of her leather jacket where she had put the letter. "It just so happens that I've received something I want to look into."

"What is it?"

"I'm not sure yet. I need to investigate it further before I can tell you whether or not there's a story there."

"Right, then get to work. And make sure to keep me posted."

* * *

When Heloise returned to the investigative section, Mogens Bøttger was nowhere in sight, but several reporters from the other sections had arrived at their desks in the open-plan office, and Heloise could feel them staring at her and sense the questions they were silently asking themselves and each other:

What's she doing here? I thought she'd been suspended.

She sank deeply into her office chair so that their faces disappeared behind the low partition wall and entered the number of the research department. She let the phone ring until it was picked up by her favorite colleague, the morbidly obese and permanently sweating Morten Munk.

"Kaldan, what the hell? I thought you were grounded." As always, Munk sounded wheezy and breathless though he never engaged in activities that could cause his pulse to rise.

"Oh, you know me," Heloise said warmly. "I can't stay away, and Mikkelsen can't manage without me. Neither can you, by the way."

"Touché, *ma chérie*. To what do I owe this pleasure?"

"Are you at your desk?"

"Where else would I be?"

"Do you have time to dig out some information for me?"

"About the Skriver case?" Munk sounded equally excited and skeptical.

"No, I'm done with that. This is something else. Does the name Anna Kiel mean anything to you?"

"Is the Pope Catholic? What about her?"

"I need everything you can find on her. Articles we've published in the paper, contributions from other media, background information—the whole shebang."

Munk was quiet, and Heloise could hear the metallic sound of a pen quickly scribbling down notes on a piece of paper.

"I'll get to work straightaway," he said. "I'll email you when I have something. It shouldn't be long."

The first documents arrived in Heloise's in-box ten minutes later. Rather than reading them right away, she put her laptop in her bag and left the building. She needed fresh air, a chance to work without everyone staring at her, and more importantly, a decent meal. Outside the rain had stopped, so she left her bicycle where it was and walked briskly past the French embassy up to Bistro Royal on Kongens Nytorv—her regular Friday lunch restaurant. Today was Monday, but that didn't matter. Today, everything seemed out of the ordinary.

The restaurant manager was a hearty, robust man. He greeted her warmly. "Why, it's my favorite reporter," he said, getting ready to kiss her cheek.

Heloise had a strong suspicion that he had never read anything she'd written, but she appreciated the welcome and greeted him politely in return.

"I'm certainly a *hungry* reporter," she said with a smile.

"Are you alone today, or . . . ?" He held up two menus.

The last few times she had come here, she had been with Martin. A week and a half ago, they had spent the whole night sitting in the bar eating mussels and sharing a bottle of Chardonnay. For once they hadn't talked shop. Well, a couple of times she had tried to turn the conversation to Skriver, but he had stopped her.

Leave it, Helo. I don't want to talk about work tonight. I'd rather talk about you.

She had just shaken her head and looked at him with a smile until he started talking about himself. About his childhood, his parents, his first love, and his divorce.

She didn't want children, I did. I still do. It ended badly. Doesn't it always?

After dinner, they had gone home together, and he had been rougher with her than she'd expected. She'd let him, and to her surprise, she had kind of liked it. But he'd also scared her a little.

Heloise smiled at the restaurant manager. "It'll be just me today."

She was shown to one of the best tables in the restaurant with a view of Kongens Nytorv and the Royal Theater. She ordered a prawn sandwich and a bottle of mineral water, opened her laptop, and read the first of the emails that Morten Munk had sent her.

She spent the next hour eating, reading, and taking notes. When she was done, she called Ulrich Andersson.

"Hello?"

"Hi, I'm looking for Ulrich."

"Who is calling?"

"This is Heloise Kaldan from *Demokratisk Dagblad*."

"Kaldan? Right. Long time, no see. What's up?"

It was midafternoon, but Heloise sensed that she had woken him up. There was a pause; she heard the flicking of a lighter, followed by a hiss and the sound of a toilet seat being flipped up.

"I'm sorry to disturb you, but I think I need your help."

"My help?" The spray hit the bowl hard, almost drowning out his voice. "With what?"

"Well, I've sort of taken over a story that you used to cover. I'm calling to see if you can help me fill in some blanks."

There was silence on the other end, and Heloise continued, "It's about the murder of that lawyer in Taarbæk. Christoffer Mossing. I've been reading all your old work on the case, and I would like to know a little more about who—"

"I can't help you with that." His voice was suddenly cold and wide awake.

"Oh, but it'll only take, like, half an hour. I'll buy you a cup of coffee; I really won't take up much of your time. I just want to know if back then you spoke to—"

"I'm sorry, I can't help you." Ulrich Andersson hung up.

Heloise stared at her cell phone in disbelief. She tried calling him back, but he didn't pick up. The third time, she let it ring until it went to voice mail.

"Hi, Ulrich, it's Heloise Kaldan again. I just wanted to tell you that I've received a letter from Anna Kiel, and I thought that perhaps you'd like to read it. Call me."

She found it hard to believe that a journalist who'd been eating crime stories for breakfast for years would be able to resist an opportunity like that.

Of course he'd call.

She unfolded the letter, trying not to touch it unnecessarily, and placed it on the table in front of her. She had probably destroyed any potential evidence already, but she still treated it with care. If the letter was genuine, she was breaking the law by keeping it to herself. But she didn't want to tell the police about it.

Not yet.

Heloise's job was to find and investigate stories. She knew she would never see the letter again if she reported it. The police would bench her for sure; that was what usually happened. It was very rare for there to be a genuine quid pro quo. But as far as she could see from the media coverage, there had been no developments in the case recently, and the letter could be the first new lead in a long time.

She would have to report it.

She looked through her notes to find the name of the police officer mentioned in the articles as heading the investigation.

She wrote *Detective Sergeant Erik Schäfer, Violent Crimes Unit, Copenhagen Police* in her notebook and underlined it twice.

Then she asked for the check.

6

UNLESS HELOISE WAS traveling or had an early-morning meeting, she never set her alarm clock. On weekdays, the Marble Church bells would toll at eight, and they were loud enough to rouse her from a slumber that had been superficial and restless for as long as she could remember.

Today she swung her legs out of the bed on the first stroke, even though she had been up half the night plowing through Munk's research and could easily have used a few more hours of sleep.

She checked her cell phone on her bedside table and saw that Martin had tried calling her at four AM. He had sent her three text messages as well, all saying, *Call me!*

There was also a text message from Gerda with a heart. Heloise sent her an emoji kiss and walked barefoot through the living room to the bathroom. She stepped around the many documents and notes she had spread out on the wooden floor last night in order to construct a timeline.

After a quick shower, she sat down at the oak table in the living room in her bathrobe and ate a big bowl of porridge with raisins and cinnamon and drank a cup of coffee.

She was reading her summary of the events when her entry phone buzzed. From the sound, she could tell that every other entry phone in the building was also being called.

On the video display from street level, she could see the top third of a balding head.

"Yes?" she spoke into the intercom.

"Newspapers," said a man with a thick, Arabic accent.

Heloise pressed the buzzer to let him into the stairwell. Soon she heard him scramble up the stairs and the letter boxes on the floors below clatter one after the other.

She surveyed the pile of junk mail that had accumulated in her hallway during the week. She bent down to pick it up and was flicking through it to see if there were any bills hidden in the inferno of special offers and pointless local news when she heard the newspaper guy reach the fifth floor and stop outside her front door. Her letter box was pushed open, and a supermarket promotion was shoved into her hallway, where it landed softly on the dirty welcome mat.

Heloise was expecting to hear the man's footfalls disappear quickly downstairs, but nothing happened. She remained by her front door, listening for several seconds.

Nothing.

She dumped the junk mail in her arms and quickly opened the door.

On the top step outside, a small, middle-aged man was trying on one of the mint-green Nike Air trainers Heloise had stepped out of after going running at the Citadel two days earlier. He froze midmotion, as if he thought he'd avoid detection if he sat perfectly still.

"Erm . . ." Heloise said, smiling awkwardly. She felt embarrassed for the guy. She gathered the top of her bathrobe tightly across her chest and said, "Would you mind leaving those where you found them?"

The man nodded, but he didn't say anything.

He put down the trainers carefully, picked up his own down-at-heel shoes, and made his way down the stairs in stockinged feet.

Heloise waited in the stairwell until she could hear the front door close behind him at street level. She shook her head, smiling, and was on her way into her apartment when her eye caught the junk mail she had just dropped.

The colorful leaflets were scattered across the floor like confetti catapulted from a party popper. The corner of a pale-blue envelope was sticking out from under a Sephora catalog.

Even before she had picked it up, Heloise knew who the letter was from.

*   *   *

"When did you get these?" Karen Aagaard pointed to the two letters in front of her on the table in the conference room.

Heloise had set up an early-morning meeting with her editor and Mogens Bøttger. So far, Aagaard had been the only one to arrive.

"The first letter was sent to me here at the paper. I found it in my pigeonhole yesterday. I don't know how long it's been there. A couple of days, maybe? A week? I can see from the postmark that it was sent from Cannes one and a half weeks ago, and the second letter was posted five days ago from Lyon," Heloise said. "It must have been delivered to my home on Saturday. Only I didn't notice it until today. It was mixed in with junk mail in my hallway."

They heard a single, hard knock on the door, and Mogens Bøttger entered the room. He was carrying a cupholder tray with three cups bearing the logo from the café across the street.

"Morning," he said in a surly voice.

Heloise and Aagaard looked at him and exchanged glances. A white, crumpled shirt was hanging over his trousers' waistline, and his hair was strangely flat and upended on one side of his head. Normally he was the epitome of good grooming, bordering on the nauseating, but today he looked like someone who would rather not be noticed. Quite a challenge for someone almost seven feet tall.

"I'm sorry I'm late, but I had to drop off Fernanda at day care, and she threw a tantrum when I said good-bye. It's easier to get a comment on the record from a tax evader than it is to get a one-year-old to stop howling. Or to go to sleep when it's her bedtime, for that matter. I don't know how people who live with their children full-time do it." He looked resentfully at both of them and flopped down on the chair next to Aagaard.

Mogens Bøttger's daughter was the result of a summer fling with a forty-one-year-old fitness instructor. After two dinner dates she was pregnant, and he was screwed. Consequently, he was now a single parent three days every two weeks, and his relationship with the child's mother was strained, to say the least.

"Don't look at *me*," Heloise said. "I've yet to discover the joys of parenthood."

"Right, anyway, that's why I'm late, and why I look like the living dead." Bøttger distributed the coffee cups between them. "So, what's up? What did I miss?"

"I got another one," Heloise said.

"Another what?"

"A letter."

Bøttger noticed the letters on the table and reached out his hand. "May I?"

"Yes, it's that one," Heloise said, pointing to the most recent.

He pinched the corners of the letter carefully and read out loud:

Dear Heloise

Mine is 4, yours is 13.
If I say *Amorphophallus titanum*, you will reply *Lupinus*.
My middle name starts with an 'E'—how about yours?

I know so much about you.
You know a lot less about me.

But we are connected through him, I understand that now.

Do you see?
Do you see it now?

While I am denied your presence, Heloise, give me at least through your words some sweet semblance of yourself.

Anna Kiel

"Holy shit," Bøttger said, looking up at the other two. His eyebrows had shot right up to his already receding hairline. "Are you absolutely sure you don't know her?"

"One hundred percent," Heloise insisted. "I have no idea why she's chosen me. 'Connected'—us? It makes no sense. But she knows me, or at least she knows some personal things about me." Heloise pointed to the letter sent to her home. "Thirteen is my lucky number, so I presume that hers is four, and *Lupinus* is the Latin term for *lupine*—my favorite flower. How the hell does she know that?"

"Maybe she sat next to you in primary school? In her next letter she'll probably write that your favorite color is pink and that your favorite food is mac 'n' cheese." Bøttger was the only one to laugh at his joke.

"What's your middle name?" Aagaard asked.

"Eleanor," Heloise said. "And Anna's full name is Anna Elisabeth Kiel."

"Eleanor . . ." Bøttger said, as if tasting the name.

Heloise held up her hand. "Mogens, I'm warning you!"

"And what's this *amor*-something or other . . ." Aagaard continued. "She says it's her favorite flower. Does it have something to do with love? *Amor*?"

"Funny you should ask that," Heloise said, opening her notebook. "That was my guess too, but no. *Amorphophallus titanum*—more commonly known as the corpse flower—is pretty much as far as you can get from a plant symbolizing love."

Aagaard and Bøttger both stared at her.

"Corpse flower?" Bøttger echoed.

"Yes. It's a giant plant that in the wild grows only in Sumatra in western Indonesia and in a handful of botanical gardens across the world. There's currently one in Copenhagen. What's unique about it is that its smell can be easily mistaken for that of a rotting corpse."

Heloise found her notes from the botanical reference website and read aloud: " 'The flower's purple-red leaves and texture also contribute to the illusion that it's a piece of decaying meat, and it helps the plant attract carrion beetles, which are lured into the plant where they pollinate it. The literal translation of the plant's Latin name is "malformed giant penis"—' "

Bøttger raised an eyebrow.

" '—and it is sometimes referred to as "the penis flower," presumably due to its phallic shape. However, because of its revolting stench of death, it's also known as a corpse flower.' "

"Right . . ." Mogens Bøttger said. "And Anna Kiel's favorite flower is this corpse-like penis plant?"

"So it would seem." Heloise nodded.

"Charming," he said, pushing aside his coffee.

Silence descended upon the room.

"All right," Aagaard said, "let's discuss practicalities for a second. Have you told the police what you've been sent?"

Heloise shook her head.

"No, fuck the police," Bøttger exclaimed. "They'll just snatch the letters from her and tell her to mind her own business."

"I have to tell them," Heloise said. "Anna Kiel killed a guy. If I can help the police put her behind bars, I will, regardless of how 'connected' she thinks the two of us are."

"So then why haven't you called them yet?" Bøttger asked.

"Because you're right, they'll probably try to sideline me. But I can't sit on this much longer. I just have to work out a strategy first, so I don't lose the story."

"Okay, stop!" Karen Aagaard said. "Would one of you please rewind to the beginning? Remind me again what happened to the lawyer. I'm a bit rusty when it comes to crime reporting." She blew away some milk foam and sipped her coffee.

"A lawyer at Orleff and Plessner returns home to his house in Taarbæk after playing tennis with some friends one spring evening," Heloise said. "He has a late-night snack and goes to bed. At some point between midnight and three AM, Anna Kiel gains access to his home—allegedly. She has brought with her a brand-new Codexx filleting knife. It's a medium-length kitchen knife used by many professional chefs, and you can buy it in most high-end kitchen shops. She attacks Mossing while he's in bed sleeping, cuts his throat, and leaves the murder weapon in the house. Cameras outside his house capture her leaving the scene, and no one has seen her since."

"Had the lawyer represented her or any of her family members in a trial that had gone wrong? Was this about revenge?" Aagaard asked.

"No. According to family members and friends of the victim and the killer, there was nothing to link them. They appear not to have known one another," Heloise said.

"Incidentally, Christoffer Mossing—the guy who was killed—was the son of Johannes Mossing. The real estate tycoon," Bøttger explained.

The Mossing family was the very definition of old money. Only four generations ago, the family fortune had been of Downton Abbey proportions, and although the family's current net worth was less impressive, it was still of such size that Heloise had whistled when she'd seen the numbers.

From Morten Munk's research she had learned that Christoffer Mossing's enterprising father's personal property included a house valued in double-digit millions in swanky Vedbæk, a listed country house with a stud farm on South

Funen, and a huge château south of Bordeaux complete with moat and vineyard.

"On the one hand, we have this super wealthy family. On the other, we have Anna Kiel, who grew up under much more modest circumstances," Heloise explained. "Her mother owns a pub called the Lantern, and we know nothing about her father."

"What do the police think?" Aagaard said.

"They seem to have no idea why she killed him. A lot has been written about her mental state and how she might have acted in a moment of sheer madness. The police think she picked a random victim and killed him."

"And nothing was found in the lawyer's house or at his place of work to suggest that Anna Kiel might have been in touch with him before the murder? Letters she sent him, anything like that?"

A wave of unease rolled over Heloise.

"If they did, it was never made public," she replied. "And that's another reason I want to talk to the police. I have to know who I'm dealing with here, and why she's so eager to talk to me."

"Who is this *he* she refers to?" Aagaard pointed to the letter in front of her. "The man you supposedly have in common?"

Heloise shrugged.

"It must be the lawyer," Bøttger said. "Somehow you must have crossed his path."

"I really don't see how I could have."

"Could you have used him as a source once? Or maybe you met him on a night out a long time ago and forgot all about it?" he suggested.

Heloise raised an eyebrow. "Met him on a night out?"

"Yeah, what do I know? It could have happened."

"No, it really couldn't!"

Again, there was silence around the table.

It was Aagaard who broke it. "She uses the same closing line in both letters. She writes: 'While I am denied your presence, Heloise, give me at least through your words some sweet semblance of yourself.' "

Heloise nodded and placed the letters alongside each other so that Bøttger could see the similarity.

"It's a strangely pretentious way of expressing oneself," Aagaard said. "What does it even mean?"

"I've no idea. After the first letter, I tried Googling the sentence to see if I got any hits. I didn't, so I came up with my own home-baked analysis instead," Heloise said, opening her notebook. She showed them what she had written:

I am denied your presence = I'm on the run and can't meet you face to face.
Give me through your words = write my story!
A sweet semblance of yourself = you're a journalist, which makes you objective.

"But I really can't be sure." She closed the notebook. "It's not my most insightful work, so your guess is as good as mine."

" 'A sweet semblance.' *Sweet?*" Bøttger said. "What an odd thing to write."

Aagaard zoned out of the conversation for a moment and gazed into the distance. Then she said, "If what she's really saying is that you must be objective and write the story, then by definition she's also saying that what we think we know isn't true."

"You're not saying you believe she might be innocent, are you?" Heloise asked.

"I wouldn't know anything about that. I'm just saying that you have to start at the beginning, as if you were new to the case. For instance, which sources were the old coverage based on?"

"Lots of sources."

"Such as?"

"Such as Anna Kiel's mother, friends and colleagues of both Christoffer Mossing and Anna Kiel, representatives of the Mossing family, a couple of her old teachers. It's a long list."

"Okay, then you ought to start there. Speak to them individually and don't worry about the question of guilt. Leave that to the courts. Just follow the story and see where it takes you."

Heloise could feel her cell phone buzz in her inside pocket. It was a text message from the research department.

"You tell me not to worry," she said, reading the message. "But my home address has been unlisted since I started working as a journalist, and when I asked Munk this morning to search for my address online, he found nothing." She looked up and asked with a shrug, "So how does Anna Kiel know where I live?"

7

THE DRIVE UP Strandvejen to Vedbæk gave Heloise time to
gather her thoughts. The palatial villas along the coast were
lined up like dominoes behind wrought-iron gates with ornate
monograms heavy enough to keep out uninvited guests but
transparent enough to let passersby admire the opulent gardens.

The pea shingle crunched under the wheels of the Ford
Focus she had borrowed from the newspaper when she pulled
into the courtyard in front of the huge, pale-gray house. It
looked nothing like the soulless art deco buildings or the
ridiculously pompous mansions that surrounded it. Rather,
it reminded Heloise of those luxurious summer houses you
always saw in American feel-good movies. It was made from
wood and built in Nantucket style with shutters and white
casement windows, with a large porch going around the
whole house. Insert Diane Keaton wearing a straw hat, light-
colored linen clothes, a kitchen filled with fruit and vegeta-
bles and plenty of sunshine, and you'd get the picture. It was
that kind of house, Heloise thought.

She parked next to a silver Jaguar gleaming in the afternoon sunshine and walked up to the front door. There was
no bell at the entrance, only a brass doorknob shaped like an
anchor. Seconds after Heloise knocked, the door was opened

by a young Thai woman wearing a dark knee-length dress. She sized up Heloise from head to toe—twice.

"Can I help you?"

"Yes, hello, my name is Heloise Kaldan, and I'm looking for Ellen or Johannes Mossing."

"I'm afraid Mr. Mossing is not at home, but Mrs. Mossing is here. Do you have an appointment?"

"No, this is a surprise visit, I'm afraid." Heloise smiled.

"May I ask what it's in regard to?"

"It's about her son."

Heloise had been expecting a reaction from the young woman, but none came. She merely opened the door further and invited Heloise inside.

"Please wait here."

The woman disappeared.

Heloise could hear rock 'n' roll music playing somewhere in the house, an odd choice of soundtrack for the setting. She looked around the hall. There was a big open fireplace that didn't look as if it had ever been used, and a broad staircase curved its way up to the second floor. Framed photographs of the family and friends of the residents hung on the wall along the stairs as evidence of their famous circle of acquaintances. Heloise recognized a former Copenhagen mayor, two aging tennis stars, Tony Blair, an American music producer complete with diamond necklaces and gold teeth, and a long list of Danish jet set types whose main achievement in life was being born to the right parents.

Heloise walked a few steps up the stairs and took a closer look at one of the pictures. She recognized Christoffer Mossing from the news coverage, although he was at least ten years younger in the picture than he had been at the time of his death. He was wearing an American mortarboard with a tassel, and champagne flowed from the bottle he was holding up in triumph to the photographer.

The young housekeeper cleared her throat behind her. "It's this way," she said.

Heloise followed her through two spacious connecting living rooms furnished with white sofas and armchairs upholstered in brandy-colored leather. Walls and bookcases were decorated with maritime motifs, horse racing cups, and other collector's items. The music grew louder as they approached an open set of double doors that led to a large conservatory at the back of the house and overlooking the Øresund Strait.

A woman was standing in there. She wore a cap and a white wrap dress and was busy deadheading a New Dawn rosebush with a small pair of gold secateurs as a loud, squealing guitar solo made the windows in the conservatory rattle.

The woman turned to Heloise with a smile. "Hello."

"Hi!" Heloise had to raise her voice to drown out the music. She stuck out a hand and introduced herself. "Cool music. Who is playing?"

Ellen Mossing stared at her as though Heloise had just asked her which planet they were on. "Why, Led Zeppelin, of course. Do you really not know them?"

Heloise nodded while she thought about it. "It's some LSD-type band, yes?"

Ellen laughed—a bright, silvery laughter—and Heloise warmed to her instinctively. Mrs. Mossing went over to the old record player in the corner and turned down the volume. Then she addressed the housekeeper.

"Noy, may we have some coffee, please? Or perhaps you prefer tea?" She looked at Heloise.

"No, coffee is fine, thank you."

"Sometimes I fear I drink too much coffee. Every now and then it causes my pulse to spike. It feels dreadful. But it's pretty much the only vice I've left, so to hell with it." She winked conspiratorially at Heloise, as though she had just revealed some naughty secret about herself.

She waved Heloise over to a rectangular teak table in the middle of the conservatory and asked her to sit down.

"You have a very beautiful name. *Heloise*." Mrs. Mossing spoke the name in a singing French accent. She took off her cap, and her long, silver hair cascaded down her back. "Far more exotic than Ellen."

"Thank you," Heloise said. "Then again, I bet you've never had to spell or explain your name to anyone."

"Well, you can't have everything."

"I guess not," Heloise said, sitting down opposite her. "I should probably explain why I'm here."

"Noy said you had some questions about Christoffer?"

"Yes, that's right. But I need to tell you that I'm a reporter. I work for *Demokratisk Dagblad*, and I'm looking into your son's death."

Ellen studied her for a while without saying anything.

"Why now?" she then asked. "Has something happened that I don't know about?"

"No, nothing specific. But I'm trying to found out whether something might have been overlooked during the original investigation. I'm here to ask you to tell me about your son."

"No one ever talks about him anymore." Mrs. Mossing gazed out at the water. "Not even my husband. It's as if people think it won't hurt if they pretend it never happened. My son is dead, and now the world is acting as though he never existed." She turned to Heloise and smiled sadly. "I don't want you to quote me, but I don't mind telling you about Christoffer."

The housekeeper appeared with a tray and served the coffee. She placed a small plate of cookies in front of Heloise before leaving the room.

"Help yourself." Mrs. Mossing nodded in the direction of the cookies.

"I saw a picture of Christoffer in the hall. Did he study in the States?" Heloise took a cookie and bit into it. It had a strangely salty taste.

"Yes, he graduated from Harvard Law. I believe those were some of the best years of his life. He would always have a special tone in his voice whenever he talked about his time there," Ellen said. "I have a grandchild in America, did you know?"

Heloise shook her head.

"A woman reached out to us after Christoffer's death. Someone he'd been seeing. It can't have been anything serious, though; we'd certainly never heard of her. But then again, he had so many girls. He was very popular." She took a cube of sugar from a bowl on the table and dropped it into her coffee. "She called us a few months after the funeral. She had heard what had happened and was very upset, as I'm sure you can imagine. She told us that she had gotten pregnant back then, and that there was a child—a young boy."

"Didn't that make you suspicious?" Heloise asked.

"Because of the inheritance, you mean?"

"Yes."

"Well, we wondered whether she might be a con artist, sure. You know, someone who reads international obituaries and tries to make money out of people's misfortune. But she sent us a picture."

"A picture?"

"Yes, a photo. Of the boy. When we saw him, we knew she was telling the truth. She offered to send us a DNA sample, but we had no doubts at all. He's Christoffer's son."

"What's his name?"

"Jack. He's fourteen years old now. A handsome boy."

Heloise could easily imagine. With his bright-white smile and well-proportioned build, Christoffer Mossing had been almost a caricature of beauty. Not Heloise's type, definitely not, but clearly someone all the overprivileged daddies' girls north of Copenhagen would have lined up to date: young, wealthy, successful, and looking like a Greek god. The perfect eligible bachelor.

"Have you met Jack?" Heloise asked.

"Yes, he came to visit last summer. Before then we had been emailing, getting to know one another in writing, as you do, and then we bought him a plane ticket. We had to meet him."

"What was that like?"

"It was . . ." Mrs. Mossing struggled to find the right words. "It was a nightmare, quite frankly. You can't imagine what it feels like to lose a son and then meet a total stranger who looks like him, moves like him, speaks with his voice . . ."

"I'd rather think it would be like getting some of Christoffer back," Heloise ventured.

"Yes, you'd think so, wouldn't you? But it felt more like my mind was playing tricks on me. My eyes were telling me that I was looking at something that wasn't there at all. Like a cruel trompe l'oeil."

"How did Jack react?"

"Oh, the poor boy didn't know what to do with himself. I was falling apart, and he tried his best to help, but in the end, he went back home. We send him presents for Christmas and birthdays, and Johannes has opened an account with a considerable amount of money which he'll get when he turns twenty-one. He's our flesh and blood and we want what's best for him. But it seems unlikely that we'll see him again."

Heloise was puzzled by Ellen Mossing's frankness. It was as if there were no barriers between them. The woman acted as if she were talking to a close friend rather than a reporter. Heloise wondered if she was just lonely and caught herself feeling sorry for the woman.

The pickup needle on the turntable had gotten stuck in a groove, and Ellen got up and carefully lifted it from the record. She flicked through a pile of old records, picked one, took it out of the cover, and blew across it. Then she put it on, and Billie Holiday's "All of Me" poured out of the speakers.

"Now that's my kind of music." Heloise smiled and pressed her hands together to show her appreciation.

"She's Johannes's favorite singer. I can't think of a single morning for the more than forty years we've known each other that he hasn't played her at the breakfast table."

They sat for a while listening without speaking. Mrs. Mossing closed her eyes and appeared to lose herself in the music.

"Where were we?" she asked, without opening her eyes.

"You told me that Christoffer was popular with the ladies. Did he have a girlfriend at the time of his death?"

"A girlfriend?" Ellen laughed and looked at Heloise. "No, that wasn't Christoffer's style. He had many women; there was never just one."

"Did he ever introduce you to any of the women he was seeing?"

"No, God no. I don't think he believed in that sort of thing."

"What sort of thing?"

"Love, I mean. The committed exclusive relationship. I don't think that appealed to him."

"Why not? Didn't he have an excellent role model in you and your husband?"

Mrs. Mossing pursed her lips and exhaled heavily through her nose. "I guess," she said in a voice that suggested the opposite. "We had many good years, Johannes and I. But I was very young when we met, nothing but a big kid really, and old age can be so cruel." She smiled awkwardly and straightened the belt around her fine, feminine waist. "Perhaps passionate love doesn't last as long as one would like it to. But we're wonderful friends, Johannes and I, and in the end, that's what really matters."

Heloise studied Ellen Mossing with a furrowed brow. True, she was no longer a young girl, but she still looked amazing at sixty-one. Christoffer hadn't inherited his attractive nose, his impressive bone structure, and his big hazelnut eyes from his father. According to the pictures Heloise had seen of Mossing Senior, he was at least fifteen years older than his wife and nowhere near as attractive.

"I think you look great, if you don't mind me saying so," Heloise said. "If I look like you when I'm sixty—or forty, for that matter—I'll be thrilled."

"Oh, you're sweet." Ellen smiled.

"No, seriously, you are very beautiful. And Christoffer took after you."

"He did." She nodded proudly. "But only on the outside. He had his father's mind, incredibly bright and hardworking like you wouldn't believe. We were so proud of him. He made partner in record time at Orleff and Plessner, and did brilliantly until . . ." Her eyes filled with tears. She let them roll down her cheeks, making no attempt to stop them or wipe them away.

Heloise felt she ought to get up and hug her or something, but she stayed put. She understood Ellen Mossing's open, raw emotions, but what could she say to a woman who had lost her child, lost the person closest to her?

Everything will be all right?

No, it damn well wouldn't. Nothing would ever be all right again.

Heloise reached out her hand and placed it on top of Mrs. Mossing's. "Did you know her? Did you know Anna Kiel?"

Ellen shook her head and withdrew her hand. She got up and walked up to a small chest of drawers in the corner of the conservatory and found an old, yellowing handkerchief from the top drawer.

"No." She dabbed her eyes with the handkerchief. "But I think that—"

"Ellen? What's going on?"

Mrs. Mossing was so startled that she dropped the handkerchief, and Heloise turned in the direction of the voice.

Johannes Mossing was standing in the doorway. He was carrying a fig tree in a terra-cotta pot, which he put on the floor, and he looked anxiously at his wife. "Are you crying?"

"No, it's nothing." Ellen walked up to her husband and let him embrace her. "I was just going down memory lane, and that makes me sentimental, as you know."

He looked at her quizzically. "You're all right, then?"

"Yes, yes. I'm just being silly." She dismissed the question as though it were an insect that had flown too close to her face. "Come, I want you to meet my guest."

Heloise got up.

"Hello," Mr. Mossing said, holding out his hand. "I'm Ellen's husband. I apologize for interrupting the girl talk, but I thought something serious had happened."

Heloise shook his hand and nodded politely. "Heloise Kaldan."

"Kaldan?" He smiled and looked at her through narrowed eyes without letting go of her hand. "Have we met before?"

"I don't think so."

"Are you a local girl?"

"No, I'm from Copenhagen."

"Heloise is a journalist," Ellen said. "She has come to talk about Christoffer."

The smile disappeared from Johannes Mossing's face, and he let go of Heloise's hand as if he had burned himself on it.

"A journalist," he echoed. He looked like someone who had just sucked a lemon.

Ellen came to Heloise's rescue.

"I invited her in, Johannes. I don't mind talking about what happened." She patted his arm softly. "You should try it. It might make you feel better."

Mr. Mossing looked at his wife for a moment without saying anything. Then he turned to Heloise and said, in a neutral voice, "Please leave."

The housekeeper appeared in the doorway as if by magic.

"I'll see you out," she announced with mechanical solemnity.

Heloise didn't budge.

She and Johannes looked hard at one another.

"I work for *Demokratisk Dagblad*," Heloise said. "I'm here because I've reason to believe that your son's killer is trying to contact me."

Ellen looked at her in shock and sat down. She opened and closed her mouth several times without making a sound, but Heloise registered no reaction in the face of Johannes Mossing.

"It would be very helpful if you could tell me everything you know about the night he was murdered," she went on. "Anything that can help me track down Anna Kiel."

With the exception of Billie Holiday's tormented voice, there was silence in the room.

Ellen reached out for her husband's hand, but he snatched it away. "Johannes, I think we have to—"

"We don't have to do anything," he said, without breaking eye contact with Heloise. "Good-bye, Miss Kaldan."

"Call me if you change your mind," Heloise said, and left the conservatory.

* * *

The Ford beeped twice when Heloise unlocked it. She got into the driver's seat and looked in the rearview mirror. Ellen Mossing was standing in one of the big drawing room windows looking out at her. Heloise could see that she was crying again.

What the hell was going on?

There was something about the story of Christoffer Mossing that didn't add up. Were his parents trying to hide the truth about him? Was there anything *to* hide, or did they genuinely not know anything? You could live a lifetime with someone without ever truly knowing them; Heloise knew that all too well. But was there a secret here? Had Christoffer Mossing lived a parallel life alongside his impressive legal career, a life his parents knew nothing about? What about Anna Kiel—where did she fit in? And last but not least: what did any of it have to do with Heloise?

She started the car, drove along the drive, and turned left down Vedbæk Strandvej. She had decided to swing by Christoffer Mossing's house in Taarbæk on her way home. She knew that the property had probably been sold since the murder and that she was unlikely to discover anything significant, but she needed to see the scene of the crime. She *wanted* to see it.

She got out her cell phone to find the address and saw that she had yet another missed call from Martin. There was also an Instagram notification. When she stopped at a red light, she could see that she had been tagged in a photo eight minutes ago. The notification said *@Anna_kiel has mentioned you in a comment: "Your door was open, @heloisekaldan, so I took the liberty of going in."*

The light changed to green, but Heloise stayed put and clicked the link.

"I don't fucking believe it," she said through clenched teeth, while the cars behind her started sounding their horns.

She pulled over and slammed on the brakes as the skin tightened across her knuckles.

The picture that had appeared on the screen was a snapshot of Copenhagen's red and black roofs. The dome of the Marble Church dominated the frame, and Heloise recognized the terrace from where the picture had been taken, the ripped dark-green windbreak.

She typed a number and waited while the phone rang.

"Hello, is this the police? Someone is breaking into my apartment. Yes, now! She's in there right now."

8

THE 150-YEAR-OLD WOODEN staircase creaked loudly under Detective Sergeant Erik Schäfer's feet as he climbed the 127 steps to the fifth floor. On the top landing, the apartment door stood open, and he knocked on the door-frame with a gloved hand before entering.

"Hey," he said, nodding at a dactyloscopy tech from NFC, the National Forensics Center, who was dusting the small foyer for fingerprints with a fine brush and a container of aluminum powder. "Are you finding anything?"

"Yeah." The man offered his fist to Schäfer for a fist bump, a form of greeting that made Schäfer feel older and dustier than the building they were in. "This place is prac-tically crawling with both partial and complete hand- and fingerprints," the tech guy said.

"Ah, well, then I guess you know what you'll be doing for the rest of the day," Schäfer said, and patted him on the back in encouragement.

Schäfer edged around him and stepped into the living room. It was a large room with panoramic windows and a door leading out to a little balcony, and he could see that a number of fingerprints had already been lifted from the glass door.

He peered around.

There was a brown apple core and a half-empty cup of coffee with some dried-up milk foam down its sides sitting on the windowsill, and the coffee table was covered with papers, dirty plates, and bread crumbs. With the exception of what he would categorize as everyday clutter, there was no real mess, nothing that screamed *break-in* or *vandalism*.

He heard voices from an adjoining room and walked over to the coffee table and glanced at the stack of papers lying there. With one quick motion, he spread the documents on the table out like a fan of playing cards and studied the contents. They were printouts of old articles about Christoffer Mossing's murder case. His eyes scanned the documents, stopping at a quote he himself had made to the press a couple of weeks into the investigation:

> *We have reason to believe that Anna Kiel has left the country, and Interpol is now searching for her internationally.*

He stacked the papers back up and went to the kitchen, where two plainclothes officers from the Burglary Unit were talking to a woman seated at the kitchen table. Schäfer didn't know the officers' names, but he had seen one of them a couple times before, a pale, redheaded young man. The other guy looked Middle Eastern and his stature was not dissimilar to that of a Dubai skyscraper, Schäfer thought. It hurt his back to even look at the man, who had to bend his neck to walk around the low-ceilinged attic apartment.

All three of them turned to look at Schäfer when he entered the room.

"Hello," Schäfer said, stepping over to the table. He looked at the woman. "Are you the resident?" he asked.

She nodded.

"Erik Schäfer." He held out his hand, and she shook it.

"Heloise Kaldan," she said.

"Were you two the first ones here?" Schäfer asked, looking at his colleagues.

"Yes, we received the call at two thirty-two PM and arrived here at two forty-four PM, but there was no one in the apartment when we arrived," the pale one said. "We called the NFC right after we talked to you, and one of their men has been here for half an hour now dusting for prints. It looks like he's already had some luck." The officer nodded contentedly.

"Yeah, well, let's wait and see what he finds before we pop the champagne," Schäfer said dryly. "You guys can pack it up. I'll take it from here. Just make sure there's a report on my desk before you go home tonight."

"We can stay, if you'd like," Dubai said. He glanced back and forth between Schäfer and the woman at the table. Schäfer got the sense that the officer's eagerness to remain might be due to the woman's white T-shirt, which was tight in all the right places, more than the investigative work per se.

"Why, that's mighty chivalrous of you, but clear out." Schäfer gave the officers a look that made them say their good-byes and exit the room.

"May I?" He pointed to the seat across from the woman.

"Of course."

He pulled out the chair and sat down.

"I'm sure you've already told everything you know to Riggs and Murtaugh there." He pointed toward the open front door, where he could hear the officers exchanging obscenities with the fingerprint tech on their way down the stairs.

The woman pressed her lips together to stifle a smile.

"But I'm afraid that if I'm to help you, you're going to have to start at the beginning," Schäfer said. "I understand that when my colleagues showed up, you asked to speak to me specifically?"

"Yes, that's right."

"Why is that?"

"Because you're the lead investigator on the Mossing case."

"The Mossing case?"

"Yes."

"What does that have to do with this?"

"I know it sounds a little nuts," she said, "but as your colleagues told you on the phone, I think Anna Kiel was in my apartment today."

Schäfer rubbed his chin with two fingers as he looked at her. Even though his regular morning routine included a thorough shave, his stubble was already visible by this time of day, and the scratching sound was audible.

"I've gotta say that I find that highly unlikely." He had been aiming for empathetic, but the words that came out of his mouth had more of a patronizing sound to them.

"But likely enough that you sent a forensics guy over here as soon as you received the call. Surely it's not standard procedure to start dusting for fingerprints so quickly after an illegal entry. Especially when nothing was missing."

Schäfer shrugged and gave her a look that said *Touché*. "But then again, you're not talking about any old random person here, and I thought it'd be better to be on the safe side," he said. "But why in the world would Anna Kiel break into your apartment?"

"I don't know, but she was here today, and she took a picture from my balcony and posted it on Instagram. Check out the username!" Heloise Kaldan held her phone up to Schäfer, who took it and looked at the picture.

He stood up and walked over to the doorway into the living room.

"And this couldn't be an old photo of yours that someone just copied?" He looked alternately down at the phone and over at the balcony.

"No, I've never seen this picture before."

Schäfer clicked on the profile of the person who had uploaded the picture. There was only the one post. No other pictures or any information about the user besides the profile name. Zero followers, zero following.

"You wouldn't believe how much harassment takes place through social media these days," he said. "Have you had anyone over to your place who might have taken the picture and who's just messing with you? It could easily be a photo one of your friends took last week or even last year."

"No. The only friends who ever come here to the apartment are people I trust."

"What about a romantic interest, perhaps? Or a bitter ex-boyfriend trying to scare you."

"No, I can't imagine that." An uncertainty crept into Heloise's voice.

"You're a reporter, right?" Schäfer asked, glancing at her.

"Yes, I work for *Demokratisk Dagblad*."

"Yeah, I thought I had seen your name in the paper. You're a pretty good writer."

"Thanks," she said with a shrug.

"Those papers over there." Schäfer nodded at the stack on the coffee table in the living room. "Are you working on a story about Mossing? Is that why you're seeing ghosts?"

"I've taken an interest in the case, yes, but this isn't just another day in the office for me. Something is going on here, and I—"

"Listen." He held up a hand to cut her off. "You don't have anything to worry about. There are strong indications that Anna Kiel isn't even in Denmark at the moment."

"I'm well aware of that," Heloise Kaldan said, standing up. "Only a week and a half ago she was in France, but I am telling you: she is here now."

That stopped Schäfer dead in his tracks.

He watched Heloise Kaldan in silence as she walked over to a black shoulder bag hanging on a hook next to her refrigerator and pulled something out of it.

"I'm not seeing ghosts." She came over to him and handed him two light-blue envelopes. "Anna Kiel is trying to tell me something."

9

ANNA HAD TO wait a long time before she heard his voice over the phone. She had managed to find one of the few old-time phone booths that still remained in Dijon. Most of the others had been decommissioned a long time ago and replaced with, well, nothing. All over the city were empty, ugly street corners with withered wires, cut off and sticking out of the concrete like ghastly artworks from a bygone era.

"Nick?"

"Yes."

"It's me."

"Yeah, I figured. No one else calls me."

"I've moved on. North. I think someone saw me."

"Someone saw you? Who, him?" He sounded concerned.

"No, some woman. It's probably nothing, but I couldn't stay there any longer."

"Anna, if you see him—or anyone who even looks like him—you get the hell out of Dodge, you've got that?"

"Yes."

"I'm serious. He won't hesitate for a second to kill you. You have no idea how dangerous that man is."

"Yes, Nick, I do." Her tone was icy. "Maybe even better than you, so quit talking to me as if it's your job to take care of me. I'm not your daughter."

There was a pause before he cautiously asked, "So what else is new? Did you send the letter?"

"I've sent two."

"Okay, good. Good."

"You promised me the information about the hotel?"

"Yes. It's a place called the Grand Hyatt Martinez. It's in Cannes."

"When does he stay there?"

"The first three weeks of June. It's the same every year."

"Alone?"

"In principle, yes. He travels alone, but I don't know whether or not he sees anyone while he's there . . ."

An uncomfortable silence arose between them.

"And the files?" Anna asked.

"You'll get the rest of yours once I have mine," he said. "Just make sure to get Heloise to Paris."

"Hey, Nick?"

"Yes?"

"How's your conscience?"

He laughed, a sad, hollow laughter.

"Not so good," he admitted. "How about yours?"

She thought about it for a second.

"Fine," she said, and hung up.

10

H ELOISE STOOD AT the kitchen sink, scrubbing black ink off her fingers with a hard nail brush. The guy from the National Forensics Center had asked for her fingerprints before he left. "Just for elimination," he'd said. With nearly clean fingers, she got a bunch of tomatoes and two peaches out of a bowl on the windowsill and took a big ball of buffalo mozzarella out of the fridge.

"I've had virtually nothing to eat all day, and if this lasts much longer, I'm going to die hungry," she told Schäfer.

Without taking his eyes off the letters on the table in front of him, he waved his hand to signal *Knock yourself out.*

Heloise watched him on the sly as she rinsed the tomatoes and peaches and cut them up. There was something about his overwhelmingly masculine presence that made her feel like Tony Soprano was sitting in her kitchen. She almost expected him to switch from speaking Danish to speaking English with a Jersey accent. He seemed at once violently authoritarian, potentially fear inspiring, and—most of all—extremely charming.

"What about you? Are you hungry?" she asked. "Can I offer you a bit of an early dinner?"

She set a bunch of basil and a handful of mint leaves onto the big wooden cutting board in front of her and started chopping up the herbs.

Schäfer glanced at the food she had set out on the kitchen table and shook his head regretfully. "I'd love to, but my doctor told me I should be thinking a little more about what I eat."

"And let me guess." Heloise looked at him with a raised eyebrow. "Your thoughts mostly revolve around big, juicy steaks?"

"Bingo!"

Heloise nodded.

His gut and ruddy skin suggested eating habits that were anything but healthy. And he smoked. She could smell the nicotine from all the way across the kitchen.

"But I'll bet you could drink one of these." She opened a cold Heineken and handed it to him.

"Well, since it's already open," he said, accepting it.

Heloise arranged all the ingredients on a plate. She drizzled cold-pressed virgin olive oil on them, ground a little salt and pepper over the plate, and sprinkled the finely chopped herbs on top. Then she sat down across from Schäfer and started eating it right out of the serving dish.

"What's your theory about Christoffer Mossing?" she asked. "Everything in his life seemed like it was all sunshine and vintage wine until Anna Kiel took it all away from him. Do you believe the glamour-shot version, or do you think there's more to it than that?"

"Well, for starters, there's no indication that he was anything but a nice guy—as nice a guy as any lawyer can be, that is." Schäfer's gaze fell on the salad. "Say, is that what you eat when you're famished? A little fruit salad and a lump of cheese? No meat, no bread—nothing?"

Heloise shrugged. "I'm not a big fan of meat."

Schäfer wrinkled his nose in disapproval. Then he shook his head and continued. "Anyways. Mossing was a criminal defense lawyer, so he obviously represented a lot of assholes—*rich* assholes, mind you—and he was good at it too."

"Then there must have been a lot of people who had a grudge against him. His competitors, for example. Wouldn't a man like him have a lot of enemies?"

"Oh, there were a lot of people who didn't like him for a variety of reasons. But there was only one who murdered him."

Heloise thought as she chewed. "Is it really true that after the murder she stood in front of the security camera in his driveway and stared into the lens for several minutes?"

"Mm-hmm." Schäfer took a swig of the beer without taking his eyes off her.

"And there's no chance that you're wrong? That Anna Kiel was framed and that someone is just trying to make it look like she's the murderer?"

"If we imagine that someone forced her into the house against her will, killed Christoffer Mossing while she protested, planted her fingerprints on the murder weapon, *and* covered her in his blood, then yes."

"Hmm."

Schäfer shook his head. "Let me put it like this: I would be amazed if we were wrong."

Heloise nodded hesitantly. "But why in the world did she do it?" she asked.

"Why did she do any of it? Why did she kill him, why did she gaze enigmatically into the camera, and why is she sending you letters now, so long after the fact—assuming that the letters really are from her, that is?"

"Don't you have any theories?" Heloise asked. "About the motive, I mean."

"Nothing concrete. Maybe the voices in her head made her do it; maybe she had seen Mossing on the street or in line at the grocery store and deluded herself into believing he was a threat to be eliminated. She must have had *some* reason to do what she did, but there doesn't seem to have been a *rational* reason. As I'm sure you read in the tabloids' coverage of the case, Anna had been ill for a long time, and a number of different school psychologists confirmed that she was a deeply troubled young woman who had shown signs of psychopathy at an early age. They don't call it that anymore, by the way—now it's called 'antisocial personality disorder,'—but whatever you name it, it's still a real shit show."

"Antisocial personality disorder," Heloise repeated. She opened a notepad lying on the table and clicked a ballpoint pen. "What does that mean, specifically?"

"You can put that away," Schäfer said, nodding at the pen. "What we're discussing here is off the record."

"Okay, off the record." Heloise clapped her notepad closed again and pushed it aside. "What does antisocial personality disorder mean?"

"People who suffer from it become aggressive easily, and they treat other people with callous indifference. They react violently to their emotions and simply don't understand that their actions have consequences. *Nothing* is their fault—it's *always* someone else's fault. In other words, they're completely insane."

"And you said that Anna's school psychologist supported the diagnosis?"

"Psychologists, plural. She was expelled from a number of different schools. She threatened a math teacher at one of them. Called his wife at their home and said she was going to shoot him when he biked to school the next day. Apparently she wasn't fond of algebra."

"And at the next school?"

"At the next school, she hit a classmate in the face with a tennis racket during PE. He'd allegedly been peeping into the girls' locker room while they were changing." Schäfer finished his beer. "It cost him a broken nose."

Heloise instinctively reached for the bridge of her nose.

"Well yeah, that *does* sound crazy," she said. "Why didn't she end up in a psychiatric ward or something like that?"

"Because she was only twelve years old at the time, and because the police weren't involved. No one reported it. No one spoke up. Everything was dealt with in-house with a little guitar playing and sitting in a circle and talking about feelings."

"Dealt with? It doesn't sound like anything was dealt with."

"Really, you think?"

"What about her parents? Where were they?"

"I didn't get the impression that they took much of an interest in their daughter. The father took a job in Greenland when Anna was eight or nine, and then he hooked up with a hot young gal up there. He and the mother got divorced, and he had a new litter of kids. He completely vanished from Anna's life after that."

"And the mother? There was something about her owning a pub in Herlev?"

"Yes, the Lantern."

"What's she like?"

"Pretty lady, a philosophy professor."

"Seriously?"

"No, not seriously. She's a pub owner. Use your imagination."

Heloise sat up straighter, somewhat baffled. On the one hand, she appreciated his dry, undiplomatic style. She had always preferred people who called it as they saw it. In her opinion, an honest insult was far preferable to a polite lie. At the same time, she was kind of stunned that a man in his position would label people so carelessly.

"If there's anything I've learned over twenty-eight years of police work, it's how to read people," Schäfer said, as if he could read her too. "And they usually live down to my expectations."

"What's that supposed to mean?"

"It means that people rarely diverge from the stereotypes. The happy hooker, the honest politician, the gold medalist who doesn't use performance-enhancing drugs? Forget about it. They don't exist."

"What about the objective journalist?"

"Objectivity doesn't exist, particularly not among journalists," Schäfer said, suppressing a grin. "For that, you are
all—forgive me for saying this—too self-absorbed. Don't get
me wrong, I have no doubt that you believe that your pursuit
of the truth is impartial. But when a murder suspect starts
sending you personalized messages, it's not *her* role in the
case that interests you the most, it's yours. And don't tell me
that you don't get off on seeing your byline in the newspaper."

"Is there something wrong with that?" Heloise crossed
her arms.

"No, not in the least, but it is ego driven."

"And when you throw a criminal behind bars, you do
it exclusively for the sake of maintaining order in society? It
doesn't do anything for your ego?"

"Yeah, sure, it makes me feel like I'm a hell of a guy,"
he nodded. "My point is really just that most of us meet the
expectations other people have of us. And there's a reason
very few people trust journalists. You almost always have
your own agendas."

Heloise pushed the plate aside.

"Ellen Mossing didn't seem to have any reservations," she
said, standing up. "Would you like another beer? Or a cup
of coffee?"

Schäfer shook his head.

"Ellen Mossing?" he asked. "You talked to her?"

"Yes, today. I had just left her house when the picture
appeared on Instagram."

"Well, I'll be damned!?" Schäfer said, leaning back in his
chair and folding his hands behind his head. "I'm amazed she
let you in. Johannes Mossing has been a complete nightmare
to work with."

"In what way?"

"In every way."

"Well, he wasn't particularly excited to see me either, I'll
tell you that much."

"What did you and Mrs. Mossing talk about?"

"Not that much. We didn't get very far in our conversation before Johannes Mossing came home and had the housekeeper show me out to my car."

"That sounds more like him," Schäfer said with a nod.

"Why hasn't he been cooperative? That seems so odd. Surely he's just as interested in getting his son's killer convicted as you are, right?"

Schäfer didn't answer the question. He pointed instead to the two letters on the table in front of him. "Do you have a couple of freezer bags I could put these in?"

Heloise was about to protest, but he held up a hand to stop her.

"They're probably already covered in fingerprints from all kinds of other people, but they should be checked anyway. There is also a chance that the sender's DNA is in the glue strip closure."

Heloise had already taken pictures of the letters with her iPhone and uploaded copies to the cloud. She got him a couple of plastic bags.

Schäfer put his gloves back on and placed each of the letters into its own bag.

"What should I do now?" Heloise asked.

Schäfer got up and zipped up his caramel-colored suede jacket. He pulled his wallet out of his back pocket and handed her his card.

"Let me know if you get any more letters or any other mysterious Instagram posts, but other than that? Just take it easy and keep your eyes and your ears open." He glanced around. "Do you have a boyfriend or someplace else you could stay tonight?"

Heloise shook her head.

"Then make sure you keep your door closed and locked the whole time." He held out his hand to say good-bye, and Heloise took it.

"You didn't answer my question about Johannes Mossing," she said. "Why doesn't he want to cooperate with the police?"

Schäfer hesitated a moment. Then he said, "I think he's got his own people looking for her."

"Are you serious?" The idea was so absurd that it almost made Heloise laugh. "What do you think he's planning to do if he finds her?"

Schäfer started moving toward the front hall.

"Just make sure you keep your door locked," he repeated, and left the apartment.

Heloise walked out onto the balcony and watched as he crossed the street in front of her building and got into a black Opel Astra, which was parked half up on the sidewalk.

After he drove away, she started cleaning up after her dinner, but her head felt like a pinball machine with a hundred balls zipping around at the same time, so she left the dishes and went to bed with her clothes on even though it was still light out.

Sleep didn't find her right away, though. The late-summer bird calls outside cut through the air like stray bullets, disturbing the peace. She pressed a pillow over her ear and waiting until the roiling surf in her inner sea slowly but surely started to subside.

11

A NOISE FROM SOMEWHERE outside woke her up. Or was it the strangely prevalent silence in the building that had awakened her? Heloise lay there for a moment, sleepily blinking with her eyes half open, as she listened.

Ten heartbeats ticked by.

Nothing.

Her eyes closed, and she was starting to doze off when she heard it again. Something moving. A quiet, scraping sound.

She sat up in bed.

What's that? Was the sound coming from the stairwell? Or from the living room?

She swung her legs over the edge of the bed, touched down quietly, and walked over to grab the baseball bat leaning in its regular spot in the corner.

In the open doorway to the living room, she tried to get her bearings in the darkness. She could sense all the contours of the room; nothing seemed out of place. There wasn't anything that stuck out.

She stood in silence and listened for a bit. Then she cautiously stepped into the living room with the bat raised high over her shoulder, ready to swing.

Nothing in here. What about the kitchen?

Heloise noticed a little light under the door in the front hall and a shadow moving on the other side of the door. She was so quiet that she could hear her pulse in her ears as she slowly walked across the floorboards, trying to avoid the ones that creaked.

Her face was only a few inches from the peephole when there was a firm knock on her door.

She took a frightened step back and tripped over her computer bag. The baseball bat hit the bare wood floor with a bang, and she fumbled frantically after it in the dark.

"Heloise?"

The voice on the other side of the door brought her to a sudden stop.

"Heloise, I can hear you in there. Open the door!"

Relief and then anger welled up inside her.

She got up and turned on the light. Then she decisively undid the lock and flung open the door.

"What the hell are you doing here in the middle of the night?" Her voice sounded three octaves higher than usual— hysterical and aggrieved. "For crying out loud, I thought someone was breaking into my apartment."

Martin Duvall gazed at her blankly, his eyes looking her over.

"It's only ten fifteen. You were asleep already?" He reached out a hand to touch her face. "You have pillow marks on your cheek."

Heloise pulled her head away. "What do you want?" she asked, her arms around herself. She was cold and tired and all too aware that she looked like someone who had slept in her clothes, while he stood there in his tailor-made suit, clean and pleasant smelling and just . . . handsome. He was always so infuriatingly handsome.

Fuck.

"I really want to talk to you," he replied. "Can I come in?"

"No." She grabbed the doorknob and blocked him from entering with her body.

"I've called and texted you a hundred times. Why don't you answer your phone?"

"Because you can't possibly have anything to say that I want to hear."

"Heloise, I swear. I didn't know anything about those documents being—"

"It doesn't matter."

"Just *listen*, would you? I didn't know—"

"No, you listen to *me*," she said in a calm, icy voice. "It doesn't *matter* why you did what you did. I don't care. Do you understand? I don't care about your explanation, and I don't care about you. Go home, Martin."

"You don't care?" His eyes sought to make eye contact with hers.

Heloise didn't look at him.

Martin shook his head. "You *do* care."

"Just go home," she repeated, and started closing the door.

He put a hand on the outside of it.

"I quit my job," he said.

His words stopped Heloise.

"That's what I've been trying to tell you," he continued. "You're not the only one who got screwed over. You're not the only one who was used."

He sounded tired, not like he had given up or been beaten, just exhausted.

When Heloise finally spoke, it was through the half-closed door. "Did you really quit your job?"

"Yes."

"Why?"

"Because I realized what had happened when your story got shot down last Thursday." He carefully pushed the door open a couple of inches so he could see her.

Their eyes met.

"I wasn't lying to you," he said. "I didn't know."

There was a long moment of silence between them.

Then she took a step back and opened the door all the way.

12

ONE OF HIS front teeth was crooked. It was also a little bit bigger and darker than the other one. It was the only feature of Martin Duvall's face that wasn't completely symmetrical. Maybe that was why Heloise liked that tooth so much; there was something so disarming about his imperfect smile.

"Are you planning to come forward with what you know?" she asked as they sat together over the tea tray in her kitchen having coffee the next morning.

"Publicly, you mean?"

"Yes."

Martin turned toward the window, and a ray of sunlight hit his face and his bare chest. He closed his eyes for a second. "I don't really see that I have any other choice."

"It wouldn't be particularly good for your career," she reminded him.

"If I were worried about that kind of thing, I would have stayed at the ministry."

"How high up do you think this goes? Who gave you the documents?"

"Carsten Holm," he replied, finishing the last of the coffee in his cup.

"The Sun King?"

Holm was the Danish secretary of commerce's right-hand man and spin doctor. A tall and seemingly perpetually suntanned man who was almost as well known in journalistic circles for his fondness for cocaine and women as for being an unmatched strategist.

"What are the chances that the secretary knew?" she asked.

"Oh, he must have known," Martin said. "He might even be the one who thought the whole thing up. Who knows?"

Heloise contemplated the potential ramifications if that theory proved true. If the secretary of commerce had fed the press fake documents to cause trouble for one of the country's largest corporations in order to save Danish jobs, that would be the biggest political scandal of the year. He would be forced to step down—if he didn't sacrifice his next-in-command instead.

"How was Holm even aware that you and I know each other?" she asked. "Why would he ask you to bring me, specifically, those papers?"

Martin coughed into his fist and got up from the table. "Is it okay if I make some more coffee?" he asked. "Would you like another cup too?"

"Yes, please."

He walked over to the machine and made two espressos. He poured a splash of 2 percent milk into the frother and turned it on without putting the lid on. Little white splatters flew through the air, landing on the skin of his stomach.

He took a teaspoon and put a little of the foam into Heloise's cup, just the way she liked it, then walked back to the table and handed it to her.

"Here you go."

"Thank you." She drank a sip. "Martin?"

"Yes?" He glanced down at her.

"I asked you a question."

"Christ, Helo, you ask so many questions." He squirmed a little and smiled at her. "Holm was aware that we knew each other because I told him, okay?"

"Why did you do that?" Heloise eyed him perplexedly.

"Why do you think?" He flung up his arms. "Because I'm crazy about you."

"Oh." She blinked a couple of times.

Martin sat down across from her. Her chair scraped across the wooden floor as he pulled it closer. "For an investigative journalist, you can be pretty slow on the uptake. You know that, right?"

He leaned forward and kissed her.

Heloise didn't know what to say. So many thoughts were flying around in her head.

"Well, if you're planning to go public with that story, then we'd better get a move on it," she said, straightening up in her chair.

"Okay."

Martin stood up and vanished into the bedroom for a minute. When he came back, he had put most of his clothes on.

"How should we approach this?" He leaned against the kitchen doorframe as he buttoned up his shirt. "Should we just sit down and go through the whole thing word for word, or what were you planning?"

"Well, for starters, I can't write the story," Heloise said. "We have to find another journalist."

"Why?"

"Because I'm too involved in the Skriver case, and my credibility is already shot to shit." She ran her eyes up and down his body as he tucked his shirt into his trousers. "It also doesn't help that I'm sleeping with the main source."

"Well, when you put it that way . . ." Martin shrugged in acceptance.

Heloise stood up and carried the coffee cups over to the kitchen sink and the tower of dirty dishes that were already there.

"There's another investigative journalist on my team," she said. "Mogens Bøttger. He's really good, and you can trust him."

"Okay."

Martin was on his way over to her when he noticed something on the floor.

He bent down and picked it up.

" 'Sergeant Detective Erik Schäfer, Copenhagen Police, Violent Crimes Unit,' " he read aloud, and gave Heloise a questioning look. "Why do you have this lying around?"

Heloise hesitated for a moment. Then she shook her head and shooed him out of the kitchen.

"I'll tell you about that later. First we need to see if we can catch Mogens at the paper."

* * *

Martin's hand found hers on the ride up to the third floor. Heloise pulled her hand away as soon as the elevator doors opened.

"It's this way," she said, leading him down the editorial office's hallway.

"Is this where you work every day?" He peered around.

Heloise nodded. "Well, I stop by almost every day," she clarified. "I do most of my work out in the world, meeting with sources, visits to various archives—you know, generally sniffing around in places where I'm not wanted. The people's watchdog and all that."

Seeing Martin here at the paper felt strange and far more intimate than lying in bed with him at home had. It was as if the whole building were holding its breath, as if the portraits of the old editors in chief were following them with their eyes as they walked down the hallway.

They found Bøttger sitting in his usual spot, leaning back with his legs crossed, propped up on his desk. He was busy impressing a young intern, who was standing in front of him hugging a case file, with an anecdote from his life as a prizewinning reporter. When he saw Heloise approaching, he instantly lost interest in the young woman and shooed her away.

Heloise stopped at her own desk and raised her eyebrows as she watched the woman walk away. Then she turned her attention to Bøttger.

"You do know you're supposed to keep your mitts off the interns, don't you, Mogens?"

"What, her? Please," he scoffed. "I'd hoped you would think more highly of me than that, Kaldan."

Heloise decided to drop the collegial teasing—a game they both really enjoyed playing and would normally keep at for hours.

Heloise pointed to Martin beside her. "Mogens, I'd like to introduce you to Martin Duvall."

Bøttger stood up and held out a hairy paw the size of a baseball mitt.

"Hi," he said. "Mogens."

"Martin Duvall."

"Martin is the head of communications at the Ministry of Commerce," Heloise explained. "Or rather, he *was* up until a few days ago. He just quit."

"Oh?"

"Yeah, it turns out that something really suspicious has been going on in the ministry lately, something that could potentially bring down the secretary of commerce, or at least knock his sunburned number two off his high horse."

"Oh?" Bøttger's expression revealed a growing interest in the story.

"That's why it occurred to me that—since I'm busy on a case that would normally fall under your area of expertise—maybe you could be convinced to take on one of my stories?"

Bøttger closed one eye and zoomed in on her with the other.

"What is this about, exactly?"

Heloise looked over her shoulder before answering, "The Skriver case."

* * *

In the lobby, Heloise was given a key to one of the company cars. She had left Martin in a room with Mogens Bøttger, a pot of coffee, and a Dictaphone. She knew Bøttger well enough to know they wouldn't come back out again until he had vacuumed every conceivable speck of thought or detail about the case out of the remotest corners of Martin's mind.

Heloise left the paper and walked over toward St. Ann's Square, where the Ford was parked. She had tried to reach Anna Kiel's mother by phone, to no avail. Now she wanted to see if she could catch her at her pub in Herlev.

It was still pretty early, but Store Strandstræde was already buzzing with life. The café across from the paper was teeming with young guys, who sat in the sun drinking hipster juice while admiring each other's tattooed toothpick arms and unruly beards. Heloise didn't understand how that kind of exaggerated facial hairiness could have become popular among men in their twenties. To her it was the equivalent of shaving out a bald spot or emphasizing the age lines on your face with a Sharpie.

She walked quickly down the street and didn't notice Ulrich Andersson until he came right up beside her and grabbed her by the arm.

"Keep walking," he said, guiding her firmly down Store Strandstræde.

Heloise instinctively looked over her shoulder but kept going without resisting. "Ulrich? What's wrong?"

She had almost forgotten about her call to him the other day. She hadn't seen him since he'd quit the paper and hadn't had much to do with him when they did work together. But she remembered him as a headstrong macho guy, the type who didn't give a shit about the newspaper's smoking rules or ethical guidelines and basically did as he pleased.

Now he seemed more like a draft beer that had been sitting out in the sun for too long. His reddish-blond hair was gathered together at the nape of his neck in a loose ponytail under a faded blue New York Yankees baseball cap, which covered his balding head, and his clothes hung, threadbare and far too big, off his bony body.

"Where's the car?" He looked down at the keys in Heloise's hand.

"Right up here," she replied, gesturing up ahead with a nod.

"Okay, we're going for a ride." He held out his hand.

"I'll drive," Heloise clarified, clutching the car keys.

CHAPTER

13

THE PAIN ZIGZAGGED up through Stefan's arm as he lit the lighter. He swore under his breath and exhaled the smoke hard through his nose. The radiologist had called it a "fracture of the fourth metacarpal" and asked how it had happened. "A work injury," he had replied, secretly amused.

Three weeks ago, a high school teacher from Risskov had become a problem, suddenly remorseful and falling apart. Stefan had been assigned to take care of it, and at first he had tried to talk some sense into the guy, appealing to his inner demons. When that didn't work, he had threatened the man's family.

Initially, it had seemed to have had an effect. It always did. But Stefan had sensed that the man was still having doubts, and they quite simply couldn't afford to gamble with the business. There was too much money at stake, too many lives that would be ruined by a defector with moral scruples. If he wasn't onboard, he'd be thrown overboard. Simple as that.

The man had fought for his life.

Who would have thought that an elf of a man with such long, flimsy fingers could put up so much resistance and fight back so well? He had flailed wildly in the air and hit Stefan with a couple of decent blows before Stefan had pacified him with a closed-fist punch right under the jaw.

The man had folded like a defective beach chair and hit the ground with a dull thump.

Stefan had observed him, unconscious, vulnerable. He'd looked so fragile, like a newly laid egg. A single blow in the right place would have cracked his skull open.

Stefan had felt a desire bubble up in his chest, the desire to place the man's head at a particularly vulnerable angle, fetch the sledgehammer from the toolbox in his pickup, and swing it in a fireworks display of blood, brain matter, and shards of cranium, but no. That would've have made too much of a mess, and there hadn't been time for that.

Instead he had tied the rope around the man's neck, tightened it, and waited.

When he had sailed out of the Aarhus marina a half hour later, he'd pushed the lifeless body over the side of the boat and stared down into the water for a long time after the man with the iron chain wound around his torso had sunk so far down into the dark water that he couldn't be seen anymore.

The media had been all over it at first. Now the East Jutland Police had decided to shelve the investigation pending new leads or evidence, but the man's family hadn't given up. A support group had been set up on Facebook, where the family asked people to help search for him. Hundreds of volunteers had wandered the streets of Aarhus, combing through cellars, wells, dumpsters, and harbor basins in the hopes of finding him.

In the beginning, Stefan had followed the news and "liked" every update and every photo the family posted. Now he only thought about the man when his hand hurt.

He put out his cigarette and was about to pull out a fresh pack when the front door of the *Demokratisk Dagblad* offices opened and the journalist stepped out onto the sidewalk.

It hadn't been more than twenty minutes since he'd watched her go in. She had been with a man then, a boy-friend perhaps? At any rate, Stefan had watched them leave her place earlier that morning, not hand in hand but *together* all the same.

Now she stood there alone. She looked so strong and self-assured. He didn't relish the thought of hurting her if things went that far. But he would do it all the same.

He stuck the pack of cigarettes back into the pocket of his denim jacket and followed her as she began to make her way down Store Strandstræde. He stayed a good distance behind her and stuck to the other side of the street as he watched her. She had an aura about her that made him think of an old painting he had seen as a child in a religious book at school, of Moses parting the Red Sea. In the picture, the waters had divided and looked like they were bowing in submission so that Moses could walk across the seafloor. In the same way, people now seemed to be moving out of the woman's way.

At first, he didn't recognize the man who appeared by her side and grabbed her arm. If it hadn't been for the baffled expression that briefly flashed over her face, he would have assumed the man was a friend, because she didn't slow down or break the rhythm of her stride. Instead, the two of them proceeded down the street, arm in arm.

Stefan followed them down to St. Ann's Square and watched them get into a dark-blue Ford Focus. It wasn't until the car pulled out into the lane of traffic and the man in the passenger's seat turned his face toward the windshield that Stefan recognized him.

He felt his pulse speed up as rage and euphoria flapped like frightened birds inside his rib cage.

He pulled his work phone out of his pants pocket and called. The call was answered after two rings, not with a greeting but with resounding silence.

"Hello?" Stefan said.

"Yes?"

"Yeah, hi. It's me. I'm standing here watching—"

"I'm busy. What do you want?"

"It's about the woman, the reporter."

"What about her?"

"The police were at her apartment last night."

Nothing.

"A couple of officers arrived first—nothing special," Stefan continued. "But then Schäfer turned up too. He wasn't there very long, but he was there."

"Where's the woman now?"

"I just saw her leave the newspaper. She got into a car and drove away. She was with Ulrich Andersson."

There was silence on the other end of the line for a few seconds. Then: "Goddamned journalists."

"Right. Him."

"Find out what he told her."

"Should I do anything else?" Stefan made a fist with his right hand, one finger at a time, and closed his eyes as the pain sliced upward through his arm.

With the exception of heavy, accelerated breathing, the line went silent again. And then: "I was under the impression that you had already had a serious talk with him?"

"I did."

"Hmm. It doesn't quite appear to have had the desired effect."

"Clearly not."

"That's a real shame."

"Yes," Stefan said. He had to bite his lip to keep from smiling. "A real shame."

*   *   *

Heloise unbuckled her seat belt and turned to Ulrich Andersson.

"Ulrich, honestly, you look like shit. What is going on here? Are you on drugs?"

She had parked the car on a deserted street down by the water at the easternmost point on Refshale Island, where they were surrounded by nothing but gravel, trees, and the gray-black sea. Ulrich had directed her there with succinct, breathless driving directions.

Take a right, go straight, turn here.

Those were the only things he had said the whole way there.

He now peered tiredly through the windshield. "You said she had written a letter to you."

"Anna Kiel?" Heloise asked. "Yes, two letters, actually."

"How do you know it's her?"

"I guess I don't," Heloise said with a shrug. "Not yet, anyway. The police have the letters and are examining them for fingerprints and DNA. But they were signed with her name and they referred to the murder case from Taarbæk."

"What did she say?"

"Ulrich, what's going on with you? Are you okay?"

"Just tell me what she wrote." He turned and looked at Heloise, his eyes vacant.

"Not a whole lot," she replied. "Mostly just incoherent nonsense, riddles, something about flowers and lucky numbers. She says that we're connected and that I need to write her story."

"Did she write anything about Mossing?"

"Just that he bled to death and that she had enjoyed watching it happen."

"No, not Christoffer Mossing. I'm talking about the father—Johannes. Did she write anything about him?"

"No," Heloise said, puzzled. "Why would she write about him?"

"I don't know, but there's something there," he mumbled, shaking his head in confusion. He seemed lost for a moment, and Heloise noticed that his shirt collar had grown dark blue with sweat.

"You mean that stuff about him having his own people looking for her?" she asked, leaning toward him.

Ulrich Andersson looked up. "Heloise, I need you to listen to me." He took a firm hold of her shoulder. "Stay far away from those people. Stay away from that case!"

Heloise twisted away from his grasp. "You're going to have to use a few more words here, Ulrich," she said, annoyed. "You're not making any sense."

A motorcycle appeared out of nowhere and roared past the parked car.

Ulrich jumped an inch or two off the Ford's dark-gray polyester seat, and he peered around, panic-stricken.

"Whoa, Ulrich, relax." Heloise tried speaking to him in a soothing voice. It was like approaching a startled horse at the far end of a paddock. His eyes seemed feverish and disoriented, and every muscle in his body looked tense, ready to flee.

"Calm down, man. It's just you and me here," she said. "It's just the two of us—there's nothing to be afraid of."

"I don't know what it is, but something is going on." He almost seemed to be talking to himself. "I was on the case back then, and I just followed the clues."

"What clues?"

"He might be getting old now, but there was a time when he was calling all the shots."

"Who?"

"Mossing, dammit! It's Mossing, don't you get it?"

"Johannes Mossing?"

"He loaned them money, and when they couldn't pay . . ." He started laughing—a nervous, borderline-hysterical laughter. "It's was like something straight out of *The Godfather*, Heloise. Pure fucking *Godfather*."

"Who did he loan money to?"

"Players, gamblers, at the track."

"Horse racing?" Heloise knew nothing about that sort of thing.

"Yes, in Klampenborg. He loaned people money in exchange for a percentage of the winnings—with interest, of course—and we're talking large sums, Heloise, not just chump change. And when people couldn't pay what they owed . . ." He closed his eyes and shook his head. "Then they disappeared."

"What do you mean?"

"People *disappeared*," he repeated. "Do you understand what I'm telling you?"

Heloise sat silently in her seat.

"How do you know all this?" she asked.

"I received a tip one day at the paper, while I was writing about the son's murder."

"A tip from who?"

"I don't know. It was an anonymous call, just a few catch-words: *Check out the racetrack, ask about Mossing, you'll see.* I went out there and asked around a little, but no one knew anything. At least no one who would talk."

"What did you do then?"

"I knew one of the old jockeys from Andy's Bar—you know the five o'clock dive on Gothersgade?"

Heloise nodded.

"I got in touch with him, and I assured him that he could talk to me off the record . . ."

"And?"

He looked straight into Heloise's eyes. "He told me the sickest things. Things you couldn't imagine even in your most fucked-up nightmare."

Heloise tried to swallow, but her mouth was dry. "What did he say?"

"You don't want to know," Ulrich said, shaking his head.

"No, I *do* want to know," Heloise insisted.

"No," he repeated. "If they find out that I talked to you . . . The less you know, the safer you are."

"But what does this gambling operation have to do with the son's murder?" Heloise asked.

"I don't know, maybe nothing. Maybe Mossing just doesn't want the police sniffing around his business activities."

Heloise thought again about Schäfer's theory that Mossing had assigned his own people to search for Anna Kiel.

"Do you think he's willing to let his own son's murderer go free in order to avoid that?"

"I don't know, but one thing is for sure," Ulrich said. "He is a raving lunatic. I went straight home from Klampenborg that day, and the next thing I know, I wake up in the middle of the night and there's a man standing next to my bed, jamming a gun into my mouth." A suppressed sob slipped from his lips. "It left abrasions way down inside my throat."

"Jesus Christ, Ulrich." Heloise held a hand up in front of her mouth. "Who was it? Mossing?"

"No, I'd never seen him before. He had dark hair, a stocky build. He said that my family would have to scrape me off the headboard if I didn't stop asking questions about Mossing and his son's murder."

"Did you go to the police?"

"No, hell no. I just tried to put all this shit behind me. I quit my job and I thought that would help, but . . ." His voice broke. "It has fucked me up. I can't sleep at night. I take pills to . . ." He searched for words for a moment and then gave up without finishing whatever he had started to say. "You have to forget all about this case, Heloise. Do not contact Mossing."

"But I can't—"

"Stay away from those people, I'm telling you! They're fucking insane!" Then he opened the car door without warning and got out without closing it behind him.

Heloise called after him. "Ulrich, where are you going? Come back!"

He had already started walking away down the dirt road.

Heloise leaned across the passenger seat, grabbed hold of the door, and slammed it closed. She pulled up alongside him and rolled the window down.

"Come on, get in. You've got to go to the police with this."

Ulrich Andersson didn't respond. Instead he turned off the road and walked away across a stubbly meadow, heading for a wooded area on the far side.

When Heloise called out to him again, he sped up.

14

THE SERVE HIT the net for the third time in a row, and the boy kicked the sand in frustration, stirring up a big cloud of dust around himself. The beige-colored particles landed on his long, moist eyelashes and in his frizzy hair.

He picked up the volleyball again and walked back over to position himself behind the line in the serving zone. He calmly looked straight ahead and composed himself for a moment. Then he threw the ball high into the air and leapt up, with both feet off the ground, before hitting the ball with a hard, overhand serve.

The ball flew through the air and landed inside the lines on the opposite side of the net.

"You did it, champ! Well done." Stefan cheered loudly and clapped despite the pain in his hand.

The boy jumped, turning in the direction the voice had come from and looking for the source of the cheering. He squinted and held his hand up to shield him from the evening sun, which hung low in a sky filled with soft cauliflower clouds.

Most of the other kids had left Amager Beach Park along with the experienced recreational athletes and kitesurfers, and there weren't any other beach volleyball players on the court aside from the boy. He hadn't noticed his audience until now and slowly nodded in appreciation. Then he walked over to a neon-green sports bag that lay in the sand to the right of the court.

Stefan watched while the boy packed his water bottle and a black Ninjago beach towel into it. Then the boy tossed the bag over his shoulder and hurried over to retrieve his white Spalding ball from the sand. He jogged over to a mountain bike, which was parked parallel to the bike path, close to the bench where Stefan had sat down to watch him.

When he knelt down in the grass to fumble with his bike lock, Stefan got up and strolled over there with his hands in his pocket and a filterless King's hanging loosely from his sun-cracked lips.

"You're really something with that volleyball there, huh?"

"Thank you." The boy stood up and secured the ball to his rear rack.

"What's your name?"

"Daniel."

"Daniel," Stefan repeated, looking the boy over. He was a handsome little guy with green eyes, suntanned skin, and fine freckles on his nose and cheeks.

"Where are you headed, Daniel?"

"Home." The boy looked down at his shoes as he spoke.

"Aw, that's too bad." Stefan took a puff from his cigarette and spit a fiber of tobacco out of his mouth. "It was so much fun watching you play."

"I promised my mom I'd be home for dinner."

"You live around here?" Stefan asked, looking around. He put his hand on the boy's shoulder.

"I promised my mom I'd be home by now," the boy repeated, and started pulling his bike down the bike path.

"What grade are you in?" Stefan continued. "Fourth? Fifth?" He accompanied the boy down the path without removing his hand from the boy's shoulder.

"Fifth."

"Fifth grade." Stefan whistled, impressed.

The boy twisted free and jumped on his bike. He pedaled hard without looking back.

"Well, have a good one, Daniel," Stefan called after him. "Catch you next time, huh?"

He kept watching the boy until he was nothing more than a dot far away down Amager Strandvej. Then he walked back to the bench and settled back down.

There still wasn't any sign of life in the apartment across the street. The building's glass facade allowed an unimpeded view of both the kitchen and living room, and both rooms were dark and empty. It didn't look anywhere near as cozy as the single-story house in Amager's Greektown neighborhood where Ulrich Andersson had been living the last time Stefan visited him. In fact, it didn't look at all cozy. Everything about the apartment was cold and modern, and it didn't seem like Andersson paid much attention to interior decorating now that his wife had left him.

Not that it mattered now, Stefan thought, looking at his watch.

When he looked up again, the light in the kitchen was on.

15

"HE SEEMED TOTALLY out of it," Heloise said. "I mean, almost crazy."

She squeezed the bottle tightly between her knees and, with a long, persistent tug, managed to get the cork out. She walked into the kitchen, grabbed two wineglasses, and returned to the balcony.

"Chardonnay?"

"Don't mind if I do," Gerda replied, drumming her chopsticks to the beat of Bruno Mars's "Treasure," which was pouring out of Heloise's iPhone on the folding table in front of them.

"Do you think we drink too much?" Heloise asked as she poured the wine. "In general, I mean."

"Yes," Gerda said promptly and without even a hint of shame.

Sometimes happiness was having a friend with the same vices as you, Heloise thought, and Gerda was her best—and in fact only—friend. The only person left in the world who knew her, really *knew* her.

For the first many years of their lives, they had lived next door to each other in the Yellow Houses—an ingenious moniker they'd come up with for some townhouses in Copenhagen's Frederiksstaden neighborhood that were—insert drum roll—yellow. On their first day at Nyboder Elementary School as six-year-olds, they had walked to school together hand in hand in matching pigtails and matching Danish-mailbox-red backpacks the size of little chest freezers on their backs.

Inseparable from day one.

At age ten they had smoked their first cigarette together, hidden away inside the cavernous beech-hedge-lined paths in King's Garden, the park surrounding Rosenborg Castle, and throughout their school days they had taken turns falling in love with the same boys. They had hated each other's enemies with great fervor, loved each other's families twice as passionately, and they had both cried (and cried and cried) the summer between second and third grade when Heloise's parents told her they were getting a divorce. "The two of us will never part," Gerda had said, and they'd sworn on it. Twenty-seven years later, that still held true.

"Maybe he *is* crazy," Gerda said, and started dividing the contents of an Onassis box from Sticks'n'Sushi between the two of them. "What did you say his name was?"

"Ulrich. And yeah, maybe. At any rate, Bøttger says he's been out on sick leave for a long time with stress or something like that."

"Yeah, but that doesn't make a person crazy."

"Then maybe it's anxiety or a depression or something."

"Again, that does not a crazy person make."

Gerda worked as a trauma psychologist for the Danish military, and she didn't let people play fast and loose with diagnoses—not even in jest. If out of frustration Heloise happened to call an exasperating source a schizophrenic douchebag or crack a joke about how she felt like she was suffering from PTSD after having completed a particularly demanding work assignment, Gerda would raise an eyebrow in a way that said *You have no idea what you're talking about.*

Gerda had been deployed multiple times to both Afghanistan and Iraq, and Heloise knew that five days a week Gerda listened to tales from the bottom of existence on down. She had seen and heard about more horrors in her six years with the military than most people did in a lifetime.

"All right, but he looked like someone who was on the verge of shitting himself, then. He had clearly worked himself up, and he seemed really terrified. I couldn't talk him down again," Heloise said.

"What is he afraid of?"

Heloise hadn't told Gerda what Ulrich had said about the man with the gun.

"He had the impression that they wanted him to mind his own business, or else . . ."

"They? Who's they?"

"I don't know. Johannes Mossing and his people, I guess."

Heloise arranged a little heap of pickled ginger on top of a big piece of shrimp tempura, dipped her masterpiece in soy sauce, and bit into it. She chewed for a long time before she was able to speak again.

"I can see that Mossing started investing in thoroughbreds back in 1982, and I know he has his own stud farm on the island of Funen. There are also a bunch of pictures of him at the racetrack in the newspaper's photographic archives, so he's definitely spent a lot of time out there."

"Thoroughbreds? That's what they use for harness racing at Klampenborg?"

"Yes, but Klampenborg is flat racing," Heloise said.

Gerda stared at her blankly from across the table.

"The track at Klampenborg is for flat racing, not harness racing," Heloise said. "Okay, so it's like this: There are nine racetracks in Denmark. Eight of them are for harness racing, but the ninth one is Klampenborg, which is a flat racing track."

"What's the difference?"

"In harness racing, the horse pulls a sulky with the driver sitting in it. Flat racing, on the other hand, is where a jockey sits on the horse's back. *That's* what they do at Klampenborg, like at Ascot or the Kentucky Derby. Anyway, Mossing's investments don't reveal anything other than him being interested in horses. Anything beyond that is baseless nonsense. For the time being, anyway."

"But this guy Ulrich thinks that Mossing has been acting as a loan shark, and that he—what—offs people who can't pay their debt?"

"Pretty much."

"Huh."

"Not a very realistic scenario, though, right?"

"I don't know about that," Gerda said with a shrug. "Every day I'm amazed at how fucked up the world actually is. While people are sitting around Instagramming their avocado toasts from a variety of lunch places in Copenhagen, the most grotesque things are happening in the apartments right above them."

"Surely not in all of them."

"No, but in too many of them." Gerda pushed her plate aside and leaned back in her chair. "What does all this have to do with his son's murder? Was Christoffer Mossing involved in the horse racing scene too?"

"No, according to the police, his murder was a fluke. They think Anna Kiel targeted a random person. She reportedly suffers from psychopathy."

"It's not called that anymore," Gerda said.

"Oh, come on. You know what I mean."

"What are they basing this on?"

"Statements from her school psychologists. Apparently, she has been pretty aggressive and unpredictable since she was about twelve years old."

"But again: what does harness racing have to do with Christoffer Mossing's murder?"

"Flat racing."

"Oh, come on. You know what I mean." Gerda smiled at Heloise.

"I don't know if there's a connection," Heloise said. "But Johannes Mossing hasn't been willing to cooperate with the police."

"No, and of course he wouldn't if he had something to hide."

"The policeman I talked to—"

"The one who looks like a mobster?"

"Yeah, that's the one. His theory is that Mossing has his own people searching for Anna Kiel."

"What do the police have to say about Ulrich Andersson's story?"

"He hasn't told them about it."

"Why not?" Gerda looked surprised.

"Because he's scared. But I'm going to talk to him again tomorrow and try to talk some sense into him."

"But if he's so scared, then why did he call you? Why get involved at all?"

"He didn't. I was the one who called him, and I think . . ." Heloise contemplated which words to use. "I think he just wanted to warn me."

"Huh." Gerda gathered her dark hair into a ponytail as she watched Heloise probingly. "But *you're* not scared, are you?"

"Me?" Heloise shrugged. "Do you think I should be?"

"I don't know. But maybe we should find you a man just to be on the safe side—a big, strong one. Big!" she repeated, holding out her hands in front of her with a considerable amount of space between them.

Heloise coughed into her fist and shifted in her chair.

"What?" Gerda raised her eyebrows.

"Nothing."

"Bullshit. What?"

"Martin spent the night here last night." Heloise bit her cheek a little.

Gerda smiled in a way that left her looking like a cat that had just swallowed a canary.

"He quit his job," Heloise continued. "He says he didn't know anything about the documents being forged and that it was probably the secretary of commerce or one of his top guys who was behind it." Heloise took a large drink of her wine and cleared her throat. "He says that he's, um, *crazy* about me." She made air quotes with her fingers. "But I don't know . . . I don't think I'm up for it, you know what I mean?"

"Can I be blunt?" Gerda asked.

"Aren't you always?"

"Maybe you should start letting someone in."

"What are you talking about?" Heloise tried to laugh, but it sounded more like a grunt. "I let *you* in, don't I?"

"I mean someone besides me. You need to start believing that life can be good again, and maybe Martin's just the ticket. 'Cause, honestly, you're becoming a little too cynical, hon. Let this guy in a little."

Heloise turned her face away from Gerda and looked out at the Marble Church. She took a deep breath and exhaled heavily.

"I miss the old days," she said.

"I know."

"I miss the life I once had, where everything just . . . made sense."

"I know." Gerda put her hand on Heloise's.

When Heloise's mother had died five years ago, it had been hard on her, sure. But truth be told, they hadn't really been all that close, and her mom had been sick for so long that it had almost been a relief that she was finally at peace.

But when she lost her father the following year, her world had stopped turning altogether.

For some reason, she hadn't been able to cry for him, though, hadn't shed a single tear. Instead, she had hardened, closed off. Made herself numb. It was like an underwater bomb had detonated inside her, and on the surface, it had made only a slight ripple, but in her inner abyss, the blast had destroyed everything.

"Mommy! Hello!" A high-pitched voice called loudly through the neighborhood.

Heloise and Gerda both turned toward the street and looked over the edge of the balcony.

On the fourth floor of the building across the street, a tan little hand stuck out of a window that was ajar.

"Hi, honey," Gerda yelled back.

"Hi, Lulu-mouse." Heloise waved with both arms. "Are you going to bed?"

"Yes. What are you doing?"

"We're eating sushi," Heloise replied.

"When are you coming home, Mommy?"

"I won't be long," Gerda yelled.

"Okay. Good night!"

"Good night, sweetie." Gerda blew a kiss to her six-year-old daughter.

"Is Christian home?" Heloise asked as the window across the street closed.

"No, he's in Singapore."

"Who's watching Lulu, then?"

"My mom, God bless her."

"Oh, sweet old Kamma," Heloise said, and put her hand over her heart. "I don't think I've seen her since—what—Christmas?"

"Sounds about right."

"Maybe we could all get together for a Sunday thing sometime soon?"

Gerda nodded.

Heloise loved that she and Gerda still lived so close to each other.

When Gerda had married Christian, Heloise had worried that they would become like every other married couple and move out into the suburban trenches into a soulless bunker of a single-family home with a chest freezer in the basement and an attic room filled with boxed-up memories from their youth together, but no. They had invested in a condo diagonally across from Heloise's. *Lulu needs her auntie,* they had said, and Heloise had wept with joy.

"By the way, did I tell you about my client who fell in love with me?" Gerda exclaimed.

"Aren't they *all* in love with you?"

The sight of Gerda routinely reduced people into gawking apes. Heloise had seen it happen more times than she could count. It wasn't just that Gerda was ridiculously good-looking—as in gorgeous in a drop-dead, otherworldly, you've-got-to-be-kidding-me kinda way. She was also somewhat like the riddle about the boy and his dad who've been in a car accident: The ambulance takes them to the hospital. The child is taken into one operating room and the father into another. Then the doctor comes into the boy's room, looks down at him, and says, "I can't operate on him—he's my son!" And then people rack their brains and wonder *How in the world can that be?*, when the obvious answer is that the doctor is the boy's mother.

Oh my God, a female surgeon? Shocking . . .

That's how it was with Gerda, too. People's expectations were always totally off, and it was because of her name. People simply couldn't imagine someone named Gerda being a complete knockout any more than they could image someone named Angelina being a five hundred-pound sumo wrestler with a goatee.

"No, they are not all in love with me; far from it," Gerda said. "Most of them are too busy having nightmares about IEDs and buddies who have to be shipped home in twelve pieces to even think about that kind of thing."

"IEDs?"

"Improvised explosive devices. Roadside bombs."

"Okay, so what about this client, then?"

"Well, he's been in therapy for about six months now, and last week he told me he was in love with me."

"Awkward."

"Yeah, a little. He doesn't know anything about me, of course, so it's just a projection. None of my clients know that I'm married, that I have Lulu, where I live, how old I am—nothing."

"How old is the guy?"

"Young. Ten years younger than us." Gerda pulled a pack of Camel Lights out of the inside pocket of her leather jacket and held up a hand before Heloise even had a chance to react. "I only smoke one a day, and that's okay," she announced in a tone that emphasized that the subject was not open for debate.

She struck a match and lit a cigarette.

"Well, so now this client has started *cyberstalking* me. He sent me a long declaration of his love on Facebook. I was forced to block him." She took a drag, inhaled deeply, and then continued as the smoke seeped out of her mouth and nostrils. "What about you? Any more mysterious pictures on Instagram?" She reached for Heloise's cell phone. "I wasn't able to find the one you told me about."

"It's under the username Anna underscore Kiel," Heloise said.

She retrieved a little copper bowl from the shelf over the stove and set it in front of Gerda.

"Here, you can use this as an ashtray."

"You said *underscore*, right?"

"Yeah."

"There's no profile with that name."

"Let me see," Heloise said, looking puzzled.

She took the phone and searched for the notification she had received. She clicked on the link. It led her to a blank page that said *No results found*.

"It looks like the profile was deleted. But I took a screen shot of the picture . . . wait a sec."

"Do you really think Anna Kiel was here in your apartment yesterday?"

Heloise found the picture and passed Gerda her phone.

"Well, *I* didn't take this picture and post it online, so who else would have done it?"

Gerda looked at the picture, her brow furrowed like she needed reading glasses.

"That is a damn good question," she said.

Then her expression changed. Her eyebrows rose a little and her lips parted, but she didn't say anything.

"What is it?"

"This picture . . ." Gerda said without taking her eyes off the screen. "It wasn't taken yesterday."

"What do you mean?" Heloise leaned toward her.

"See this right there . . ." She pointed to a little pink square in a window at the bottom of the picture, the same window Lulu had just waved good-night from. "That was a night-light Christian bought for Lulu on a business trip to Paris just after she was born. Don't you remember? It looked like the Arc de Triomphe and it was so beautiful, but then it fell—"

"—out the window and broke." Heloise finished Gerda's sentence for her.

"Exactly." Gerda nodded and held the phone up. "Heloise, this picture is at least five years old."

16

THE BUTTER WAS still out when Schäfer walked into the kitchen after his morning shower. He had forgotten to put it back in the fridge when he had responded to an insistent rumbling in his gut with a midnight snack consisting of a generously buttered cinnamon bagel, which he had eaten standing at the kitchen sink in the dark.

"Oh, for crying out loud," he snapped hoarsely, and stuck his nose down to sniff the butter. It had gotten soft overnight and smelled sour.

He opened the cupboard door under the sink and tossed the package in the trash.

"What are you barking about in there, babe?" Connie asked sleepily as she walked into the room.

After twenty-eight years in Denmark, her Danish still had an exotic lilt to it that made Schäfer's ears tingle with delight. She was wearing a white bathrobe and a pair of slippers, and her makeup-free face was shiny and jet black, like the volcanic sand beaches of the Caribbean island she had been born on, Saint Lucia.

"The butter was left out all night, and now it's ruined," he said, irritated.

"It was left out?"

"Yes. Don't we have any more?"

"Try looking in the fridge. Why was it out?"

Schäfer pretended not to hear her question and opened the door to the refrigerator. He clattered around noisily, clinking jars of jam and pickles and homemade marmalade to find an extra container of butter.

"Aha!" he exclaimed, a little too excitedly, holding his discovery triumphantly up in the air.

"Didn't your doctor say that you should cut down on your butter consumption?" Connie eyed him reproachfully.

"No, and if he had, he wouldn't be my doctor anymore."

Connie shook her head. Then she happened to think of something.

"Did you remember to renew your passport?" she asked.

"Yes," Schäfer replied. "I *did* actually almost remember to do that. That's the very first thing I'm planning to do at some point today."

"You're impossible, you know that?" She nudged him affectionately. "It expired several months ago, and if we're going to visit my mom in October, you need to get that taken care of now. Otherwise we're not going anywhere. Or rather, *you* won't be going."

Erik Schäfer's mother-in-law—a mountain of a woman, full of love and joie de vivre—was turning seventy-five, and the whole family was going to gather at Jalousie Beach on Saint Lucia for her birthday. He and Connie did their best to visit Connie's hometown at least once a year, and every time they were there, Schäfer secretly started planning for his retirement, which was still a good ten to fifteen years away. It was the only place he had ever really been able to unplug. Or, to be more precise, it was where he happily poured gasoline over whatever the plug was supplying power to and burned that shit to the ground.

"I'll do it today, honey, I promise," he said.

"Thanks, baby."

He started toasting bagels and put plates, Gruyère, and honey out on the table while humming an old Dire Straits tune.

He sat down as his cell phone rang in his pocket.

"Y'ello?" he said, pressing the phone to his left ear with his shoulder as he began buttering a bagel for his breakfast.

"Good morning. I'm calling from Forensics," a woman's voice said.

"Well, hello. Top of the morning to you," Schäfer said with exaggerated cheerfulness, glancing at the clock on the wall over the stove. It was 8:17. "You're certainly up and at it early this morning."

"You said it was urgent."

"Yeah, well, I say that all the time, and it rarely makes a difference with you guys."

If the woman took offense at his comment, she didn't let it show. Instead she got down to business. "We ran the tests you requested."

"And?"

"And there were no hits for Anna Kiel among the fingerprints that were lifted from the apartment on Olfert Fischers Gade."

"Damn it." Schäfer made a fist.

Connie came over and kissed him on the back of the head, communicating with a gesture that she was going to take a quick shower. He winked at her and put his hand on her left buttock and gave it a gentle squeeze.

The woman on the phone continued, "So there's no evidence to suggest she was in the apartment. On the other hand, the results are back from Forensic Genetics, and the DNA in the secretion in the envelopes' glue is a match."

"With Anna Kiel?"

"Yes."

"On both envelopes?"

"Yes."

Schäfer chuckled in satisfaction.

"That's good news." He took a bite of his bagel. "Okay, so we have a DNA match but nothing from the fingerprints," he summarized, smacking his lips and breathing heavily through his nose.

"Both yes and no."

"I'm sorry?"

"I didn't say that we didn't find a match for the finger-prints. I just said they weren't a match with Anna Kiel."

"Then who did they match?" Schäfer's brow furrowed.

"A guy by the name of . . ."

Schäfer could hear clicking on a keyboard.

"Duvall."

"Duvall?"

"Yes, a Martin Duvall."

Schäfer leaned back in his chair. The name didn't mean anything to him.

"What do we have on him?"

"A conviction for assault from last year. A thirty-day sentence."

"All right," Schäfer said. "I'll look into that. Anything else?"

"Not right now."

"Could you please send me an email with the test results as soon as possible?"

"I already have," she replied.

Schäfer thanked her and concluded the call. He sat for a moment, drumming his fingers on the kitchen table while he thought. He could hear the water in the shower running, and when the citrusy scent of Connie's shampoo reached his nostrils, he looked up at the clock again. He didn't have to leave for work for another hour.

He got up and started walking down the hallway toward the bathroom.

* * *

The door opened on the second knock, no more than an inch or two, but enough that Heloise dared to give it an extra push.

She leaned into the hallway.

"Hello? Anybody home?"

Nothing.

She could see the yellow Nikes he had been wearing yesterday sitting next to the doormat.

"Ulrich?" Heloise took a step into the apartment. "You here?"

She had managed to sweet-talk his address out of the central switchboard at *Ekspressen* by playing the coworker card and especially by feeding them a shameless lie about a scoop of a story they were working on together: "It's a tell-all story about the crown princess. I can't reveal anything except that it's going to make a lot of noise when it breaks. Ulrich and I have a meeting at his place with a source for the piece today, but I misplaced his address, so . . ."

She had felt her toes curl in shame and had been astonished at how easily they bought it. Now she couldn't help but wonder if it had been as easy for Anna Kiel to sniff out her address.

She took a couple of steps farther into the apartment.

She could hear a humming sound somewhere and had started moving toward it when it suddenly occurred to her that she might be about to surprise Ulrich in a, um, private situation. A look of disgust crossed her face, and she shook the image out of her head. She walked farther into the apartment, making sure her footsteps were audible so as to draw attention to her presence, and repeated loudly, "Ulrich? Are you here? It's me, Heloise!"

She peered into the living room.

It was empty. Not only in the sense that Ulrich wasn't there but also in that the room itself was sparsely furnished and uninviting. She moved on, opening a door that led to a room with an unmade bed. A harsh smell of tobacco and sweat hung heavily in the air, even though an electric ceiling fan spun around and around above the bed.

Heloise pulled on the metal cord. The fan gradually slowed down until it came to a complete stop.

She glanced over at the nightstand, where there was a full ashtray and a pill container. She walked over and picked up the pill container and looked at the label. It was American and said, *Dramamine Original Formula*. The label said the pills prevented motion sickness and that a side effect was severe drowsiness. Heloise remembered Ulrich telling her he was having trouble sleeping, and since the pills were by his bed instead of in a toiletry bag, she assumed he was interested in the side effect rather than the medication's primary effect.

Heloise walked through the kitchen, crossed the living room again, and ended up back in the front hall.

Why had Ulrich left his apartment without closing and locking his front door properly behind him? That didn't make any sense, considering how paranoid he had seemed the day before.

Heloise pulled her phone out of her inside pocket and dialed his cell phone again. When the call went through, there was a slight delay between the sound of the ring tone she heard through her phone and the remixed version of Queen's "We Will Rock You" she could hear from somewhere in the apartment.

Heloise held her phone away from her ear as she slowly followed the sound.

We will, we will rock you!

She walked through the kitchen, the sound growing louder, and stopped at the door to a bathroom she apparently had overlooked during her inspection of the apartment. She caught a glimpse of a sink behind the door, which was about a quarter of the way open, and a gray towel hanging on the far wall.

We will, we will rock you!

Heloise gave the door a push, and it opened slowly.

She didn't scream. Her mouth was shaped like a perfect O for a moment, but no sound came out of it.

She silently scanned the room with her eyes as an icy sensation spread from the base of her neck up through the nerves in the back of her head.

The footstool was tipped over and lying on its side on the white marble bathroom floor. A thin stream of blood had trickled down and spread out in the grout channels between the tiles.

We will, we will rock you!

Ulrich Andersson's lifeless body hung limply from a rope tied to a pipe near the ceiling as Freddie Mercury sang rhythmically in his pants pocket.

CHAPTER

17

"WHAT ARE YOU doing?" Augustin looked over at Schäfer as he pulled the car over. "Why are we stopping here?"

"I've gotta do this thing—it'll only take a second."

He opened the car door and nearly caused a pileup of hipsters on Tokyobikes when he crossed the bike path.

The glass door slid open automatically as he approached the entrance to the local Municipal Services office, and he pulled his expired passport out of his back pocket. It was bent from having been sat on all morning.

"Good morning!" he exclaimed in his friendliest, most cheerful tone. The new lead in the investigation meant he was in a better mood than he'd been in for months. He felt all bubbly inside, a feeling he always had when a case started to unfold.

Despite the fact that his greeting echoed through the deserted office space, the woman behind the counter completely ignored him. Schäfer leaned his hefty body against the counter and studied her intently. After a quick inspection, he determined that she was neither blind nor visibly hearing impaired and concluded that it was probably a classic case of unmotivated animosity.

Ah, well.

One one thousand, two one thousand, three one thousand . . .

"Yes?" barked the woman, still not looking up.

Schäfer politely told her why he was there, and she made a big production out of demonstrating that she got off her ass exclusively at a pace that suited her, underlining that she cared neither about him nor her job.

Under normal circumstances, he would have responded to this type of nonservice with a snarky comment of sorts, but today he just smiled through clenched teeth, thinking of Connie, who'd tell him to try to kill that kind of rude behavior with something as un-Danish as friendliness.

Smile, baby. Just smile.

"Did you fill out the right form?" the woman snapped.

"Yup, it's right here."

Schäfer pushed the document and his old passport across the counter to her.

She typed on the computer in front of her, making a point of doing it slowly, one finger at a time, provokingly calmly and methodically.

Click . . . click . . . click . . .

"Good thing we're not in a hurry," Schäfer smiled.

"Look into the camera."

She pushed the trigger, and his fleshy face appeared on the screen in front of her.

He leaned over the counter to look at the picture. His strained smile made him look like someone who was getting his teeth whitened.

"Again. And this time, close your mouth!"

Schäfer did as she asked.

"Is that it?" he asked.

"Yes."

"Thanks for your help, ma'am. Have a nice day." He patted the counter a couple of times by way of good-bye before turning and proceeding toward the exit.

"Oh, please. Spare me," the woman hissed quietly from behind him.

Schäfer stopped and looked back. "I'm sorry?"

"Just how old do you think I am? Don't be calling me ma'am."

Schäfer blinked a couple of times as he stared at her blankly.

"I apologize," he said. "Given the balls you've got on you, that was clearly a mistake."

He stormed out of the building, fuming, got in the car, and slammed the door shut behind him.

Augustin took in the aggressive attitude and raised a curious eyebrow.

"Uh, what were you doing in there?"

"Making sure that I'll soon be able to escape this shithole of a country and all its petty fucking bureaucrats."

"Okay, okay. Easy, tiger." Augustin patted him on the shoulder in solidarity as Schäfer pulled out into the lane.

He turned right on Nørre Søgade and snorted in irritation when he saw that the traffic was crawling at a snail's pace past the swan paddle boats and that the cars were being passed by joggers wearing neon-colored sweatbands.

Schäfer's phone made a few beeps, and the car's intercom system crackled. He answered the call, and Heloise Kaldan's voice filled the car.

"Schäfer? He . . . he's dead," she stammered. "You have to come now! You have to hurry!"

She gave them an address somewhere in Amager and hung up.

"Come on, damn it," Schäfer growled at the traffic as he prepared to do a U-turn in the middle of the road. "Move it!"

Then he turned on his siren.

* * *

Heloise had sat down on a chair next to Ulrich's shoe rack and was leaning against a jacket hanging from a coat hook above her. She could smell his sweat on the fabric and suddenly felt like she was going to throw up.

She dropped her head forward, down between her knees, and took a couple of deep breaths to settle the turmoil in her stomach and make the images in her head go away.

She got up and walked slowly to the bathroom door. She peered into the room, where Schäfer was squatting under Ulrich's body. He was wearing a surgical mask and a body suit, blue booties on his feet and white latex gloves on his hands, the same outfit he had asked Heloise to hop into when he arrived at the scene.

A flash went off each time the police photographer took a picture: of the black stool and the crooked toilet seat, of the blood on the floor, of Ulrich's purple feet hanging motionless above.

A young woman stood beside Schäfer. Heloise had said hello to her when they arrived. She had blond hair and muscular arms, and Schäfer had introduced her to Heloise as Sergeant Lisa Augustin.

The woman bent over the toilet tank and picked up something with a pair of long tweezers. She got out a little Ziploc bag with her other hand, shook it open with a quick motion, and deposited what she had found into the bag.

"The skin is punctured here," Schäfer said to Augustin, pointing with the end of a ballpoint pen to the sole of one of Ulrich's feet.

Heloise couldn't make herself look at Ulrich's distorted face again and limited her observations to his torso on down.

"This is where the blood is coming from," Schäfer continued. "If it was suicide, he would have to have been bleeding from his foot before he kicked the stool aside."

"There's no blood on the stool," Augustin said.

"How the hell did he get up there?" Schäfer stood up and looked around the room. "There's the stool, the toilet, the edge of the tub . . ." He pointed to the things as he spoke. "If he was bleeding from his foot when he came into the bathroom, there would be spatter or prints on the floor, and there should be blood on the furniture or whatever high point he jumped from."

"There isn't," Augustin said.

"He certainly didn't suffer the injury *after* he jumped."

"Well, maybe he was thrashing around and kicking vigorously as the noose tightened around his neck."

"Changed his mind at the last minute?"

"Yes, that always happens. The body automatically fights to survive."

"And then—what? Then he hit something or other and hurt his foot before he lost consciousness?"

Lisa Augustin shrugged.

"Okay, what would that be, then?" Schäfer asked, looking around. "What could he have hit from here, given the distance from where he's hanging?"

They both stood and looked around the bathroom for a moment.

Then Schäfer shook his head. "There isn't anything he could have reached from here, not from that height."

Heloise sensed a warm breath on the back of her neck, and when she turned around, she was hit by a scent she recognized as Pierre Cardin aftershave. It reminded her of standing in the bathroom of her childhood home and singing into the microphone-like glass bottle with the convex mirrored lid that had made her face look like it bulged out weirdly and her nose appear huge. Like the Snapchat filter of its day.

A friendly-looking man with a thick moustache, like Thomson and Thompson from the Tintin comics, stood behind her. He politely gestured that he would like to get by her. "May I?"

The man's voice caused Schäfer to peek down the hall toward the door, where he noticed Heloise.

"Kaldan," he barked. "Out!"

Heloise hurried away from the bathroom doorway and pretended she was going into the living room. But she stayed in the hallway, out of view but within earshot.

"Now, what have we got here?" she heard the man with the moustache ask as he entered the bathroom. Schäfer amicably greeted the man, whom he called Oppermann, and Heloise could tell from the jargon he used that he was the medical examiner.

She took a step closer to the door just as Lisa Augustin stuck her head around the corner and looked at her.

Heloise jumped at the sight.

"Why don't you just have a seat in the living room and wait until we're done here?"

Heloise nodded reluctantly.

She walked into the living area and took a seat on the hard sofa, which sat by itself in the middle of the room. It wasn't until most of the police folks and the medical examiner had left the apartment and Ulrich Andersson's body had been cut down from the rope and taken away in a body bag that Schäfer and his young colleague came in to see her.

"Are you okay?" Schäfer asked, putting a cigarette between his lips without lighting it.

Heloise nodded.

"We're going to stop by police headquarters now."

"You need me to come too?" she asked.

"Yup."

Heloise nodded again and stood up.

* * *

Heloise had been to police headquarters many times, but the closest she had ever come to sitting in an interrogation room was when she had been caught cheating on a test in high school and was sent to the principal's office.

Now she was sitting at a table across from Schäfer and Sergeant Lisa Augustin in a stuffy, windowless room and was about to tell them about her conversation with Ulrich by the water the day before.

"As far as we know, you were the last one to see him alive, so your account of your meeting could be important to the investigation," Lisa Augustin said. "I need to inform you that you are being formally questioned and that you have the rights of a suspect. That means that you are under no obligation to speak to the police and that you have the right to have an attorney present during the questioning if you want one. Do you understand?"

Heloise furrowed her brow. "The rights of a *suspect*?"

"Yes, of course you're not a suspect at the moment, but we can't rule out the possibility that you could become one, so anything you tell us today—if you choose to say anything— can only be used in court of law if we inform you of your rights. As I have just done."

"I'm sorry, but aren't we talking about a suicide here?" Heloise looked at each of them in turn.

Schäfer and Augustin said nothing, just eyed her expectantly.

Heloise took a deep breath and started from the beginning. She told them about the letters and about her very first phone call to Ulrich from the restaurant in Kongens Nytorv. About the message she had left on his answering machine and about how he had turned up unannounced on the street in front of the newspaper's offices.

Schäfer and Augustin listened without interrupting while she repeated all of Ulrich's speculations about Johannes Mossing. Schäfer didn't say anything until she had finished telling the story about the man with the gun.

"Did he describe the guy's appearance in any way?"

"Dark hair, tough guy," Heloise said with a shrug.

"Ethnicity?"

"I don't know. Caucasian, I think."

"When did Ulrich say this took place?"

"A couple of months after Christoffer Mossing's murder, I think."

"Why didn't he report it to the police?"

"He said he was scared."

"Huh," Schäfer said, chewing on his lower lip.

"He really was scared," Heloise repeated. "He also looked totally different from how I remembered him when we worked together at the paper, and he seemed really paranoid."

"And it didn't occur to you that he might be suicidal?" Augustin asked.

Heloise glanced over at her. She didn't care for the insinuation.

"I thought he seemed a little crazy, but no. It didn't occur to me that he would go home and kill himself."

"He wasn't crazy," Schäfer said.

Heloise looked at him.

"And we're not so sure that he killed himself either," he continued. "There's nothing in what he told you about Johannes Mossing that we haven't heard before."

"Well, then . . ." Heloise began, looking from one to the other. "Why is the guy still walking around?"

"Because for all the years of rumors about Mossing, we haven't obtained a single piece of evidence that there's anything to it."

"What about up at the racetrack? Ulrich said he had talked to—"

"We have examined and turned over every stone," Schäfer said, calmly. "We've dragged Johannes Mossing in for questioning once a year since the early 2000s, up until a few years ago when his lawyer put an end to the 'police harassment,' as he called it. The fact is that Johannes Mossing is a successful businessman who runs a legitimate business and who, in his spare time, likes betting on horse racing. He has a reputable social circle, a delightful wife, several beautiful homes, and a dead son." Schäfer flung up his arms. "There's nothing more to it than that."

"Until proven otherwise, right?"

Schäfer nodded and said, "Exactly."

Heloise stared straight ahead for several seconds. Then she said, "If Johannes Mossing really is the person you suspect him of being, and if Ulrich was murdered because he got too close, then what are the chances that Christoffer Mossing's murder was a random incident?" she asked. "Maybe Anna also found out about something she wasn't supposed to know. Maybe Mossing's people threatened her too?"

The room was quiet for a moment, and Heloise had the strange sense that there was something Schäfer and his colleague weren't saying.

"What?" she asked. "What am I missing?"

"Maybe it's you," Augustin said. She had gotten up from her chair and was now leaning against the wall in the back of the room.

"Maybe *what* is me?" Heloise looked confused and glanced over at Schäfer, who remained silent.

His eyes were calm, attentive.

"What ties *you* to this case?" Augustin continued. "A murder suspect sends you letters and seems to know personal things about you. And now Ulrich Andersson is dead, probably because he talked to you. And yet you claim that you've never met Anna Kiel and that you have no idea why she's reaching out to you."

"Claim?" Anger trembled in Heloise's body. "I'm not making this shit up. I've never met Anna Kiel, and I have no idea why she sent me those letters. Besides, we still don't know they're even from her. Maybe someone is—"

"Her DNA is on the envelopes," Schäfer said.

Heloise didn't know why she was so surprised. Maybe because up until this point it had been only a theoretical possibility and now it was real. Her collar felt tight at her throat, and she reached for the glass of water sitting on the table in front of her.

"We also got the results back on the fingerprints," Schäfer said.

Heloise looked at him.

"Who is Martin Duvall?"

The question hit her like a wrecking ball.

"One of the fingerprints we lifted in your apartment belongs to him," Schäfer continued.

It took Heloise a few seconds to collect herself. "Why do you have Martin's fingerprints in your database?" she asked.

"He has a conviction from last year."

"A conviction?"

"Yes."

"For what?"

"For assault."

"Assault?" Heloise repeated, stunned.

"He received a thirty-day sentence for knocking out four teeth of the victim in the case."

"So, he's been to prison? Is that what you're telling me?" Heloise leaned back in her chair.

Schäfer nodded slowly. "I take it you know him?"

"Yes."

"What is the nature of your relationship with him?"

"I've used him as a source for a few different stories, and we're, um . . . sort of seeing each other."

"You're dating?"

"No. No, not exactly."

"Have you ever known him to be violent?"

Heloise hesitated.

She thought about that night they had eaten at Bistro Royal. Remembered how he had held her hands firmly behind her back and pushed her up against the wall of her bedroom, hard, as he pulled down her panties . . .

Had he crossed the line? Had she really enjoyed that? Had she considered the marks on her wrists the next day a souvenir from a night of rough play or evidence of an . . . assault?

Schäfer continued before Heloise had a chance to respond. "Could it be that Martin Duvall has something to do with all this?"

Heloise felt dizzy and closed her eyes. "No, I don't think—"

"Could it be that he's the one who took the picture from your balcony?"

"No." Heloise looked up. "I didn't know him when that picture was taken."

"Come again?" Schäfer cocked his head to the side, and Augustin came back over and sat down at the table.

Heloise's hand trembled as she took her phone out of her pocket.

CHAPTER

18

Anna had visited Nick earlier in the day. She had rented a small apartment through Airbnb on Avenue de la Liberté, which ironically enough—considering the situation—was close to him.

She hadn't told Nick she had arrived in Paris, and when he saw her sitting there on the metal bench, his face had crumpled like a failed soufflé. He had been hoping for someone else, and Anna almost pitied him.

Almost.

"I want access to the files," she demanded.

"No, not yet. That wasn't the agreement."

"I don't care. If you want me to help you, then you'll give me what I'm asking for. Otherwise we don't have an agreement anymore."

She had expected him to put up a fight and was prepared to hit him with a whole range of colorful threats, but he surrendered to her demands in mere seconds. He had given up a long time ago, she could tell. There was no resistance left in his body.

He gave her the name of the website and a password and said, "Watch out for yourself now, okay?"

"It won't be long now," she responded, and gave him the number of the burner phone she had gotten herself.

"I won't be coming back here, so the next time you hear something, it'll be Heloise. Then you call me right away, you understand?"

He nodded. "Do you really think she'll come?" he asked.

"She'll come," Anna replied.

19

THERE WASN'T A soul by the main entrance of the Department of Forensic Medicine, which was located between Copenhagen City Hospital and Fælled Park. Sometimes the lobby was jam-packed with medical students from the Medical Sciences Faculty, but today it was dark and so quiet that Schäfer could hear his own breathing as he moved down the dark-brown brick hallway to the elevator.

On the second floor he passed a line of lab technicians in white coats who were studying tissue samples under microscopes. He nodded to the ones he knew before crossing the walkway at the end of the floor and pushing open the door into the autopsy room.

The air felt cold and the smell wasn't overwhelming today. Most of the tables were empty, and the morning's cadavers were down in the morgue drawers in the basement, but the slightest hint of death lingered in your clothes and hair after you'd been in there, sometimes as a clear mineral odor of rust, other times like the nauseating stench of over-ripe apples. Both of those could be washed away with soap and water, but on bad days you reeked, as if you had been stirring in a sun-warmed barrel of week-old fish, and then it took more than a shower to get rid of the stench of decay.

Schäfer passed the first of the autopsy room's five open bays, which were each equipped with a big stainless-steel sink and a docking station, and joined the team working in the rearmost and largest of the bays.

"Hello, boys and girls," he said, and took a couple of steps closer to the autopsy table with his hands in his pockets.

"Ah, there you are," the department chair and medical examiner John Oppermann said affably, scratching his moustache with his shoulder as he held his rubber-glove-covered hands out in front of him. "We're just getting started."

Schäfer and Opperman weren't what one would call friends, because they didn't socialize outside of work. But they felt a great deal of sympathy for each other. Their jobs had brought them to disaster-stricken parts of the world and war-torn regions far from the relatively safe duck pond of Scandinavia. They'd had shared experiences, which for better or worse—mostly worse—had brought them together.

In 2000, they had both been in Kosovo with the UN to do practical autopsy and identification work immediately after NATO kicked out the Serbs. What they found waiting for them down there were Milosevic's mass graves—a sight that still sometimes haunted the insides of Schäfer's eyelids late at night.

Schäfer regarded the body of Ulrich Andersson on the autopsy table as a forensics tech started cutting his clothing off and placing the items into separate plastic bags. His face was bluish and swollen, and his tongue, which was sticking out of his mouth, looked unnaturally large. There were dark livor mortis blotches on his feet, lower legs, hands, and underarms, whereas the rest of his body was pale.

When Schäfer was present at an autopsy, his primary concern wasn't the *cause* of death. Whether the person lying on the table had died from a fall, from suffocation, a heart attack or from a shot from a sawed-off shotgun—that wasn't his main interest. He wanted to know about the *manner* of death. Had it been a natural death, an accident, a suicide, or a homicide? He had been in the job long enough to know that first impressions weren't always right.

For the next hour, Schäfer watched while Ulrich Andersson was cut open with a Y-shaped incision from the neck down to his pubic bone. His ribs were cut, his organs removed and examined one by one.

"The face is cyanotic with numerous punctate hemorrhages," the medical examiner said to the pathology tech next to him. Then he waved Schäfer over to the autopsy table.

"This wasn't visible in the dim lighting at the scene, but here it's very clear: there are pinpoint bleeds in the eyes and in the eyelids and here—can you see?"

He pointed with a pinkie finger behind the ears.

"And they are also inside in the mucosa of the mouth. If he hung himself with sufficient distance above the floor, which appeared at first glance to be the case, then we shouldn't find petechiae like this," Oppermann said. "On the other hand, if we're talking about something tied around his neck—for example, let's say someone tied a rope or a cord around his neck and pulled—then that would close off the veins bringing the blood from the head back to the heart but not the arteries taking the blood up to the head. In other words, the pressure in the blood vessels in the head would rise, which causes the thin little blood vessels—the capillaries—to burst, which results in the petechiae, which you can see here."

Schäfer nodded.

"On the other hand, if he hung himself and was hanging freely," the medical examiner continued, "then there would be so much weight on the rope that it would close off both the veins and the arteries, and then you wouldn't see this petechia pattern."

"So, you don't normally see this with hangings?" Schäfer asked, scratching his neck.

"Well . . . only if someone has hung himself from, say, a doorknob and is lying relatively horizontally on the floor.

Autoerotic asphyxiation deaths would result in these same punctate petechiae, but I've never seen it like this. Not when the individual in question has been hanging freely."

Schäfer took a step back as John Oppermann made an incision from ear to ear over Ulrich Andersson's scalp and rolled the skin back over the skull, turning the face inside out. The procedure, which Schäfer had seen done several times, always made him think of those reversible dolls that portrayed Little Red Riding Hood one way and then, when you tipped her over the other way and pulled the skirt down over her head, the Big Bad Wolf from underneath. Peaceful from one angle, nightmarish from the other.

The medical examiner got out a Stryker saw designed to spare soft tissue and started to open the skull. Ulrich Andersson's brain and the blue rope around his neck were removed, and both of them were examined.

"There is a very obvious brownish groove in the shape of an inverted V on his neck where the rope tightened," Oppermann stated into a Dictaphone. "But there also appears to be a horizontal mark on his neck, a skin abrasion just under the groove from the rope."

He picked up a fine scalpel and started slowly and carefully dissecting the musculature layer by layer around Ulrich Andersson's trachea and esophagus.

Schäfer waited patiently until the autopsy was completed and Oppermann had thrown away his gloves.

"So, what's the verdict, Doc?"

The medical examiner stood at the sink, lathering his hands thoroughly with soap.

"There's no doubt," he said. "We have the petechiae, a horizontal abrasion on the neck. There are hemorrhages in the tissue around the larynx and fractures of the thyroid cartilage horns and hyoid bone. The deceased did not suffer those by hanging himself in his bathroom."

"So, we've got ourselves a homicide?"

"The cause of death must be assumed to be strangulation by ligature of the neck. Yes, a homicide." Oppermann nodded.

"All right, just send the autopsy report my way when it's done," Schäfer said. He gave Oppermann a friendly slap on the back and started walking toward the exit.

"Given how much trouble the perpetrator went to in order to make this seem like a suicide, it wasn't particularly cleverly performed," Oppermann said to Schäfer's back. "The killer could have easily camouflaged this better if he had done his homework."

"It's an amateur, then?" Schäfer asked, looking back over his shoulder.

"I can't comment on that. But he's no forensic pathologist, I can tell you that much."

* * *

Back at police headquarters in the Violent Crimes Unit, Schäfer filled the chief superintendent in on the medical examiner's assessment, and an investigative team was formed. In addition to Augustin and Schäfer, it consisted of Lars Bro and Nils Petter Bertelsen from Violent Crimes Section 1.

"Listen up," Schäfer said, tapping the edge of the big table in the meeting room where they were all sitting. "As you already know, I've just returned from Forensics, where the good Dr. Oppermann confirmed that we are dealing with a homicide."

"Based on what findings?" asked Nils Petter Bertelsen.

"The physical trauma on the vic isn't consistent with this type of hanging. Everything suggests that he was strangled first and then hung up afterward."

"Is there a suspect in the case? A motive?"

"He worked for a tabloid, so I'll bet a lot of people would have liked to string him up," Lars Bro interjected with a knowing smile.

Schäfer ignored that comment and said, "We know that the victim, one Ulrich Andersson, had been on sick leave from his job at *Ekspressen* for a while. We also know that he had been in touch with another journalist the day before we found him, a former colleague of his who currently works at *Demokratisk Dagblad* by the name of Heloise Kaldan. The medical examiner estimates that Andersson had been hanging there for at least twelve hours when we cut him down, and Heloise Kaldan says she saw him sometime before noon the day before yesterday. This means that the victim was killed at some point between noon and ten PM the day before yesterday. According to Kaldan's statement, the victim told her he had covered the Taarbæk murder case—the killing of Christoffer Mossing—and that he had poked around into Johannes Mossing's business up at Klampenborg Racecourse. When he had asked one or two questions too many, he was reportedly threatened in his home by some goon with a handgun."

"The Mossing murder? That was several years ago, right?" Lars Bro said, his eyebrows raised. "How is that relevant to what's going on now?"

Schäfer briefed them on Heloise's involvement in the case, the letters containing Anna Kiel's DNA, Martin Duvall's fingerprints, and the old photo on Instagram.

"This Kaldan woman is an important piece to this puzzle," Augustin emphasized. "We need to find out how she fits in."

"But she's not a suspect?" Nils Petter Bertelsen asked.

"Not at the current time," Schäfer said, taking the plastic pouches with the letters out of the case folder, which he had brought to the meeting. "Another one of these arrived this morning."

Augustin looked up. "A third letter?"

"Yes," Schäfer said. "Kaldan called me when I was on my way over to the Forensic Medicine Department, and I picked the letter up from her on my way back."

"Pass me that," Augustin said, snapping her fingers eagerly.

Schäfer handed her the middle plastic pouch.

Dear Heloise,

Why don't you have any children? I know why I don't, but what about you? You must be getting that question all the time, and I am sure that you have a scripted response for it by now, because, well, you're no spring chicken.

No spring chicken. Not quite so . . . fertile anymore.

TICK. TOCK. TICK. TOCK.

My mother. She was not a good mother.

Maybe it's hereditary. Anyway, my own clock never ticked.

Maybe I was born defective.

Maybe I am that way because of her.

There's so much I want to tell you.

While I am denied your presence, Heloise, give me at least through your words some sweet semblance of yourself.

Anna Kiel

"Ouch, that's gotta sting, right?" Augustin looked up. "She's basically saying, 'Hey, you're old and dried up and may have lost your chance of ever having children.' "

Bertelsen asked, "How old is Kaldan?"

"She's thirty-six," Schäfer replied. "So still very much a spring chicken, if you ask me."

"What did she say to the development in Andersson's case?" Augustin asked.

"That it's a homicide, you mean?"

"Yes."

"I haven't told her." Schäfer said. "That's not something we want the press to know until we know a little more about what we're dealing with here."

No one said anything for a while. Then Lars Bro broke the silence. "Okay, so who's doing what here?"

"I want you and Bertelsen to look into Ulrich Andersson's coworkers and friends and find out if he talked to anyone besides Heloise about the Mossings," Schäfer said. He took Andersson's byline photo from *Ekspressen* out of the case file and pushed it across the table. "Take this and drive up to the racetrack in Klampenborg. Show it around and see if anyone remembers him. We need to know who he talked to and what they said to him."

"What about me?" Augustin asked.

"You go talk to the ex-wife again."

Augustin made a face and winced. She and Schäfer had driven out to Ulrich Andersson's ex-wife's house in Amager the day before. The couple's two children, a girl of seven and a boy of nine with unruly, rust-colored curls, had been eating pasta with meatballs and watching an old episode of *Hannah Montana* on an oversized flat screen in their small living room. The children hadn't even looked up when Andersson's ex-wife invited Schäfer and Augustin in.

She had asked them to follow her into the kitchen, where they had conveyed the tragic news to her. She had cried in silence, her mouth open and her eyes full of fear, with the canned laughter from the TV in the living room and Miley Cyrus's affected voice serving as an absurd soundtrack.

"What am I gonna tell the children?" she had asked in a voice that came from deep down in her throat. "How am I going to tell them that their father committed suicide? How can they live with that knowledge?"

Now August had to go back out there again and inform the woman that her children's father hadn't hanged himself after all. The children would have to live with the knowledge that his death had been a much more violent one.

"What about you?" Augustin asked. "What are you going to do?"

Schäfer stood up and straightened his belt.

"I think I'm going to go have a chat with Mossing."

CHAPTER

20

B Y COUNTING THE seconds between a flash of lightning zigzagging across the sky and the thunderclap that followed, it was possible to determine how far away a storm was. In much the same way, Heloise had a theory that she could measure how far away from Copenhagen's Stork Fountain she was by counting the number of Solarium & Spray Tanning storefronts she passed on her way: the farther she got from the bustling heart of the Danish capital, the shorter the distance between the tanning salons on her route.

She parked in front of what must have been the twelfth tanning salon she had passed in the last ten minutes and looked around.

Herlev Main Street was not the quaint provincial pedestrian shopping street she had pictured but rather a large, two-lane road flanked by what looked like recently built senior housing and a cavalcade of classic suburban businesses: a pizzeria, three women's hair salons, two newsstands, the tanning place, and the Lantern pub.

She had tried to find the pub's opening hours online, but the establishment didn't have a website. Apparently, the clientele wasn't really of the iPad/smartphone/Internet-surfing variety. It was almost two o'clock in the afternoon, and she figured that people in pubs around the city must surely have already opened their breakfast and lunch beers.

The Lantern was on a corner and had a rather confused sense of style: orangy-brown benches, Tyrolean half-timbering in the walls, cemetery flowers in vases on the tables, a Norwegian flag hanging from the ceiling, and an American rockabilly jukebox just inside the door next to a life-size cardboard cutout of Tom Jones.

Heloise skimmed the jukebox's playlist: Big Fat Snake, Smokie, Bonnie Tyler, Dodo and the Dodos. She smiled at how predictable the selection was for a Danish pub like this and then turned her attention to an older man with a goatee and nicotine-gray skin, who was sitting at the end of the bar with his fist wrapped solidly around a bottle of beer. There wasn't anyone else in the place, not even behind the bar.

"Huh." He nodded to Heloise. "You look new."

"I'm looking for the owner," Heloise said, smiling at him. "Jonna?"

"Yes, Jonna Kiel. Do you know where she is?"

The man got up and walked around behind the counter. He stuck his head into the back room and bellowed, "*Jonna!*"

A whiskey voice from somewhere back there replied, "*What?*"

"Got a customer," the man called, and shuffled back to his barstool.

Heloise could hear the sound of a glass or a bottle falling over someone back there.

A lanky woman with turquoise hoop earrings appeared in the doorway. Her hair was short and red, and her skin was a lunar landscape of acne scars.

"You need something?" she said to Mr. Goatee.

"You've got a customer," he repeated, nodding at Heloise.

"Jonna Kiel?" Heloise asked.

The woman leaned her head back as if she were looking at Heloise through her nostrils.

"Who wants to know?"

"Are you Jonna Kiel?"

The woman nodded one time and crossed her arms.

"My name's Heloise Kaldan. I'm a journalist. I work for *Demokratisk Dagblad*."

"Uh-huh, that sounds fancy." The woman smiled. "Have we been nominated for Pub of the Year or something?"

She and Mr. Goatee snickered.

"No, I was just wondering if I could ask you a couple of questions," Heloise said, walking over to the bar.

"As long as you order something, you can ask me anything you want, sweetheart," the woman said, gesturing to the bottles behind her. "Then we'll see if I can answer."

Heloise shrugged and looked up at the selection. "I'll have a mineral water."

"Oh, come on." The woman shook her head as she made a *tsk-tsk* sound. "You can do better than that."

"Well then, make it a . . . a beer."

Heloise sat down at the bar while the draft beer was poured.

"That'll be five hundred kroner," the woman said with an encouraging smile, and set the glass down so hard that the foam sloshed over the edge and ran down onto the bar.

Heloise looked her in the eye.

The women shrugged in a way that said, *Pay or be gone.*

"I'm here because I'd like to ask you a few questions about your daughter." Heloise pulled a five-hundred-kroner note out of her wallet and set it in front of her.

The color drained from the woman's face. The playful smile she had given Heloise when she asked for the money was gone too.

"My daughter?" she asked, her voice timid.

"Yes, Anna."

"Did they find her?" The woman blinked a couple of times.

"No." Heloise hurriedly shook her head.

The woman closed her eyes and exhaled heavily, and Heloise couldn't decipher whether she was expressing relief or annoyance.

Maybe it was both.

When the woman opened her eyes again, she nodded slightly. Then she slowly reached forward and took the money. Heloise thought for a second that Jonna Kiel was going to ask her to leave, but she didn't say anything.

"When did you last hear from her?" Heloise asked.

The woman shrugged uncertainly.

"Have you been in touch with her at all since the police started looking for her?"

The woman still didn't say anything, so Heloise tried again. "When was the last time you saw her?"

"I . . . I don't know. It was a long time ago."

Heloise briefly considered how she should approach this and decided to tell the truth. "I'm here because Anna has sent me some letters."

The woman looked up and shook her head, confused. "Letters?"

"Yes."

"Why? What did she write?"

"She says that she and I are connected."

The woman looked Heloise over, as if she were searching for something tangible—a concrete, physical connection. "In what way?"

"That's what I was hoping you could help me figure out."

"Well, you don't really . . . look alike," the woman said. "You're not her type."

"No? What's her type then? What kind of friends did she have?" Heloise asked.

"She didn't really have any, I don't think."

"She didn't hang out with anyone?"

"No. No one besides Kenneth." The woman shook her head.

"Who's Kenneth."

"Just some boy she went to school with. He was a couple of years older than her, this handicapped kid."

"Handicapped?"

"Yeah, he was in a wheelchair, something about a car accident. Anna was always pushing him around town; they were together almost every day. They always sat and read books together, wrote secret notes to each other, that kind of thing."

"Were they, like, dating?" Heloise asked.

"I don't know," the woman said with a shrug.

"But they were friends as kids?"

"Yes."

"What was Anna like back then?"

The woman got a faraway look in her eyes, and for a long time she said nothing. "Her teachers said she was a strange child," she began. "She was withdrawn, always so angry, so I had a lot of problems with her."

"What was she angry about?"

The woman turned and walked over to the cash register and reached for a pack of cigarettes that was sitting on top of it. She lit a cigarette and took a few deep drags before responding.

"Her father wasn't a good father. He left us when she was little." She stuck out her lower lip and exhaled the smoke upward in a vertical column toward the ceiling. The she shrugged indifferently. "Maybe she was angry about that."

"And what about you?"

"What do you mean?"

"Were you a good mother?"

The woman gave Heloise a vague look, and her eyes filled with tears. "Do you have any children?" she asked.

Heloise shook her head.

"Then you don't know how hard it is." She put out her cigarette in a glass of water that was sitting on the bar before it had even burned halfway down. "You try to be the best mother you can be to your child. Was I good enough? I don't know . . . but Frank just went on his way. He left us. At least I gave our daughter a place to live and a bed to sleep in."

"Did you have a close relationship?"

"Me and Anna?"

"Yes."

The woman stared right past Heloise, lost in her own thoughts. "No, not really."

"Why not?"

She didn't answer the question but instead said, "I don't think I've seen her since she moved out."

"When was that?"

"When she was sixteen."

"And you haven't seen her at all since then?" Heloise raised her eyebrows in surprise.

The woman shook her head.

"What about the case against her? Do you have any idea why she killed Christoffer Mossing?"

"Yes."

Heloise looked up, attentive.

"The police say she's crazy," the woman said. "Not right in her head."

"And do you also think that?" Heloise asked. "That she just snapped?"

"Maybe." The woman shrugged.

"Do you know anything about corpse flowers? Does that mean anything to you?"

"About what?"

"Corpse flowers," Heloise repeated. "In one of her letters, Anna wrote about a corpse flower."

"You mean, like, the flower arrangements they have at a funeral? On top of the coffin?"

Heloise glanced inadvertently at the "decorations" in the vases on the tables.

"No, it doesn't have anything to do with funerals. It's a flower that grows in Sumatra."

The woman's face was blank.

"The flower lures beetles into its petals by emitting an odor of death," Heloise continued. "Does that mean anything to you?"

The woman wrinkled her nose and shook her head.

Heloise scratched her chin and shifted gears. "How long have you had this pub?"

"I took over in 1994. It was my father's, and when he died, I carried the torch, I guess you could say." She held a bottle of beer up in the air symbolically.

"What did you do before?"

"Before the Lantern?"

"Yes."

"I ran a cleaning company, Kiel Cleaning."

"Did you sell that company when you took over this place?"

"Something like that." The woman gave a half shrug with one shoulder.

"What about your ex-husband? What did he do?"

"Frank? All sorts of things. He was never around."

"Didn't he have a job?"

"Yeah, he had lots of different jobs: electrician, waiter, auto mechanic, dog walker. Like I said, he was rarely home."

"Did you guys fight a lot?"

The woman attempted a smile. "Only when we were in the same room together."

"Would you say there was violence in your relationship?"

She lit a new cigarette. "What does that have to do with anything?"

"I'm just wondering if Anna could have been affected by that kind of thing. Did she experience your being violent toward each other? Did either of you hit her? Maybe an occasional spanking that went too far?"

The woman frowned and shook her head fleetingly.

"Was there anything between you and Frank that might have contributed to Anna turning out the way she did?" Heloise continued. "To her being so difficult?"

"I don't know . . ." the woman said. "She just had trouble living life, I think."

"Did you do anything to help her?"

There was a long moment of silence between them, and Mr. Goatee started moving around uneasily on his creaking leather-upholstered barstool.

"I made sure we could pay our bills," the woman repeated. "I made sure she had clothes to wear and a roof over her head."

"Yeah, you said that already," Heloise said, unmoved.

The woman stared at her for several seconds. "Life wasn't easy for Anna, and so what? It wasn't easy for the rest of us either." She nodded toward the man at the end of the bar. "We all have things we struggle with, but we don't go around killing people, do we? Anna isn't normal. She's sick. You understand? Her mind's all twisted."

Heloise didn't say anything.

When the woman spoke again, she sounded hollow.

"Was I a good mother?" A snorting sound slipped out of her lips. "Maybe not. But I did the best I could."

* * *

Heloise Googled the number for Herlev Elementary School as she got back into the car and called the office.

"Herlev School, this is the front office, Marianne speaking. How can I help you?"

"Yes, hello. My name is Heloise Kaldan. I was wondering if you could help me. I'm looking for a former student of yours."

"Yes?"

"Unfortunately, I don't have a last name, but I know his first name is Kenneth."

"Kenneth?"

"Yes. He must have graduated around 1998, plus or minus a year or two."

"Uh-huh. That's going to be really hard for me to find."

"Don't you have a student directory you could search?"

"I do, but the digitized database only goes back to 2002. The registration information for all the students from before that is in a physical archive, and the students are listed alphabetically by last name. So, I would have to review all the class lists for the years you're looking for to find this Kenneth, and there are probably several Kenneths on the lists, so without a last name, I'd be lost, you see?"

"Yes, of course," Heloise said. "Obviously you shouldn't have to bother with all that."

The woman laughed in nervous agreement.

"Would you mind my coming in there and looking through the lists myself?" Heloise offered.

"Oh." The woman cleared her throat. "Um, I don't think I'm authorized to—"

"It won't take long. I promise no one will even know I'm there."

"Well, no, I don't think so. I'm sorry. If you had any other information about the student aside from his first name, then maybe I could—"

Heloise happened to remember something Jonna Kiel had said.

"Oh, he was in a wheelchair. He had a physical disability of sorts?"

"Ah," the woman said, and Heloise could almost sense her clasping her hands in excitement. "Well, then it must be Kenneth Vallø you're looking for."

"Do you know him?"

"Why yes, of course. Don't you?"

"No, I—"

"Kenneth Vallø is the founder of ScanCope."

"Um, that doesn't mean anything to me."

"ScanCope," the woman repeated, as if that were the most obvious explanation in the world. "The tech company."

"Okay," Heloise said. "Never heard of it."

"You're not from Herlev, are you?"

"No, Copenhagen."

"Well, that's probably why. Kenneth Vallø is sort of a local hero around here."

"A hero, really?"

"Yes, the new sports center we got here at the school a few years ago—he donated that. And the big bronze sculpture in Herlev Square and the embellishments in the new library? Kenneth Vallø paid for all of that too."

"That was mighty nice of him."

"I know, right? That's just the kind of man he is."

"Yeah, he sounds great," Heloise said. "Where did he get the money from, though?"

"He sold ScanCope to a foreign company several years ago, a Chinese company, I think it was. I can't remember how much he got for it, but it was a lot of money—somewhere in the hundreds of millions of kroner, if I remember correctly."

Heloise whistled, impressed.

"And I think he's just really proud of his hometown," the woman on the phone continued. "Kenneth Vallø hasn't forgotten where he came from," she said. She all but started humming that he was a jolly good fellow.

"Well, it must be nice to be able to give something back to your hometown," Heloise said. "How long have you been working at the school?"

"Almost six years."

"There wouldn't happen to be anyone in the office who's been working there longer, would there? Someone who could maybe remember Kenneth from when he was a student?"

"No, unfortunately not. The old school secretary retired last year, and the rest of the team up here has been gradually replaced over the last few years. What do you need to know about him?"

"There was a girl that Kenneth was friends with when he was a kid," Heloise began. "Someone he hung out with a lot when he was in elementary school."

"Oh, I'm afraid I wouldn't know anything about that," Marianne said apologetically. "But you know you could just go and ask him yourself. He's very down-to-earth."

"Do you know him personally?"

"No, but I know people who have met him and one who lives in the same neighborhood as him. They all say he's really nice."

"In the same neighborhood?"

"Yes, he has a house right here in Herlev."

Heloise frowned. The man was worth hundreds of millions of kroner and he still chose to live here in Herlev? He really *was* "Kenny From the Block."

"As I mentioned, Kenneth had a friend he went to school with," Heloise said. "I can imagine that there's been a fair amount of talk about her as well. Her name is Anna Kiel. Does that ring any bells?"

It grew quiet on the other end of the phone line.

"Hello?" Heloise said. "Are you still there?"

"Yes," the woman said, her voice suddenly out of sync with the Stepford Wives melody.

"Do you know Anna Kiel?"

"No, I don't, but of course I've heard of her."

"And you know that she's wanted for murder?"

"Yes."

"So, not exactly a local hero here in Herlev, I presume?"

"Certainly not. That woman doesn't have anything to do with our town."

"No, obviously not," Heloise said, secretly amused at people's tendency to claim credit for others' successes but never for their missteps. "The reason I mentioned Anna Kiel is that she and Kenneth Vallø were very close friends as kids. They went to school together."

"Are you saying that Kenneth Vallø was friends with . . . with *her*?"

"Yes. I know that you didn't work at the school back then, but I can imagine that Anna Kiel's story has been passed down?"

"You can say that again."

"And?"

"What do you mean?"

"I mean, what do people say about her?"

The woman paused and then said, "I'm sorry, who did you say you were again?"

"My name is Heloise Kaldan. I'm a reporter for *Demokratisk Dagblad*."

"A reporter?" The woman's voice rose two octaves, and Heloise could almost sense her pulse rising over the phone. "Oh, I don't really think I should say—"

"Oh, don't worry," Heloise said. "I'm not planning to quote you in an article or even refer to our conversation. I'm working on a story and am only calling because I need information—"

Heloise didn't get a chance to say anything else before she realized that there was no longer anyone on the other end of the line.

She stifled a sigh and hit redial. She waited patiently for a full minute while the phone rang without being answered.

Then she gave up.

Instead she Googled *ScanCope* and *Kenneth Vallø*. A series of articles showed up with headlines that indicated that the man had indeed become absurdly wealthy overnight.

Heloise clicked on the top link and read the article, dated six years back.

Sure enough, a Chinese company had bought all of Vallø's shares in the business he had built from scratch.

She skimmed the article, which was long and full of technical details about the company, scrolling down the page. At the bottom was a picture from ScanCope's initial stock exchange listing. A man, whom Heloise assumed was Kenneth Vallø, was featured in the middle of the picture. If you ignored the wheelchair he was seated in, he didn't look like a person with a physical disability. He was sitting in his chair as straight as a dancer from the Royal Danish Ballet. His torso looked healthy and muscular, and his eyes seemed powerful and confident. Several people stood around him, men in suits who were smiling and reaching out their hands to congratulate him, and just behind him—right there behind his left shoulder—stood Anna Kiel.

Heloise smiled when she saw her.

Anna was wearing her blond hair down, and it framed a narrow face with big blue eyes, a mouth with full lips, and a pretty little upturned nose that gave her a young, almost childish look, even though based on the date she must have been at least twenty-five when the picture was taken.

That was the only picture Heloise had come across in her research in which Anna Kiel didn't look indifferent. Her mouth was curled into a smile. Her blue eyes twinkled, focused on Kenneth Vallø.

She looked proud, almost happy.

Okay, so she and Vallø hadn't only been childhood friends. Their friendship had continued way into their adult lives. But could there have been more between them than that? Heloise wondered. Had they been in love?

Heloise called Morten Munk in research, and he answered after just one ring with a theatrical, "You may speak."

"Hey, it's me," Heloise said. "I need the address of a guy."

"Will any old guy do?"

"Ha-ha, very funny. His name is Kenneth Vallø, and he lives in Herlev. Can you find an address for me?"

"Give me a sec," Munk said, and hung up without saying good-bye.

Heloise sat there with the car engine turned off until she received a text from Munk.

CHAPTER

21

THE HOUSE WAS an ordinary rich person's house, the kind of house you lived in in Denmark's bigger provincial towns if you had a job that paid well, like an orthodontist living by the Vejle Fjord or a lawyer in Sønderborg. Nice looking, neat, and expensive, at least compared to the other houses in the neighborhood. But it wasn't the kind of house you normally lived in if you were worth three hundred million kroner or more, Heloise thought.

She had interviewed a number of prominent business leaders in Kenneth Vallø's league in her time as a journalist, and as a teenager she had also briefly dated a guy or two whose family name had been accompanied by a *von* or a Roman numeral. Boys whose families lived up the ritzy north coast. In Heloise's experience, even people who were less than half as rich as Kenneth Vallø almost always prioritized owning a home with tennis courts and a private dock.

But this place had neither.

She pulled into the cobblestone driveway that led right up to the brick single-story house and parked in front of the property.

She approached the front door and rang the bell and heard loud, electronic bird chirps from inside the front door, until a young woman opened it. "Yes?"

"Hi, I'm looking for Kenneth Vallø. I was wondering if he's home?"

The woman didn't ask for Heloise's name or why she had come but instead opened the door with a smile and invited her in.

"He's in the kitchen. It's this way," she said, leading Heloise through the house.

They found Kenneth Vallø sitting at the table in the kitchen. The table in front of him was set for a traditional Danish lunch with pickled herring and hard-boiled eggs and something that looked like homemade pâté in a glazed ceramic bowl.

Heloise suddenly became aware of the amount of saliva in her mouth, and her stomach reacted to the aroma of the warm pâté and the freshly baked bread by tying itself in knots of hunger.

"Oh, I'm sorry! I'm interrupting you in the middle of your meal," she said, coming to a halt.

Kenneth Vallø looked up and smiled. "Hi."

"Hello. My name is Heloise—"

"Kaldan," he said, holding out his hand. "I know. I'm Kenneth."

Heloise looked at him in astonishment and hesitantly took his hand. "Have we met before?"

He shook his head. "I recognize you from your byline photo."

"My byline photo?"

"Yes. You're a journalist, right?"

"Yeah."

"Well, please, come on in." He gestured toward the empty seat across from him and indicated that she should sit.

"Aren't I interrupting you in the middle of your lunch?" she asked. "Maybe I should come back a little later?"

Heloise was surprised at her own eagerness not to seem pushy. Normally she wasn't afraid to disturb sources, whether they were in the middle of a meal, on vacation, or at a funeral. That was part of the job—the part that gave many journalists a reputation of being like parasites—and she had never had any problem with that.

So why now?

Was the wheelchair turning her into a softy? Was she cutting him some slack merely because he was disabled?

Regardless of the reason, there was something about Kenneth Vallø that made her want to be agreeable.

"Don't be silly," he said. "Please join me."

Heloise noticed that the table was set for two people.

"You're sure you don't mind me taking your seat?" She glanced over at the woman who had let her in.

"No, please, go ahead," the woman said, gently pushing Heloise toward the empty seat. "I actually have a couple of things I need to take care of anyway."

She pulled the chair out for Heloise, who thanked her and sat down.

The woman left the kitchen, leaving Heloise alone with Kenneth Vallø.

"Is that your girlfriend?" Heloise asked, nodding after her.

Kenneth Vallø's head bobbed up and down and side to side in a way that indicated, *Both yes and no.*

"Miriam is my aide," he said. He stared intently at Heloise and was quiet for a few seconds. Then he said, "What's on your mind?"

"Nothing. Or, well, I was actually wondering how it could be that a man like yourself, a man of great wealth, has chosen to remain here in Herlev?"

"As opposed to moving where?" he asked. "To Luxembourg? Provence?"

"Well, yeah. Or to Rungsted . . ."

He laughed. "Rungsted? Why in the world would I want to move to Rungsted?"

"I don't know," Heloise said, smiling, accepting the bread basket that he held out to her. "Isn't that where people go to live once they've made some serious dough?"

She helped herself to a piece of rye bread. The middle was still a little moist and warm, and the bread smelled of malt.

"I was born and raised here," Kenneth said. "My family lives just around the corner, as do most of the people I care about. Here, try the herring. It's good," he said, and pushed the porcelain bowl over to her. "I don't see any reason to leave. Do you?"

Heloise shrugged. "Not when you put it like that, no. But most people I know dream of winning the lottery—or creating a tech start-up that they can sell to the Chinese for a fortune such as yourself—so that they can get away, away from the life they're living, away from the town they were born in."

She bit into the open-faced sandwich she had made herself and almost groaned in delight.

"Mm. Wow, this is good."

"Yes, it is, isn't it? It's the bread. Miriam trained as a baker. You should taste her raspberry muffins."

Heloise smiled. Raspberry muffins? Had Vallø chosen her as his aide for her baking skills? Almost certainly.

"I'll have to try them someday," she said, taking another mouthful of herring.

"Well, so what brings you here, Heloise Kaldan?" Kenneth asked, leaning back in his chair. "I assume that you're not here because you are interested in the tech industry."

"What makes you say that?"

He smiled and shrugged. "Just a guess," he said, reaching for a beer without taking his eyes off her.

There was a loud *tss* as he popped the top of the can open.

Heloise hesitated for a moment. Then she said, "I'm here because I'm writing a story about Anna Kiel."

Vallø nodded. His facial expression didn't change. He still seemed open and accommodating.

Heloise squinted and regarded him skeptically.

"Why do I get the sense that that doesn't surprise you?"

"Probably because you're right: it doesn't surprise me. Any journalist worth a damn would be interested in Anna's story."

"But you knew that I would contact you?"

"Well, I'm definitely not surprised."

"Why not?"

"I just told you."

"Yes, any journalist worth a damn, you said. But now I'm asking you: did you know that *I* was going to contact you?"

He took a drink of his beer and wiped the foam from his mouth with the back of his hand before setting the can down again.

"No, but I figured you might."

"Why?"

"Because she wants to talk to you."

"Anna?"

"Yes."

"How do you know that?"

He smiled but didn't respond.

"Why me?" Heloise asked.

"I can't answer that."

"Can't or won't?"

Kenneth chuckled. "Does that really matter?"

Heloise set her utensils down and pushed her plate away a little. "So, you were friends, you and Anna?"

"We're still friends. Best friends."

"You're friends with a murderer?" Heloise raised one eyebrow.

"Anna's not a murderer. She's . . . misunderstood."

"She's a murderer."

"Semantics."

"No, it's not a question of semantics. It's not subject to interpretation, and it doesn't matter what angle you look at it from. Anna Kiel murdered Christoffer Mossing in cold blood. She's a murderer. Period."

"I think you'll see it differently one day."

"Have you talked to the police?"

"Sure. Several times. Erik Schäfer—good man."

"What did he ask you about?"

"About the nature of Anna's and my relationship, about when I last saw her, if I had financed her getaway, that kind of thing."

"And?"

"And what?"

"Did you finance her getaway?"

"Oh, please." He smiled charitably. "Do you really think I would help a wanted murderer—wasn't that what you called her?—to escape arrest?"

"Yes."

He stifled a smile. "And do you really think I would tell anyone if that were the case?"

Heloise folded her hands in her lap. "So, you're in contact with her?"

He didn't say anything, just smiled a warm, subtle smile as he looked down at the lunch table, as if he were trying to decide what to choose from the bowls.

"Well, next time you talk to her, tell her that if she needs me, she should give me a call. I can't take any more of these cryptic letters she's been sending me. I assume you also know that she's been sending me letters?"

He smiled. "Why do you say that?"

"What?"

"That they're cryptic?"

"Because they're gibberish."

"Maybe." He smiled. "Or maybe you're just reading them wrong."

"Wrong? How so?"

"Oh, I don't know," he said, shaking his head slightly. He pushed a button on his armrest, and his large, upholstered wheelchair backed away from the table. He gestured that Heloise should get up.

Apparently, lunch was over.

"You may be right," he said as he said good-bye to her at the door. "Maybe Anna should call you—and who knows? Maybe she will."

22

H ELOISE HAD TURNED over the third letter to Schäfer before she drove out to Herlev. Now she sat at her desk at the newspaper and looked at the picture she had taken of the letter with her iPhone. She felt strangely struck by the wording Anna Kiel had used to taunt her with, but at the same time, she felt sympathy for her after having met her mother and Kenneth Vallø.

Sympathy for a murderer?

That wasn't like Heloise.

It offended her sense of justice when violent offenders received sentences that were too lenient. On the one hand, she knew that rehabilitation was the only thing that worked. On the other hand, she thought that the sentencing guidelines in Denmark were laughable: violent offenders often received a scolding, a slap on the back of the hand, and they were rewarded with very brief, college-like stays in downright comfortable surroundings. It was an insult to the victims, who all too often were forgotten in the rush to accommodate the convict's existence. Part of Heloise would have preferred to dump all the murderers, pedophiles, and rapists into a deep, soundproof pit, throw a heavy metal lid over it, and forget they ever existed. It wasn't a particularly politically correct opinion, but she just got so overwhelmed with indignation, so filled with hatred.

But there was something about Anna that made her feel . . . something *more*. An inexplicable compassion and a desire to understand what had brought her to such an extreme that she had felt compelled to take another person's life.

She pulled out her iPhone and found Schäfer's number.

"Yeah, hello?"

"Hi, it's me. Heloise."

"What's up?"

"I'm just calling to find out . . . Kenneth Vallø, you know . . ."

"What about him?"

"I visited him today."

"You went to see him? Why?"

"To get closer to Anna. I talked to her mother too."

"I hate to tell you this," Schäfer said, "but I think you're wasting your time by running around in my footsteps."

"Yes, I know, you already talked to Vallø, but the weird thing is that it seemed like he was expecting me."

"What do you mean?"

"It was as if he knew I was going to come. I think he's still in touch with Anna."

"I know they were close, the two of them. But we checked out all his bank transactions, all his outgoing and incoming phone calls, his email system, and ransacked his house. We haven't found anything."

"They're still in touch," Heloise repeated.

"That's very possible, yes. But, like I said, we haven't been able to prove it."

"How does she pay her bills?"

"I'm sorry?"

"Anna's expenses. I mean, she must sleep somewhere. She must eat something. How does she pay for it?"

"She's been on the run for several years now. And yes, unless she's out begging on a street corner somewhere, she must have money to live on. Maybe she got a job. That happens. People on the run shave their heads, change their name to something international sounding like Maria or Michelle, and get a job under the table at a beach café in Umba Umba or somewhere."

"Or maybe she has a crazy-rich friend who sends her money."

"Or maybe she has a crazy-rich friend, right," Schäfer conceded. "If they agreed on a PO box, an address, a collection time, then yes. He could easily be sending her cash in an envelope or a package."

"But wouldn't she have to show ID to receive mail like that?"

"Yeah, probably. But it's easier to get your hands on a fake driver's license than most people think. Ordinary people can rarely tell the difference between a real ID card and a fake one."

Heloise's landline rang on the desk in front of her, and she could tell from the number that the call had come from the lobby.

"Hang on for a sec," she said.

She put her call with Schäfer on hold and answered her phone. "Hello?"

"This is the switchboard. I have a call for you."

"Thanks, go ahead and put it through."

It was quiet on the line for a couple of seconds.

"Hello?" a man's voice said.

"Yes, hello," Heloise replied. "This is Heloise Kaldan. To whom am I speaking?"

"Are you the one who was in Herlev today?"

"Excuse me?"

"You were at the Lantern today."

"And you are?"

"My name is Frank Kiel."

Heloise blinked a couple of times. "Anna's father?"

"Yes."

She quickly pushed the paperwork on her desk aside, found a pen in the mess, and flipped open a notebook. "What can I help you with, Frank?"

"You talked to my ex-wife today."

"Did she tell you that?"

He began to laugh, and then it turned into a cough. "No, we don't talk anymore," he said.

"Then how did you get my name?"

"A little birdie told me."

Mr. Goatee, Heloise assumed.

"What can I do for you, Frank?"

"You can tell me what you wanted to talk to Jonna about."

"I wanted to talk about Anna."

"Why?"

"Because I'm trying to get an impression of her."

"You told Jonna that Anna writes you letters."

"That's right."

"Why does she do that?"

"I don't know," Heloise said. "That's what I'm trying to find out."

It was quiet on the other end of the line for a moment. "I think maybe I know why."

Heloise set down her pen. "You know why she writes to me?"

"Yeah. I think I can help you."

"Okay, Frank, tell me what you know."

"No, not like this," he said. "Not over the phone. Can we meet?"

"Are you in Denmark?" Heloise asked. "I thought you lived in Greenland."

"No, I haven't lived there for years." The man was quiet for a moment. "Can you meet me tonight?"

Heloise agreed and wrote down the address he gave her. She concluded the call and returned to her call with Schäfer.

"Guess who just called me! . . . Hello? Schäfer?"

But there was no one waiting on the other end of the line.

CHAPTER

23

SCHÄFER STEPPED ON a dried-out crab claw that had been dropped by a sea gull on the farthest section of dock at Rungsted Marina. He proceeded down the floating dock, heading toward a beauty of a Bavaria Yacht—one of the higher-end sailboat makes—that was moored at the end.

He used to sail himself, years ago, and as the scent of the salt water and the sea air hit his nostrils, it almost made him miss his old, scratched-up Nordic Folkboat. But that boat had been so much work that he had finally had to adopt one of his grandfather's favorite sayings: *The only thing that feels better than acquiring new stuff is getting rid of the shit later.*

Johannes Mossing was squatting on the yacht's deck with his back to the dock and hadn't seen Schäfer approaching. He was either loosening or tightening a mooring line. Schäfer took note of his preppy uniform: a yellow polo shirt, light khakis, and a pair of caramel-colored boat shoes. He smiled to himself and shook his head. Prejudices, he thought. They had a tendency to prove true.

"Are you heading out, or did you just come in?" Schäfer asked.

Johannes Mossing turned halfway around toward the voice and tilted his sunglasses up onto his forehead.

"I just came in," he said, turning his back to Schäfer again.

"That's a damn pretty yacht you've got there," Schäfer said, standing fore of the boat with his legs slightly apart and his fists planted solidly at his sides.

"What brings you here, Inspector Schäfer?" Mossing asked, still without looking at him.

"Sergeant first class now. I'm not an inspector anymore."

"Oh?" Mossing turned, giving Schäfer a sour smile. "Were you demoted?"

"No, not that. It's the police reform and all that jazz. New departments, new titles, but the work is the same: assholes break the law, I throw them in jail."

The two men regarded each other for a long moment.

"What are you doing here?" Mossing asked again, stepping out onto the dock in front of Schäfer.

"I have a problem you might be able to help me with. You see, a man was murdered the day before yesterday, a journalist."

Mossing didn't say anything.

"Ulrich Andersson. Ring any bells?"

"Should it?"

"He was strangled and then hung up in his bathroom, a murder that someone attempted to make look like suicide."

"That certainly sounds like quite the mess."

"Yes," Schäfer said, scratching behind his ear. "But what's interesting is that a couple of hours before that, he had complained that *you* had threatened his life."

Johannes Mossing chuckled. "Nonsense."

"He said he was threatened at gunpoint in his home when he was writing an article about Christoffer."

The smile disappeared from Mossing's mouth when his son was mentioned.

"Coincidentally, the journalist had heard the same stories about your activities at the racetrack as I have," Schäfer continued, "and when he started investigating the rumors more closely, he was threatened with fire and brimstone."

"Well, that all sounds very interesting," Mossing said, and started making his way down the dock. "But I'm afraid you've watched too many movies."

Schäfer followed him to the parking lot. "I don't suppose I can tempt you into taking a trip down to headquarters for a chat, then?"

"No, but you are welcome to call my lawyer at Orleff and Plessner if you have any further questions," Mossing said, climbing into the driver's seat of a black Range Rover Sentinel. "I assume you still have his number."

Schäfer put a hand on the open car door and leaned in toward Mossing.

"You know that sooner or later I'm going to find out what sort of shit you're involved in, right?" The jovial small-talk look was gone from Schäfer's face. "Maybe you think you've gotten away with whatever you've been up to. But eventually something will topple the house of cards, and when that happens, you're going to go away for a long time. And for an old guy like you . . . that might end up being for the rest of your life."

Mossing stared expressionlessly into his eyes. Then the corners of his mouth curled up into a little smile, and for a fleeting moment the look in his eyes seemed to challenge Schäfer. It didn't last more than a second—maybe two—but it was the closest Schäfer had ever come to obtaining a confession from Johannes Mossing.

Mossing made a *tsk-tsk* sound and shook his head, like a sadistic teacher reprimanding a student with intellectual disability in front of the whole class.

"As usual, you're wrong, *Sergeant* Schäfer." He turned his key, and the car's engine started to purr. "My house of cards is very solid, thank you, and now you'll have to excuse me. I'd like to get home and enjoy the rest of the day with my lovely wife."

He grasped the door handle to close the door but then stopped.

"How's it going, by the way, with that chocolate-colored woman of yours? Connie's her name, right?"

At the sound of her name, Schäfer's heart skipped a beat.

"Wowza, that's an exotic beauty you've got yourself there," Mossing continued, whistling in appreciation. "You'd better keep a close eye on her. Somebody might snatch her away from you one day when you're not looking."

A primitive rage bubbled up in Schäfer.

"How the hell do you know my wife's name?" he demanded.

"Oh, I just like to keep informed." Mossing shrugged nonchalantly.

"You stay the fuck away from her, you understand?" Schäfer rapped on the car's rear door with his knuckles—a reaction that made Johannes Mossing burst out laughing.

"You have a nice day, Schäfer." Mossing slammed his door shut and stepped on the gas pedal.

The car pulled away so fast, it kicked up gravel that ricocheted off the finish of the red Porsche Cayenne that was parked next to it in the lot while the dust from the unpaved lot swirled up and enveloped Schäfer.

He stood there watching Mossing until the car turned left onto Rungsted Strandvej and accelerated.

Then he cussed loudly and angrily kicked an empty cola can, sending it bouncing on its way.

CHAPTER

24

THE SKY THAT had been so blue earlier in the day was now covered with a doomsday-like cover of black clouds, which opened up over Copenhagen and flooded several of the city's lower-lying streets in under twenty minutes. The downpour fell so hard and in such vast quantities that even the most dedicated of atheists had to contemplate hammering some nails into a couple of boards and building an ark— or at least a raft of some sorts.

It was the third torrential rainstorm in only two months, and the city's sewer system was not up to the tremendous masses of water, which had insurance company assessors working overtime in the basement-level businesses in the city.

Outside, the rain had perforated petals and snapped stems in flower beds. But the rest of the botanical gardens just looked all the healthier, even more lush in the pouring rain: wet, green, and beautiful.

The drops drummed on the glass roof of the Palm House, where the temperature inside was near a hundred degrees. Heloise stripped her wet denim jacket off her shoulders as she walked through the greenhouse, searching for what had brought her here: the *Amorphophallus titanum*.

The corpse flower.

Her research had revealed that not only was there a specimen of the plant right here in the middle of Copenhagen, it also happened to be in bloom right now for no less than the third time in only four years. A botanical miracle, the experts called it, since normally the plant bloomed once only every ten years. It must be happy here in Scandinavia, far from its native Indonesia, since it kept flowering. Or maybe there were just more bugs here that got excited about the stench of death, Heloise thought.

She had seen photos of the plant online. It was enormous—ten feet tall—with dark-purple petals and a gigantic light-yellow inflorescence that rose right up into the air like a flagpole. She could easily see why it was also known as the "penis flower," and when she spotted the plant in the Palm House, the nickname's meaning became even clearer: the yellow spathe was no longer erect and looked like an oversized caterpillar, drooping down dead from the plant.

Flaccid, limp, and lacking *umph.*

"You're a little too late."

Heloise turned toward the nasal voice and saw a gangly young boy with long hair wearing a dark-green employee's uniform jacket.

He nodded toward the plant. "It's withering now."

"Yes, I see that." Heloise smiled. "It looks pretty done."

"You should have been here last week. It was simply magnificent then."

Magnificent?

That wasn't exactly the word that had popped into Heloise's mind when she had seen pictures of it. Fascinating, yes. Big, impressive, and crazy, yes. But magnificent? That Frankenstein's monster of a botanical specimen? No!

She walked a couple of steps up the ramp that had been set up beside the plant, leaned in close to it, and cautiously inhaled. She looked puzzled, inhaled more deeply, and then looked down at the boy.

"It doesn't smell like anything?"

"No, not anymore," he said. "It's only when the flower first opens and the temperature inside it rises to human body temperature that it smells of rotting flesh."

"Human body temperature?"

"Yes, about ninety-eight point six degrees. Then the plant emits a steam of chemical sulfur compounds, which spread through the rain forest and attract carrion beetles and flies, which land on the warm spadix and make their way down to the meat-colored spathe toward the stench and the heat."

"Gross," Heloise said, making a face.

"No, it's not gross. It's ingenious."

"Ingenious?"

"Yes, just think: it shows that the flower is intelligent. It's devious, cunning. You really can't help but admire it, right?"

"Huh." Heloise stepped back down off the podium again. "I think it's a little morbid."

"Yes, but it's not the plant's fault that it's been furnished with the need it has. It didn't choose to smell like a morgue. It's just playing the hand it was dealt by nature, and it's playing it well. It's about survival."

"Okay, whatever." Heloise gave him a smile. "I'm more into tulips, but to each his own."

The boy moved to stand between Heloise and the plant. He pushed some of his long hair behind one ear, and Heloise could just see the edge of a hearing aid clinging to the top of the cartilage in his ear.

"Tulips are pretty, but they're common flowers," he said.

Heloise was surprised to hear in his voice that he sounded hurt.

"Billions of them bloom every year. They're nothing special. But this guy here . . ." He caressed the soft sausage hanging limply down from the plant with his hand. "He's unique."

Heloise couldn't help but smile at him. Apparently, the carrion beetles weren't the only ones who were spellbound by the corpse flower's creepy scent. The boy before her was in serious need of a mouthful of fresh air. And a boyfriend.

She thanked him for his time and walked out the exit, which led her back out into the rain.

There was a little three-wheeled coffee cart parked by the stairs descending to the lawn, and Heloise bought a cappuccino. She walked down to the water and stopped in the middle of the white wooden bridge, where she observed the raindrops leaping and dancing on the water lily leaves like corn kernels in a hot frying pan as her clothes and her hair clung to her body.

Ulrich's contorted face flickered constantly through her mind, and she blinked a couple of times to chase the image away. Schäfer had told her that the results of the autopsy weren't back yet, that they still didn't know what they were dealing with. But Heloise felt unnerved.

Why would a man who had been so afraid of dying commit suicide? Wasn't that like someone with claustrophobia letting themselves be buried alive? And why in the world would Ulrich contact her to warn her and then go right home and hang himself?

No, she didn't buy it. It didn't make any sense. Someone must have gotten him out of the way, because he had come too close to something . . . but what? And why had Anna Kiel murdered Christoffer Mossing? Was it really a coincidence, like the police were telling her? No way. She didn't buy it anymore. There had to be something beyond Johannes Mossing that linked those two cases together.

And what about Martin?

Heloise still didn't know him well enough to rule out his possible involvement. The last few weeks had proved that she didn't know him that well. It was as if suddenly her life was full of criminals and violent offenders.

Her eyes fell on a mother duck that was heading for the bridge to find shelter from the rain with her ducklings. One of the little yellowish-brown balls of feathers had fallen behind and was now slogging across the water to catch up to the flock.

What was it that Anna was trying to tell her?

What was it that she wanted her to see?

In one way or another, all of the pieces seemed to come from the same puzzle, but none of the pieces Heloise had found so far fit together.

She stood there until the duckling had made it safely to its mother. Then she turned around and headed for the garden's east gate.

* * *

Schäfer found Lisa Augustin alone in their office at police headquarters. She was sitting on the floor leaning against the wood-chip-wallpapered wall behind her as she looked at a document she was holding in her hands. Papers were spread across the floor in front of her, and Schäfer could see that she had underlined things, added comments, and drawn squiggles on several of the pages.

"Where are Bro and Bertelsen?" he asked.

August glanced up briefly and said, "They went over to Forensic Unit." Then her eyes returned to the document in her hands.

"What are they doing there?" Schäfer pulled off his rain-soaked suede jacket and tossed it over the back of his desk chair. He sat down heavily and swiveled the seat from side to side as he waited, watching Augustin.

"That print from the shoe sole that was lifted off the toilet seat on Amager Strandvej, you know?"

"What about it?"

"It doesn't match the victim's size."

Schäfer nodded. "That's not a surprise. What else did they say?"

"That it's from a Puma sneaker, size seven. Ulrich Andersson wore a size eleven. I haven't heard anything else."

Schäfer didn't say anything.

"Are you okay?" Augustin asked, pushing her reading glasses up on top of her head. "You look a little grumpy."

Schäfer just grunted in response.

"Did you get ahold of Mossing?"

"Mm-hmm."

"Was he home?"

"No, down at the marina. Man, the rich really know how to live, huh?"

Augustin nodded. "What did he say?"

"The usual: nothing. He denied knowing anything about anything and referred me to his lawyer. But he's lying. I know he's lying."

They were quiet for a moment, and then Schäfer nodded to Augustin. "What about you? What are you up to?"

"I'm just looking at the letters from Anna Kiel." She pointed to the copies in front of her.

"Have you managed to make any sense of them?"

"No, none. What does she want with this Kaldan woman? Why is the whole thing so goddamn vague?" Augustin looked almost angry. "Why doesn't she just say what she wants instead of sending all this nonsense?"

"I guess the big question is: why Heloise?" Schäfer said. "What does Anna Kiel want specifically with *her*?"

"She's a relatively well-known journalist, and she works for a prominent paper," Augustin said with a shrug.

"So, she's a potential spokesperson for Anna Kiel. Is that it?"

Augustin shrugged again.

"Look at it a little more," Schäfer said. "Maybe bring Heloise in here again so you can talk to her. By the way, did you get ahold of the ex-wife?"

"Yes."

"What did she say?"

"Not that much," Augustin said, getting up off the floor with a groan of effort. "Lot of tears, not so many words."

CHAPTER

25

T HERE WERE TEA bags in the kitchen cupboard in the small apartment on Avenue de la Liberté, so Anna filled the white enameled kettle with water and lit the gas stove. She sat down at the little bistro table in the kitchen and flipped through the documents she had printed at the library earlier in the day.

The stack was two fingers thick.

Anna had created a clear summary for the journalist with dates, details, names. There were twelve in total, but only nine that she knew.

Nine, she could remember.

She had used the link and the password Nick had given her and had vomited twice. Now everything was ready. There was nothing to do now but wait, and if nothing happened, she would just have to yell louder and more clearly.

But Nick had said that it had to be "subtle." That was the word he had used. He had said that it needed to be a refined hint rather than a flashing neon sign, and that the journalist would never come if she knew why she was being summoned.

But soon, she would surely turn up.

Soon, it would all be over.

Anna gathered all the papers into a yellow folder and put it in her backpack, which was hanging out in the hall, as the kettle started whistling in the kitchen.

She sat in the kitchen window with a cup of tea in her hand and watched the A86 freeway, which ran behind the property.

"It'll be over soon," she told herself out loud, and in a way it was true.

At the same time, she knew that it would never really be the case.

26

Everything on the woman's body pointed downward. She was probably younger than she looked, but her loose skin had long ago given up on the hope of ever being stretched tightly over actual muscle mass.

Heloise watched her swing around the metal pole a couple of times with all the charm of a dead body that had washed up on a beach. The toes of her knee-high patent-leather boots looked scruffy, her nail polish was flaking off, and the look in the woman's eyes could at best be described as apathetic.

Heloise had never been to a strip club before, but she had seen the movie *Showgirls* when she was a teenager. It was about rivaling Las Vegas strippers and their perfect bodies, shimmering and sparkling with glitter as they twirled lustfully on the stage. Silly, yes, but also kind of hot. Still, it's wasn't like she had expected a go-go bar by the name of Beverly Hills located in touristy Kongens Nytorv between a McDonald's and a cell phone store to be sexy, but still. She was at a loss for words.

There were three people sitting in the bar: a woman, who with her run-down physique and week-old makeup looked like she worked there, and two men, both looking gray and worn. They were each sitting on their own with a suitable distance between them, so Heloise figured they were there alone.

The rest of the club was empty.

That was maybe the only thing about the place that didn't shock Heloise. Because it was only six thirty, it was still light out on the other side of the blackout curtains, and the mood in the place was about as exciting as yeast. Not exactly what you would call a crowd pleaser.

One of the men in the bar glanced over at the entrance and spotted Heloise. Their eyes met for a second, and then he waved her over.

He got up off his barstool as she approached. He was a small man, skinny and short, and Heloise felt oddly broad shouldered next to him.

"Frank Kiel?" she asked, holding out her hand.

He took it, his handshake limp and sweaty. "And you're Louise?"

"Heloise, yes."

"Have a seat," he said, patting the red leather chair next to him.

Heloise kept her wet jacket on. She sat down and got right down to business. "What can you tell me about your daughter?"

"Whoa, take it easy," he said, nodding toward her purse. "Let's get a drink. My throat is a little dry."

Their eyes met.

He smiled and flung up his arms. "One drink. Your newspaper can afford one drink, right?"

Heloise looked over at the bar. There was no bartender behind the counter.

"It doesn't look like there's anyone to serve us," she said.

Frank Kiel turned around in his chair and raised his voice. "Hey, June!"

The woman farther down the bar looked up.

"We're thirsty."

The woman sighed and got up slowly. She dragged her feet as she walked around the other side of the bar and then came over to them.

"What can I get you to drink?"

Her accent sounded Polish, Heloise thought, maybe Ukrainian.

"We'd like two rum and cokes," Frank said. "Double the rum and use the dark one."

"Oh, no thanks. Just one. I'm not having anything," Heloise said.

"We'll take two," Frank repeated, and then to Heloise he said, "That way she doesn't need to get up again in a couple minutes."

The woman poured the drinks and set them on the bar. Frank raked them in like a casino croupier gathering up the house winnings.

"Three hundred eighty kroner," the woman said.

Frank looked at Heloise.

She nodded faintly as she got out her Visa card and passed it across the bar.

"Cash only," the woman announced, pointing at the wall behind her, where that same message was written in marker on a piece of lined binder paper, which had been taped to the mirror. "There's a cash machine down the street if you don't have cash with you."

Heloise pulled a crumpled five-hundred-kroner bill out of her wallet and handed the bill to the woman, who threw it into the cash register without entering the amount and handed her the change.

"Okay, Frank, you're the one who called me. What can you tell me about Anna?" Heloise asked.

"What do you want to know?"

"When did you last see her?"

Frank shrugged and took a big swig of his drink. "I don't remember the exact date."

"Your ex-wife says that she hasn't seen Anna since she moved away from home. That was seventeen years ago, so she didn't have much to contribute, and as far as I know, you moved to Greenland when Anna was eight years old. Is that correct?"

"Yes."

"Have you seen her since then?"

"Yeah, yeah."

"When?"

"I saw her last year."

Heloise looked at him for several seconds without saying anything. "You saw Anna *after* Christoffer Mossing's murder?"

"Hmm . . . was that before or after? I don't remember."

"Mossing was killed more than three years ago."

"Well, then you're probably right," he said, and drained his first glass.

"Where did you see her?"

"In a bar."

"Here in Copenhagen?"

"Mm-hmm."

"What was the name of the bar?"

"I think it was . . . I think we met at Andy's."

"The dive over on Gothergade?"

Heloise thought about what Ulrich Andersson had said about his source at the racetrack. It was someone he knew from Andy's.

"Yeah."

"Do you go there often?"

"A couple of times a week."

"Does the name Ulrich Andersson ring any bells?"

Frank leaned his head back as he thought about it. "Yeah, he's one of the guys from ABBA, right?"

Heloise closed her eyes to stop herself from rolling them.

"No, he's a journalist. He works for *Ekspressen*." She watched him attentively. "He has red hair, freckles . . ."

"Maybe," Frank said. "I know so many people, so I've probably met that guy too."

"Okay, but you met Anna at Andy's last year?"

"Yes."

"When was this?"

"Oh, I don't remember the date," he said, and started on his second drink.

"Was it warm out that day? Was it snowing—what? Try to think back."

"Yeah, I think it was snowing. Yeah."

"So, it was in the wintertime?"

"Right."

"How was the meeting set up? Did she contact you?"

"Yes."

"How?"

His eyes weren't focused, and he kept looking anywhere but directly at Heloise.

"I . . . She sent me a letter."

"A letter?"

"Yeah, like the ones she writes to you."

"What did it say in the letter?"

"Uh, something like, 'Hi, Dad. Long time no see. Why don't we get together?' You know."

"And then you met at Andy's?" Heloise repeated.

"Yes."

"Did you suggest that you meet there?"

"Yes."

"And how did you communicate that message to her?"

"Huh?"

"How did you answer Anna's letter?"

Frank shifted positions in his chair and drank the rest of his second drink. He had emptied both glasses in under five minutes. "I don't really remember."

Heloise eyed him without saying anything.

"What?" he asked.

"You haven't received any letters from Anna, have you?"

"I have too."

"I don't believe you."

"Hey, I know all kinds of stuff I can tell you," he protested.

Heloise shook her head. "I don't believe that you saw her either."

"Did too!" Frank exclaimed, his eyes wide and darting around. "If you just give me five hundred kroner, I'll tell you everything I know."

"No thanks," Heloise said, getting up.

"Yeah, but I mean, you have tons of money. I know you do. You paid Jonna to talk to you too."

Heloise got it now. Mr. Goatee must have told Frank about her visit to the Lantern, and there was only one reason Frank had contacted her: he wanted to make money off his daughter's story.

He disgusted Heloise. She wasn't convinced yet that Jonna had failed as a parent, but *him*? She couldn't decide what was worse: that he had abandoned his daughter when he walked out on her when she was little, or that he was trying to capitalize on her situation now.

"Sorry, you are of no use to me," Heloise said, beginning to walk away.

Frank snorted so that snot bubbled out of his nose. "Why not? What the fuck are you talking about?"

"You walked out on your family, Frank," Heloise said. Her voice was cool, disinterested. "You left when Anna was still a kid, so you won't make a good source."

"But I had no choice, did I? Jonna, that crazy bitch, drove us into the ground. I had to work seven different jobs to make ends meet, and then that offer from Greenland came, and in the beginning I sent money home, but . . ." The arteries in his neck throbbed violently as his face turned from gray to purple. "At some point I'd had enough of her bullshit. So don't fucking blame me for leaving. Anyone would have with that bitch gambling away all our money."

Heloise felt a tingling sensation spread through her chest. She took a couple of steps back toward the bar.

"What did you say?"

"I said that you can't blame me for leaving," he sniveled. "You weren't married to her, so who are you to judge me?"

"No, you're right," Heloise said. She put a soothing hand on his shoulder. "What was it you said about her gambling away all your money?"

"Every month we were a week farther behind. We were broke. We never had enough money. Fucking compulsive gambler, man."

"What did she play?"

"Everything."

"Like what?" Heloise asked, sitting down next to him.

"The lottery and card games. She would sit in there all day playing on one of those damned slot machines at the Lantern back when her dad owned it."

"What about horses?"

He leaned his head back and inhaled through the ice cubes to get the last drops before he set the empty glass down. "Yes."

"Horse racing?"

"*Yes*, that's what I'm telling you, man. It wasn't my fucking fault that she couldn't control herself."

Heloise took her notebook out of her purse and opened it. "Frank, do you know if Jonna ever went to the racetrack at Klampenborg?"

He looked at the ballpoint pen she was holding at the ready over the page of her book and hesitated for a moment. He wiped his nose on his sleeve and smiled briefly.

"You gave five hundred kroner to Jonna, right?"

Heloise sighed and opened her wallet. "I only have a hundred and twenty kroner left in cash."

"Okay," he said, holding out his hand.

Heloise handed him the money.

"Did Jonna ever go to the racetrack?" she asked.

"If by *ever* you mean *all the time*, then yes."

The stripper on the stage behind the bar eyed the money and moved in closer. She performed a clumsy pirouette and opened the clasp of her purple lace bra and let her two heavy breasts fall out.

Frank looked up at her and smiled but didn't let go of the hundred-kroner note in his hand.

Heloise ignored the stripper and continued, "Did Jonna win money at the track?"

"Sometimes. But mostly she lost."

"What kind of amounts are we talking about here?"

He shrugged. "Sometimes she lost five thousand kroner, ten thousand kroner. Other times more, a lot more."

"How much more?"

"How the hell should I know? But I can remember the last sum I sent home from Greenland: thirty-eight thousand kroner. That was two months' salary I had saved up for her and Anna to pay the mortgage with so they could spend the summer hanging out together."

"Did she gamble away all the money then?"

"She already had, man." He cleared his throat loudly and spit into his empty glass. "The money I sent went straight into the hole she had already dug."

"Did she ever talk about a man named Johannes Mossing?"

"Who's that?"

"That's Christoffer Mossing's dad."

Frank shook his head. "I don't remember her mentioning that name. We haven't been together for more than twenty-two years."

"And yet you can remember the exact amount of money you sent home back then?"

"Believe me, if you had saved up thirty-eight thousand kroner and given it to someone, you'd remember it too if they'd spent the money paying off a gambling debt." He looked over at the bartender and waved for her to come over again. "But she didn't, though."

"She didn't what?" Heloise looked puzzled.

"Pay off her debt. Not the *whole* debt, anyway."

"What do you mean?"

"I cut off contact with her after that episode, but I heard stories from home about her owing more money, a lot more money. I don't know how she was even able to rack up a debt like that—we didn't have money like that, so she must have borrowed it from somewhere."

When people couldn't pay what they owed, they disappeared. People disappeared, Heloise. Do you understand what I'm telling you?

Heloise bit her lower lip. "All the money she owed back then . . . do you know how she managed to pay off the debt?"

Frank shook his head. "I don't know, and I don't care."

Heloise moved a little closer to him. "Frank, do you have any idea at all why Anna killed Christoffer Mossing?"

He shook his head again.

"Jonna said that she was crazy, mentally ill," Heloise said. "Do you think that?"

He didn't say anything.

"She also said that Anna was angry and withdrawn as a child . . ."

"No," he said, and for a split second Heloise made out a softness in his inebriated eyes. "She was damned cute when she was little, always warm and loving."

"Then what happened?"

He shrugged. "Like you said, I left. I have no idea what happened in Anna's life after that."

*   *   *

Heloise said good-bye to Frank Kiel and headed toward the exit as the bartender started magically transforming his newly acquired bill into a Bacardi shot.

Once she was standing in Kongens Nytorv out in front of the strip club, she called Schäfer, but it went straight to his voice mail. She left him a message and asked him to call her back as soon as possible.

She hung up and looked around.

The rain had stopped.

She started walking toward Bredgade, toward the sound of car tires racing over still-wet asphalt, as she tried to suppress the tiny nagging sensation that had begun to take shape somewhere deep within her.

27

A SMALL GROUP OF Asian teenage girls with Playmobil haircuts and DSLR cameras lit up the high-ceilinged room every time they took a picture. They whispered to each other, and every now and then they broke the silence with discreet giggles, holding their hands over their mouths and looking very naughty. They lacked only pigtails and pleated skirts, Heloise thought.

She recognized two regulars, each sitting on their own side of the aisle with their faces bowed and that particularly radiant look of suffering reserved for people whose souls were in agony.

Apart from them, the Marble Church was empty.

The attendant at the entrance to the dome was the same as when Heloise was a child. Bobo was his name, and Heloise had always thought that sounded like something right out of *Lord of the Rings*. He *looked* like it too, and hadn't changed since their first encounter: he was a pale, human version of a contented raisin with a milk-white toupee.

Every Christmas she brought him a nice bottle of port, and that was why he always turned a blind eye at times like this when she showed up outside the church dome's visiting hours. He'd let her slip behind the heavy oak door unnoticed by the other churchgoers.

She smiled at him as she passed the desk where he always sat, and he returned her greeting with a warm, conspiratorial look.

"It's wet up there this evening," he said.

Heloise nodded and continued past him.

She knew the way like she knew the lines of her own face, knew exactly which steps creaked, where the stairs were uneven, and how many steps she needed to take to cross the attic space above the dome's twelve apostle paintings.

And then, as she stepped out onto the narrow walkway that ran around the tower, Copenhagen revealed itself below her. Glinting in the gathering twilight, familiar. And safe.

She wiped off the seat with her jacket sleeve and sat down on the bench, from which she had a view of Amalienborg Palace and the Opera House. Normally at this time of day, she would have chosen the opposite side of the dome to watch the sun sink behind the city's roofs, but with the western sky still overcast, the sky was prettiest in the opposite direction.

She sat for a long time, watching the airplane traffic over the Amager skyline. The incoming aircraft weren't spaced very far apart. One by one, the planes lined up like pearls on a string in the lavender-blue evening sky, headed for the tarmac at Kastrup.

Heloise needed the peace up here to focus, to digest the week's impressions. In a matter of days, she had been on the verge of losing her job, a wanted and mentally ill murderer had become fixated on her, and she had found out that Jonna Kiel had—or at least at one time had had—a serious gambling problem. She had found Ulrich Andersson's body, and her apartment had been broken into.

Or had it?

She still couldn't seem to make all the pieces fit together. Who had taken the picture from her balcony and posted it on Instagram?

No matter what angle she tried to approach the case from, her thoughts constantly returned to the same riddle.

Martin.

Martin was the one who had given her the documents about the Skriver case that had caused problems at the newspaper. He was the one who had shown up the same night as Anna Kiel's Instagram picture, and now the police had told her he had a record, for assault. The more she thought about it, the more she was convinced that she didn't really know anything about him, just his outermost shell, the smooth facade he let the world see.

She reached for her phone.

He answered on the first ring. "Hi!"

There was a crisp freshness to his voice that made Heloise's chest feel effervescent, and she could hear that he was outside somewhere, on the go.

"Hi, where are you?" she asked.

"I'm on my way home. How about you?"

Heloise got right down to business. "Why do you have a conviction for assault on your criminal record?"

She could hear that he had stopped.

"Excuse me?"

"The police lifted your fingerprints when they were in my apartment after the break-in, and you're in their system."

After a brief pause, he replied, "Yes."

"Yes? Is that all you have to say?"

"What do you want me to say?"

"I want you to tell me why you've served time."

He was quiet for a moment. Then he said, "I punched a guy. It's not something I'm particularly proud of, but trust me when I tell you that he had it coming."

"Had it coming?" Heloise furrowed her brow. "Who deserves getting four teeth knocked out? You're going to have to explain that to me, Martin."

"It's not important who—"

"It's important to *me*."

She could hear him exhale heavily. Then he said, "A guy by the name of Thomas Berggren."

"And who's Thomas Berggren?"

"He was my best friend for twenty-four years. Until I found out that he was sleeping with my wife."

Each word landed like an ax, chopping wood.

Zak, zak, zak.

Heloise didn't say anything.

"Listen," he continued. "I didn't tell you about it because it's not relevant to the two of us. I broke the law. That was a long time ago now, and I've paid for it. My wife became my ex-wife, and my friend is now my ex-friend. They mean nothing to me—*less* than nothing. I've moved on. But I would be lying if I said I felt guilty about it or even regretted it. Like I said, he had it coming."

Heloise didn't know what to believe. Was he telling the truth now, or was this a lie he had made up on the spot? There was getting to be so much distrust between them. She had so many reasons to doubt him. Every time she demanded answers, excuses came pouring out of his mouth, far too easily, far too conveniently. Could she ever trust a man whose job for many years had primarily been about rewording, manipulating, and misleading?

"Why were you allowed to keep your job?" she asked. "Why didn't they fire you when you went to jail?"

"Because I'm the best at what I do." He didn't even try to sound the slightest bit modest.

Heloise leaned back with her eyes closed, resting her head against the verdigris copper of the wall of the dome. She contemplated how to handle the situation.

"Where are you?" Martin asked.

Heloise didn't answer.

"Why don't we just get together and talk about this? I'll come to you. Just tell me where you are."

"I think . . ." Heloise said, trying to muster up some inner determination. "I think it's best if we don't see each other anymore."

"What? No, come on. I—"

"I think it would be best if I were alone right now. So much is going on at work, and—"

"Heloise," he said. His voice had been reduced to a dark whisper. "You're going to have to start trusting me a little. I think . . . I think I'm in love with you."

She smiled sadly to herself.

"I want to believe you," she said, looking out at the city's roofs. "But I don't."

* * *

Heloise sat there for a long time after she had hung up. She had lost all sense of time as she tried to untie the knots tangling up her thoughts. She jumped when the little door in the wall next to the bench was assertively pushed open.

Bobo stuck his wrinkly face through the doorway.

"Heloise," he said, and then pointed a bony, admonishing finger toward the dome behind her. "Unless you want to lose your hearing, you come down now. It's almost eight o'clock."

Heloise jumped off the bench and looked fearfully at the giant bronze bell behind her.

"Oh, I'm sorry. I lost track of the time!"

The old man shook his head in disapproval and held the door open for her so she could quickly scurry down the little oak staircase.

They had made it only across the attic space when the clockworks began to creak and groan. The gears turned with a resounding boom, and the space was suddenly filled with a deafening, polyphonic cacophony of bells ringing.

Heloise and Bobo covered their ears as they ran down the whitewashed spiral staircase, which was so narrow that

Heloise scraped one of her elbows on a little nail jutting out of the wall.

When they had made it down to a safe distance from the noise, the old man put his hand on her arm.

"You're bleeding," he said.

Heloise turned her arm and looked down at the wound. It was just a scratch, but the blood was running down her forearm and dripping onto the white stone floor.

"Come," he said, waving her closer. "Come in here."

He pulled a tapestry aside, and Heloise followed him through a door in the wall into a small chamber.

"I . . . I've never been in here before!" she said, blinking a couple of times.

"No," he said as he rooted around in a little dresser drawer. "There are still areas of the church you haven't seen."

"Really?" Heloise was astounded. "I thought I'd been everywhere there was to go."

Bobo shook his head secretively. Then he smiled. "No, not everywhere."

"But . . ." She glanced around. "What else is there? Can't I see the other rooms I don't know about?"

Heloise felt like she had just heard a secret about a trusted friend she had thought she knew inside and out. She didn't like the feeling.

Bobo pointed and said, "Sit down, Heloise."

She sat down on a chair upholstered in moss-green velvet next to an old mahogany desk.

"Hold out your arm," he ordered kindly.

Heloise held out her arm.

With the yellowish crowns on his teeth, Bobo bit the corner of a little square plastic envelope and then pulled a moist towelette out of it. He carefully wiped away the blood. Then he stuck a bandage over the scrape and gently patted it a couple of times.

"There!" he said. "Good as new."

Heloise thanked him mechanically, even though her arm hadn't bothered her at all.

"So, what rooms haven't I seen in this place?"

"Why so curious?" Bobo chuckled softly.

Heloise shook her head gently. "Just because."

"Why?"

Heloise didn't answer.

Bobo peered at her with eyes that were completely cloudy with cataracts. His one eye was so white that Heloise wondered if he could see out of it at all.

"What is it with you and the dome?"

Heloise shrugged. "It feels safe."

"Most people are afraid of heights and feel dizzy when they go up there."

"Not me," she said, shaking her head. "It's my place."

The old man got up and gestured for her to follow suit. They started walking toward the exit, and in the heavy doorway, he put a hand on each of her shoulders so that they were standing face-to-face.

"The church is a place where many people come to find peace, Heloise. They come to seek comfort. But there are also some who come seeking absolution for their sins."

Heloise didn't say anything.

"I've seen you here in the church since you were a child, and it's been a long time since you've looked happy." He watched her intently. "What I'm trying to ask is, did you do something you need to be forgiven for? Because if that's the case, I'm sure the pastor would love to talk with you. No matter what it is, you can trust him. You know that, don't you?"

Heloise looked into his eyes. For a second she considered telling him everything, leaning into his fatherly embrace, sobbing. But the words burned in her mouth and wouldn't come out.

Instead she said, "No, Bobo. Forgiveness isn't what I need. It's what I'm having a hard time giving."

28

H ELOISE HADN'T EATEN anything since the couple of pieces of rye bread she'd had at Kenneth Vallø's place earlier that afternoon. Now her stomach was rumbling, but even so she didn't feel hungry. She just wanted to go home and go to bed, to close her eyes and for a few hours allow herself to sink into a world where everything was still possible. A world where men like Johannes Mossing didn't exist, where people around her didn't get murdered or hang themselves, and where the only mail she received was vacation postcards and Christmas cards and greetings from friends and family members.

Where everything was the way it had once been.

She walked down Bredgade and turned left on Frederi-ciagade, heading home toward Olfert Fischers Gade. The rosebushes flanking the front door of her building were still in bloom. She stopped and stuck her nose all the way down into one of the big, powder-pink blossoms. She inhaled deeply, and a couple of the delicate petals drifted down onto the ground. Then she stuck her key into the front door and started walking up the stairs to her apartment on the top floor of the building.

As she rounded the fourth floor, her phone beeped in her pocket.

A text from Karen Aagaard: *Hey! Apparently, The Shovel decided to forgive you for your Skriver article and he's recommending that we punish you only with a slap on the wrist. Rumor also has it that Mikkelsen simply didn't want to lose you, no matter what. So, congratulations! In other news: Bøttger's story about the secretary of commerce will break on Tuesday. Exciting!*

Heloise smiled.

At least that was all resolved now.

She slipped her feet out of her shoes on the welcome mat in front of her door and had just turned her key and grabbed the handle when the man appeared out of nowhere.

It all happened so fast.

Before Heloise had a chance to look back, he pounced on her from behind. He swung his right arm around her neck and held it in a deadlock with his left while he pushed her forcibly into her front hall. She dropped her purse and instinctively started hitting and clawing at his arm with both hands, but her blows bounced off him.

The man leaned back and picked her up so that she was dangling in the air for a moment. A searing pain pierced her neck as adrenaline surged through her body. It was as if time froze, as if she were hanging in the air with her legs wriggling in slow motion while all sound around her evaporated.

The man lowered her so that her feet touched the floor and loosened his hold a little—just enough that she was able to draw a gasping mouthful of air down into her lungs.

Then he tightened his hold again.

"Heloise," he said, smelling the back of her head. "I wish I didn't have to do this, but you wouldn't listen."

Her whole body was screaming; her skin, her blood, her muscles were shrieking in pain and desperation.

She opened her mouth, but nothing came out.

The man pushed her further into the apartment.

She fell over the threshold on the way into the living room, and her legs dragged limply along behind her as he pulled her to the sofa and lay her on her stomach on the light-gray cotton-covered cushions without releasing his hold on her neck.

He put a knee on her back, and a piercing pain cut through her whole body. She tried to kick, to twist free of him, but with each move she made, he gained a harder, tighter hold.

"You should have minded your own business, Heloise."

"Stop!" she managed to stammer. Her voice sounded like she was talking from inside a vacuum-sealed plastic bag.

The man didn't stop.

Instead he put a hand on the back of her head and pushed her facedown, hard, into the sofa cushion as he brought his entire body weight down on her. Her lungs burned, and it felt like her head was coming loose from her body. As if it weren't attached to her spine anymore.

Then she heard a sound, a weird sound that at first she couldn't interpret. It sounded like a sea gull crying in the distance, a burbling cackle, and she realized it was laughter. The man was *laughing*. He kept pushing her facedown into the sofa and tightened his hold around her neck, and he laughed.

She knew right then that her life was over.

It didn't flash before her eyes. There was no slide show that exploded onto her internal projector, no display of sepia-toned images of childhood highlights like homemade rhubarb juice and tetherball and camping trips along the North Sea. No regret over unfulfilled dreams or roads she had chosen not to travel.

It was just totally quiet.

I'm dying now, she thought.

Then everything went black.

CHAPTER

29

HELOISE HAD TO struggle to pull herself out of sleep. She slowly opened her eyes a crack and tried to figure out where she was, but she couldn't see anything other than blurry contours in the darkness. Her tongue was dry and rough, and she tried to swallow. The motion cut through her windpipe and neck muscles like a knife.

Where am I?

Her heavy eyelids kept slipping shut, and she rubbed her face to wake up properly. Her hand smelled strangely pungent, like ethanol, and that triggered a wave of nausea that rose through her body.

She tried to stand up. Then she sensed something that made her hold her breath as short bursts of adrenaline pumped through her arteries.

She wasn't alone.

There was someone there in the darkness with her, slowly breathing somewhere behind her.

Heloise slowly turned around. "Who's there?"

She heard the sound of footsteps. Then she felt a hand on her shoulder, a voice she recognized, deep, rasping.

"Heloise."

She quickly pulled away from his hand, trying again to stand up, but the sudden movement made her dizzy.

"Martin? What . . . what have you done?'

She felt drugged, poisoned.

"What did you give me?"

Heloise fumbled for something to hold on to, and he grabbed her by her right upper arm.

Then everything around her vanished, and she fell deep into the darkness again.

CHAPTER

30

WHEN HELOISE WOKE up again, the room was bright. Many hours had passed while she had slept, and the night's cloud cover had vanished, as had the fogginess in her mind. The room she was lying in was so clear in the morning sunlight.

There was a machine by the headboard, and she was connected to it by electrodes. It was beeping slowly and steadily. A tube connected to her nostrils was sending oxygen to her lungs, and fluid from an IV drip was running into her left hand through a soft rubber tube.

Martin was holding her right hand firmly.

He was leaning over the bed with his eyes closed. He must have felt Heloise looking at him, because he suddenly raised his head and looked right at her.

He jumped when he saw that she was awake.

"Hey," he said cautiously and let go of her hand, afraid of scaring her again. "How are you doing?"

"I'm thirsty," Heloise whispered.

He got up and took a glass from the table by her bed. He held it to her face and positioned the white straw sticking up out of the glass between her lips.

Heloise sucked the water into her mouth, swallowed, and made a face.

"Does it hurt?" he asked.

She nodded and tried to sit up in bed. "What happened?"

"Let's just ring the bell first," Martin said, and pulled the cord over her bed. "I just want the doctor to check on you."

"How did I end up here?" she asked. "Where's the man, the guy who attacked me?"

Martin gently shushed her and carefully ran his hand over her hair.

"You don't need to worry about him anymore," he said. "The police arrested him. He can't hurt you anymore."

Heloise reached for his hand. His knuckles were red, torn up.

"What happened to you?"

Before he had a chance to respond, the door to the room opened and Gerda came in. Heloise could see that she had been crying. Her cheeks were red and puffy, her eyelids swollen from crying. Tears started seeping out again as soon as she saw Heloise.

"You're awake!" she exclaimed in relief, sitting down on the edge of the bed.

Heloise let go of Martin's hand and took Gerda's. "How did you know I was here?"

"Martin called and told me what happened."

"But how . . . ?" Heloise looked over at him.

"There's not that many people in the military named Gerda, so . . ." He smiled fleetingly.

Gerda started sobbing and crying profusely, and the words tumbled out of her in half sentences.

"You were . . . And I didn't think that I would . . . What if you'd been . . ."

She leaned over close to Heloise and sobbed like a little kid. Heloise put an arm around her and held her close, but she couldn't cry herself. She felt parched and hollow inside.

"Who was he?" she asked Martin, once Gerda had calmed down again. "What happened?"

"I don't know his name, but the police are going to come talk to you about it."

"How did you know I was here?" she asked Martin.

He and Gerda exchanged a look, and he was about to respond when the door to the room opened again. An older woman walked in wearing white scrubs, a stethoscope hanging like a piece of oversized jewelry around her neck.

"Ah, you're awake," she said, just as Gerda had. She smiled with professional, distanced empathy.

She walked over to the edge of the bed, coming close to Heloise's face. She pulled something that looked like a pen out of her pocket, clicked the top of it, and shone a light into Heloise's eyes with the pen.

"Can you tell me your full name and date of birth?"

Heloise did as she was asked.

"And where do you live, Heloise?"

"Olfert Fischers Gade in Copenhagen."

"Do you know where you are?"

Heloise looked over at the window and saw the green lawns of Fælled Park outside.

"Copenhagen City Hospital?"

"Yes, that's right." The doctor turned off the flashlight and stuck it back in her pocket. "Heloise, you've suffered some injuries to your neck, so you'll be sore for the next few days. You've had a CT scan, and luckily there's no bleeding in your brain or damage to the soft tissues in your neck. But it's likely that you've suffered a concussion. Do you feel nauseous? Any headache?"

She thought for a moment. "Yes."

"Do you still feel dizzy or foggy?"

Heloise shook her head. "Not anymore. I'm just tired."

"Do you remember what happened?"

Heloise thought for a moment, trying to remember. All her thoughts were like strange echoes inside her skull. What had happened? Where had that man come from? It had all happened so fast.

"There was a man. I was on my way into my apartment, and he . . . He grabbed me here." She held a hand up in front of her throat and was startled when she felt the bandage around her neck. "He was pressing down on me, and it hurt, and I . . . I don't know how I got away. I can't remember anything else."

She glanced around at the three of them in turn.

"There's no guarantee that you will remember more," the doctor said. "You passed out and were unconscious for many hours. But you're going to recover. You just need to take it easy for a little while."

"When can I go home?"

"Let's see how you're doing tomorrow. I'd like you to spend the night. I'll be back later this evening to see how you're doing. All right?"

Heloise nodded.

The door had scarcely closed behind the doctor when there was a soft knock from the outside.

Heloise looked up.

Sergeant Erik Schäfer stuck his head discreetly into the room. He smiled when he saw her.

"Ah, it's good to see you up."

"Well, I'm not exactly up yet," Heloise said. She felt uncomfortable lying half-naked in a bed surrounded by other people.

"You know what I mean—awake!" he said. "Are you okay?"

She shrugged.

Schäfer glanced at Gerda and Martin. "Would it be all right if I speak to Heloise alone?"

"I'll be right outside," Gerda said, and squeezed Heloise's hand before she left. Martin gave Heloise a concerned smile and a nod before he followed Gerda out.

Schäfer pulled a chair over to the bed and sat down beside Heloise.

"So, how are you really doing?"

"I feel like shit."

"Well, you still look very beautiful."

Heloise attempted a little laugh, but it hurt her throat. "The guy who attacked me . . . You got him?"

Schäfer nodded.

"Who is he?"

"His name is Stefan Nielsen. He's really bad news. His rap sheet is longer than my . . . well, it's long! Aggravated assault, threatening to kill people, unlawful restraint . . ."

"Unlawful restraint?"

"Yes, a sixteen-year-old that he had locked in a boathouse for three days last year for the fun of it." Schäfer took out a picture he had found in the police database and held it up to Heloise. "This is him here. Do you remember him?"

She sat up in bed a little and closely studied the man's face. He had a wide jaw and a thickset face below his black hair.

"Ulrich said that he had been threatened by a burly, dark-haired man," she said.

Schäfer nodded. "Do you recognize him?"

"No, I didn't see him." She shook her head. "He attacked me from behind."

"Never mind," Schäfer said, sticking the picture back in his pocket. "Maybe it's for the best that you didn't see him. Then you won't have these images in your head."

"But how can you know for sure that he was the one who attacked me? Where did you find him?"

Schäfer furrowed his brow. "You don't know?"

Heloise shook her head.

"Your friend Duvall—he saved you."

Heloise blinked a couple of times.

"He came into your apartment and found you before it was too late. You should have seen this guy Stefan when Duvall was done with him. He had to go to the ER to get his face sewn back together before we could even question him. Not that he was some kind of fashion model before, but he sure as shit ain't too pretty to look at now," Schäfer said, chuckling contentedly.

A tear ran down Heloise's cheek. "Martin saved my life?"

"Yup." Schäfer nodded.

CHAPTER

31

I T HAD TAKEN twenty-eight stitches to close the gash that
ran from his forehead, down the bridge of his nose, and all
the way across his right cheekbone. He had also acquired a
broken incisor and an "eight-ball" eye, black due to bleeding
inside his eyeball.

"That's a good look for you." Erik Schäfer pointed to
the messed-up face and sat down at the table across from the
man. "Does it hurt? I mean, other than your manly pride?"

The man didn't say anything.

"It must be humiliating for a street kid like yourself to get
your ass handed to you by a yuppie with manicured nails and
neatly pressed slacks." Schäfer slapped a case file down hard on
the table. "Humiliating!" he said, making a sympathetic face.

He pulled out a chair and sat down across from the man.

"It's Stefan, right? Stefan Nielsen? We haven't met before,
but I can see that you're a regular visitor here in the building,
so you know your way around and you know how this works.
Naturally, I need to inform you that you have the right to
remain silent and to have an attorney present. But if you tell
me something I wanna know, then there's a chance that we'll
be willing to cooperate a bit at your arraignment hearing in
a couple of hours."

"You're not selling anything I need." The man leaned back in his chair and smiled smugly.

"So, you're not interested in reducing your sentence?"

"It doesn't make any difference to me. I'll be out again in no time."

"I wouldn't be so sure," Schäfer said. "The sentencing guideline for a crime of this caliber says five years to life. You can't run from that. There are witnesses to what you did. You're going down for this, and when we nail you for Ulrich Andersson's murder as well, it'll be doubled. Unless we agree on some compromise beforehand, you and me."

Schäfer opened the folder in front of him and pulled out a picture of Ulrich Andersson's dead body lying on the autopsy table. In the picture, his rib cage was open like a cardboard box being emptied of its contents, with an unobstructed view of the dark-red organs, the yellowish fat, the intestines and tendons.

Schäfer pushed the picture across the table, where it stopped a couple of inches from the man's right hand.

"This guy," he said. "Remember him? He's the one you threatened with a gun a few years ago—the guy you strangled and slung up in his apartment on Amager Strandvej the other day."

"Who, me? Nah."

The look in the man's good eye was playful, defiant. Aside from his injured face, he didn't look like someone who had met his match the day before. He rather looked like he was enjoying himself.

"Where were you last Wednesday?"

"Around," he said with a shrug.

"Where were you last Wednesday between noon and ten PM specifically?"

The man leaned back in his chair. He clasped his hands behind his head and crossed his outstretched legs.

"Go fish," the man said.

Schäfer's eyes looked the man over, coming to a stop at his feet.

"Nice kicks," he said, and nodded at the man's red sneakers, which were sticking out under the table.

The man looked up at the ceiling and exhaled heavily but otherwise remained silent.

"The price of sneakers like that is totally different now from when I was young," Schäfer continued. "These days that kind of fashion statement will set you back most of a day's pay." He flipped through the case file. Then he looked up. "It doesn't say in the paperwork here what you do for a living."

Nothing.

"You had almost eight thousand kroner in cash on you when you were arrested."

"So what?"

"Where did you get it?"

"The Tooth Fairy," the man said, and smiled so that Schäfer had an unimpeded view of his broken front tooth.

"What do you do for a living?"

"This and that."

"This and that? For whom?"

"For myself."

"So, you're self-employed?"

The man nodded as if he liked that title. "Self-employed . . . yeah."

"So, what are you, uh, self-employed at?"

"I solve problems."

"And was Heloise Kaldan a problem that needed solving? Was Ulrich Andersson?"

The man looked around the room as if he was bored.

"Did Johannes Mossing pay you to get rid of them?" Schäfer asked, leaning in across the table.

The man looked Schäfer in the eye. He smiled but didn't say anything.

"What kind of shit is he messed up in? What is he hiding?" Schäfer continued. "If you give me Johannes Mossing— if you give me something with some meat on it, something I can use against him—then you'll find that your time here with us will be significantly shorter and far more pleasant than it's going to be if you don't play along."

Schäfer was bluffing. He didn't have any authority to offer that kind of plea deal, and he had the clear sense that the man sitting across from him knew it.

"Johannes . . . who?" The man's eyebrows almost met over the bridge of his nose as he regarded Schäfer skeptically.

He and Schäfer eyed each other for a long moment. Then the man broke into a laugh, a high, cackling laugh.

"Okay," Schäfer said, nodding in agreement. "We'll do this the hard way."

The door behind Schäfer was flung open, and a short-legged man he recognized as criminal defense attorney Marcus Plessner steamrolled into the room. He was wearing a silvery-gray suit, which Schäfer guessed had been custom tailored, because as far as he knew there wasn't an off-the-rack suit anywhere in the world that would fit a body with Plessner's measurements. The man was every bit as wide as he was tall and deep, like a Rubik's cube with feet.

His hairline had, surprisingly enough, moved farther down his forehead since Schäfer had seen him last. Implanted tufts of dark-brown hair now grew like watercress from his previously bare temples.

"Get away from my client," he said, and walked over to stand on the opposite side of the table.

He put a hand on Stefan's shoulder and looked over the injuries to his face.

"I sure as hell hope you didn't have anything to do with this." He spoke quickly, which he always did, as he peered distrustfully over at Schäfer.

"No, unfortunately, I can't take credit for that."

Erik Schäfer had sat across from Marcus Plessner many times. The man had a notorious knack for making gang members, child molesters, violent criminals, and drug dealers look like poor picked-on souls—and even worse, he was good at convincing judges and juries that they were precisely that.

Schäfer had had the dubious pleasure of his company whenever he questioned Johannes Mossing. And when after yet another batch of inquiries from Schäfer, Mossing had decided to report him for harassment, Plessner was the one who had screamed, "When a civil servant harasses a good, honest citizen like Johannes Mossing, it is a traumatizing experience. There isn't a single piece of incriminating evidence against my client—not one! It is pure harassment, and if it does not cease immediately, we will need to apply for a restraining order against Mr. Schäfer."

"You are not to say another word, you understand?" Plessner said, looking down at Stefan. "Not one word without my permission."

"Whatever you do in your everyday life, Stefan, it must be going really well if you can afford to be represented by none other than Orleff and Plessner." Schäfer looked back and forth between the two men.

"Do not say anything," the defense attorney repeated to his client.

"It is kind of funny, though, that you're being represented by Johannes Mossing's people, isn't it? By Christoffer Mossing's old coworkers?"

"Yes, it's hilarious," Plessner said sarcastically. "Now, would you please leave the room? I need to speak to my client alone."

"Oh, I'm done with him." Erik Schäfer stood up. "I can inform you that your client is being charged with attempted murder of the journalist Heloise Kaldan, and that we are charging him at the same time with the murder of journalist Ulrich Andersson."

"Thank you for the information, and good-bye." Plessner nodded toward the door.

As Schäfer grabbed the handle, he turned around. "By the way, I'm going to send Forensics in here."

"What for?" Plessner gave Schäfer a distrustful look.

"We just need an impression from those shoes." Schäfer pointed to Stefan's Pumas. "They look like a size seven, and that's a serious problem for your client for two reasons. The first being that a shoe print from a similar shoe was found at the crime scene where Ulrich Andersson was murdered . . ."

Plessner sent an irritated snort through the room. "And the second?"

Schäfer opened the door. "Well, you know what they say about men with small feet."

CHAPTER

32

GERDA HAD STOPPED by Heloise's apartment earlier in the day to pack a bag of clean clothes—a couple pairs of panties, a hoodie, some sweat pants, Heloise's favorite sneakers, and a denim jacket. She had dropped it off at the hospital in the morning and asked if she should stick around.

"No, no, you go. It's fine. I'm doing fine," Heloise had said, and it was only a white lie.

Physically she was relatively okay. Her throat no longer felt like it had been through a blender, and her skull no longer weighed as much as a bowling ball. The doctor had discharged her because she had promised to spend the next few days at home in bed.

But Heloise was afraid to go home alone. No, not afraid—she wouldn't have anyone believe that of her. But she just didn't want to walk into her apartment on her own.

Not today. Not yet.

Schäfer had called and told her that the man who had attacked her had also been charged with Ulrich's murder.

Murder.

So, Heloise's hunch had been right. Ulrich had been murdered. By the same man who had attacked her.

The thought shook her.

Schäfer had said that the man had been arraigned and that the judge had decided to take him into custody. But was he the only one out there who had it in for her? Were there other people, hiding in the shadows, ready to jump her as soon as her back was turned? Would she ever feel safe again?

Heloise took the bag from Gerda into the bathroom and was happy to get out of the hospital gown. She put her hands together under the cold water from the faucet and splashed water on her face. Then she looked at herself in the mirror.

Hold your head high, she told herself. Stand up straight, pull yourself together!

In the elevator she pushed the button for the ground floor, and she felt a sinking feeling as the elevator began to move. Every time the doors opened on the way down the shaft, new patients stepped into the claustrophobic metal box, all wearing hospital garb, some bringing an oxygen supply or wheeling an IV drip stand along with them, others with obvious tumors on their neck or face, dialysis patients with yellowish skin and edema in their legs and a little girl without a hair on her head, who smiled warmly at Heloise. Heloise smiled back, but she left the elevator with a feeling of never ever having had less faith in God.

She hurried through the lobby and walked through the big revolving doors out into the freedom of a gray morning sky, where a strong wind lifted her hair away from her face.

Martin was waiting for her, as he had promised. Heloise walked over to the car and climbed in through the passenger's door.

"Hi!"

He leaned over to her and kissed her. "Are you ready to go home?"

"Yes," Heloise said. "I wasn't five minutes ago, but now I am."

They drove over Fredens Bridge with the windows open on their way to Heloise's apartment. In just a few days the leaves on the trees had turned an orange brown, and there was a freshness in the air that hadn't been there last week, a crispness.

Fall had arrived.

They parked in front of the rosebush by her front door, and Martin held her hand the whole way up the stairs.

Heloise unlocked the door and looked around her apartment.

"You can't tell at all what happened here, can you?" she said. "It actually looks nicer in here than it usually does."

"Gerda came by to tidy up and clean the place."

Heloise spotted a large bouquet of purple flowers standing on the dining table in the living room. She walked over and read the card. It was a get-well-soon card from the editorial crew, signed by Karen Aagaard and Bøttger and the rest of the investigative team.

Heloise smiled a little to herself. Then she set the card down and looked around.

"My rug is gone." She pointed to the bare wood floor under the coffee table, where she usually had a Moroccan Berber carpet with a blue diamond pattern.

"Yes," Martin put an arm around her. "Unfortunately, it couldn't be saved."

"Did it get thrown away?"

"Yes."

"Why?"

"Do you really want to hear about that?" He scratched his cheek as he watched her.

"Yes," Heloise said. She couldn't remember anything between when she ended up on the sofa with the man's knee on her back and when she woke up at the hospital with Martin's hand in hers. "I need to hear it. I need to know what happened."

"Okay," Martin said, and led her out into the kitchen. "There was blood on the rug, so it got thrown away."

"His blood?"

"Yes."

"How did you get in here that night? Why were you even here at all?" Heloise sat down at the kitchen table.

"After we talked on the phone, I decided to come over to your place." Martin opened the fridge and took out a bottle of mineral water. He grabbed a glass from the shelf over the sink and filled it. "Here, drink this. You need to stay hydrated."

Heloise reluctantly took a sip.

"You said you came over here?"

"Yes. Because . . . I know you're afraid to let anyone in and get close to them. I know that you've had a hard time trusting me. But we have something together, you and I, don't we? Something real?"

She didn't respond.

"So even though you told me that we shouldn't see each other anymore, I came over here, because I knew that you would feel differently if we were face-to-face."

Heloise nodded slightly.

"When I arrived, the front door downstairs was ajar, so I came in without buzzing you, and once I got up here, I saw him. Your door was open, and he . . ." Martin stopped. He ran his open hand over his mouth and swallowed a couple of times. "He was sitting on top of you and you were lying with your face smashed down into the sofa, and he . . . he was smiling."

Heloise looked at him but didn't say anything.

"That motherfucker was smiling, and I . . . I just lost it. I yanked him off you and started punching him. I kept hitting him until I couldn't do it any longer. I . . . I can't actually really remember what happened then. But I called the police after I tied him up. I pulled a wire out of your TV and tied his hands behind his back. Then that Erik Schäfer guy showed up with a bunch of other police officers. An ambulance came, no, two ambulances, I think . . . Anyway, there were a bunch of paramedics here. They drove you away, cuffed the man, and questioned me right here at this table."

Heloise could see that he was shook up, even though he was trying to hide it. She bit her lower lip. "Are you okay?"

"Me? You're the one who got attacked, and you're asking me if *I'm* okay?"

"It must have been pretty traumatic for you too."

He nodded. "I have a ton of questions that keep filling my head. I told the police everything I know about that night, but no one has told me anything at all."

Heloise swallowed. The movement made her throat hurt. "What do you want to know?"

"Who was he?"

"His name is Stefan Nielsen."

"Did you know him?"

"No." Heloise shook her head. "But Schäfer told me that in addition to the charges for attacking me, he was also charged for the murder of a journalist named Ulrich Andersson."

"The guy from *Ekspressen*?" Martin blinked a couple of times.

Heloise nodded. "You know him?"

"No, but in this morning's paper, it said that he had been murdered in his home."

"I'm the one who found him."

Martin's eyes widened.

"The police think it was the same man who did that," she continued.

"What the fuck, Heloise, that's . . . How did you . . . Why would a psycho like that be out to get you?"

"I think it's because I'm investigating a—"

They were interrupted by Heloise's phone. There was no number showing on the caller ID, and she answered with a simple, "Hello?"

She could hear static on the line, silence, a delay. And then:

"Heloise?"

For some reason or other, the hoarse female voice made a cold sensation trickle through Heloise's body, and her eyes went to Martin's.

"Who is this?"

"You know who this is."

". . . Anna?"

"Mm-hmm."

"Anna Kiel?"

"I told you that you knew."

A rage grew within Heloise. She had had enough now. "Why do you keep contacting me? What do you want?"

The voice sounded approachable, almost polite. "I'm not the one who wants something."

"What the hell are you talking about? Why do you keep contacting me?"

"I want to tell you, but you need to come to me if you want to know more."

"Come to you? I have no idea where you are. I don't even know *who* you are."

"I'm with him."

"With who?" Heloise yelled in frustration into her phone. "Who are you looking for?"

"If you want the story, you have to talk to him first. You're the only one who can write the story—the only one he'll tell it to."

"You know what?" Heloise shook her head. "I don't think I'm interested in your story anymore. Find someone else to harass. I'm done with this."

The voice on the other end remained unchanged, calm. "It's not just *my* story I'm talking about. It's yours. It's *your* story, Heloise. If you want to finish your story, you need to come to me now."

"I don't understand . . ." Heloise said, puzzled.

"He's waiting for you."

"Who's waiting for me, Mossing?"

"There isn't much time left, so you need to hurry now."

There was a click, then a persistent beeping.

"She hung up!" Heloise looked at the phone in her hand.

"Who was that?" Martin had stood up and was now standing very close to Heloise.

She looked up at him. "Look, that thing I said to you the other day on the phone . . ."

"About how you don't think we should see each other anymore?" Martin nodded.

"Yes," she said. "I didn't mean that."

He looked down at her and smiled briefly. "I know."

Then she told him everything that had happened since she had received Anna Kiel's first letter.

33

"I'VE GOT A story for you!" Lisa Augustin set a tall stack of books down on her table, accidentally knocking over a plastic cup of cold coffee, which quickly spread across her whole desk. "Oh, shit!"

"A story?" Schäfer looked up from the case file. He had been taking a closer look at the old crime scene photos of Christoffer Mossing's open throat.

Augustin frantically flapped her hands in front of the automatic paper towel dispenser on the wall as the machine calmly spit out one sheet at a time at an infuriatingly slow pace.

"Yes, an anecdote from the Dark Ages," she explained as she wiped up the spilled coffee. She gave him a smug look that made him clasp his hands behind his head and lean back in his chair.

"All right, I'm listening."

"Okay, so, this story takes place in Paris at the beginning of the twelfth century." She slam-dunked the used clump of paper towels into the trash and then gathered her hair into a messy bun on top of her head. "Let's set the scene. Here we meet a young girl who is none other than the niece of Fulbert, the canon of Notre Dame."

"Canon?"

"Yeah, that's . . ." She flipped through her notes and then read out loud. "That's a term used for all ecclesiastical workers in a diocese aside from the ordained priests and curates, whatever that means. They were also sometimes referred to as clerics." She tossed aside her notebook. "Anyway, the canon's young niece was looking for answers to the questions of human existence—"

"As one does." Schäfer nodded.

"—so she pesters her family for permission to be educated. It quickly becomes clear that there is only one teacher in the city that can give her the education she seeks, namely a philosopher and theologian named Pierre Abélard."

Augustin paced back and forth in front of her desk as she spoke.

"Fine, all right. So, the girl starts receiving tutelage from this guy Abélard, and he quickly discovers that she is ridiculously gifted, in other words, functioning on the same intellectual level as the scholars in the Church. So, even though he's more than twenty years her senior, he becomes wildly fascinated by and attracted to her."

"Uh-huh. I smell trouble."

"Exactly. They begin this intense love affair, and so while her mom and dad think she's sitting around contemplating the great existential questions and having her intellect stimulated in Abélard's chambers, they're really going at it like rabbits."

"You don't say."

"And that was super taboo back then, because they weren't married."

"I'm sorry." Schäfer held up his index finger. "Is this story going to be much longer? Because if it is, then I'm just going to duck out and grab a bucket of popcorn and a cold beer."

Augustin ignored him and kept going. "Well, the couple kept their relationship secret, but when the girl became pregnant, her family found out that they had had sex, and then she was kicked out of the Church in punishment for living in sin. She and Abélard decided to escape to Brittany, where she bore them a son, and at some point or other—I can't remember when—they returned to Paris and got married."

"And then they lived happily ever after?"

"Not quite, no. Because one night the girl's family breaks into Abélard's house and attacks him in his sleep. They still haven't forgiven him for bringing shame to the family, so they castrate him—they cut his pecker off."

Schäfer looked pained and moved a protective hand to his lap.

"Abélard survives and flees to a monastery north of Paris to become a monk and live in celibacy—now that he also really kinda doesn't have that many other options—and he convinces the girl to become a nun in a place nearby."

"And then?"

"And then they begin a twenty-year-long correspondence."

"A what?"

"They write love letters to each other, long, intense love letters. And in that way their love continued to flourish despite their separation, until they both died many years later. They are buried side by side in a cemetery somewhere in Paris, and their letters have been published and analyzed and studied by historians and romantics for centuries."

Augustin grabbed one of the books off the desk in front of her and waved it in front of Schäfer. A pink Post-it note stuck up from one of the pages in the middle of the book.

"And *now* . . ." she said. "Now comes the million-kroner question: what do you think the young student's name was?"

Schäfer looked into Augustin's eyes and shrugged.

"Héloïse," Augustin said. "Her name was Héloïse."

Schäfer raised an eyebrow but still said nothing.

"There's a ton of literature about their forbidden love story," Augustin continued, "but I could only find one book with a Danish translation of the couple's most popular letters."

She cracked open the book she was holding in her hands and flipped through to the page with the pink Post-it note.

She set the book in front of Schäfer.

"This is a letter from Pierre Abélard to Héloïse. Read the underlined section!"

Schäfer leaned over the book and read, " 'While I am denied your presence, Héloïse, give me at least through your words some sweet semblance of yourself.' " He looked up at Augustin in surprise. "How did you find this?"

She sat down heavily in her desk chair and smugly flung her feet up onto the desk.

"I've tried analyzing Anna Kiel's letters in a hundred different ways, but most of it is just a bunch of damned nonsense, and that sentence didn't get any hits in the search engines. But then I had the idea to run it through Google Translate. First I tried German. *Nichts*. Then Spanish. *Nada*! But then I searched for the French version of the sentence—*et voilà!*"

Schäfer smiled at her. "Well done."

He read the sentence in the book again. "So then how did you find it in Danish?"

"I checked out all the books they had on the topic at the city library and worked my way through the pile," Augustin explained with a shrug.

Schäfer leaned back. "So, Anna Kiel ends the three letters to Heloise with references to this medieval story about forbidden love?"

"Yes."

"Why?"

"Well, we need to ask the journalist about that."

"But don't you think it's pretty unlikely that she knows about this medieval couple? Isn't that the kind of thing only history buffs would know about?"

"I don't know. It is an unusual name, *Heloise*. She must get asked about it all the time. I mean, like, I went to school with this chick called Isolde, and people were always bringing up Tristan when they heard her name."

Schäfer stared at her blankly from across the desk.

"Isolde," Augustin repeated. "You know, like Tristan and Isolde."

Still nothing.

"For Christ's sake," she said, rolling her eyes. "Tristan and Isolde, like Abélard and Héloïse, are a famous pair of lovers from the Middle Ages."

"This may come as a shock to you," Schäfer said, "but that was before my time. I don't know any of these fools you're talking about."

"My point is just that Heloise must have heard about her namesake. She must know the story. At some point or other in her life, someone must have mentioned it to her."

Schäfer pulled out his phone. "Well, there's only one way to find out."

* * *

It startled Heloise when her phone rang.

She had shared a bottle of white wine with Martin while she told him about Anna Kiel, even though the doctors had advised her not to mix alcohol with the painkillers she had brought home from the hospital. They had dozed off on the sofa, intertwined and exhausted, and Heloise had fallen into a coma-like sleep. The light-colored silk pillow she had been lying on was wet with saliva, and her head felt heavy.

She pulled her phone out of the crack between the sofa cushions.

"Hello?" She spoke softly so as not to wake Martin.

"Hi! Sorry, did I wake you?" Schäfer asked.

"No. Well, a little."

"How are you doing?"

"A little groggy, sore throat."

"I'm really sorry to hear that, but it'll pass soon. I promise you."

"Yeah, maybe. I don't know . . . What's up?"

"We were just looking at the case and trying to find some sort of red thread, something that connects you and Anna Kiel, right?"

"Okay?"

Heloise suddenly remembered Anna's phone call earlier in the day.

"You don't happen to have a bachelor's degree in history, do you?" Schäfer asked.

Heloise could hear him turning pages. "No, undergrad business major and a master's in communication and journalism. Why?" She sat up on the sofa and started rubbing one of her eyes.

"Does *Abélard and Héloïse* mean anything to you?"

Heloise's hand stopped midmotion, and she stared with her one free eye at the candle's bluish-yellow flame, which was still burning on the coffee table in front of her.

A pain spread through her chest, as if Schäfer had just branded her with his words.

"Abélard and Héloïse?" Heloise repeated.

"Yeah, I had my partner analyze Kiel's letters, and it turns out that the final sentence—*While I am denied your presence, give me at least through your words some sweet semblance of yourself*—is a quote from an old love letter from the Middle Ages. It's from a letter that a theologian sent to his young lover. Her name, like yours, was Heloise, just spelled with a diaeresis over the *i*—you know, two dots like the umlaut in Schäfer?" He paused and waited several seconds for her response. "Hello?"

"No," Heloise replied.

"No, what?"

"That doesn't mean anything to me."

"You're not familiar with the story?"

"No."

"Well, all right then." Schäfer sounded disappointed. "But it is pretty weird, isn't it, for Anna Kiel to toss a reference like that into the letter, and that it was originally written in the year eleven hundred something or other to a woman named Héloïse?"

"Yes . . ."

"And you're sure that you've never heard of these medieval people before?"

"Yes."

"Okay, but it has to mean something. We just need to look at it from the right angle. Would you mind looking it up and see if it rings any bells?"

"Sure. Anything else?"

"Not right now. How about you? Any news?"

"No," Heloise lied. Her voice sounded strangely hollow to her own ears, as if she were standing above ground and hearing herself speak from the bottom of a dry well.

"You sure?"

"Yes. Could we talk some other time?"

"Of course. So, you're okay?"

"Yes."

"Are you sure? You sound a little—"

"I'm fine, okay? I'll talk to you soon."

Heloise hung up and let the phone fall from her hands as she slid off the sofa down onto the living room floor, where she lay for a long time gasping for breath in short bursts.

She felt sick. Sick and decimated and broken deep down inside.

It couldn't be true.

It had better *not* be true.

In a clear vision that filled her with fear, she understood what the letters were about—what connected her to Anna—and she didn't know what was worse: the story Anna Kiel wanted to share with her or what she had to do to hear it.

34

"Baby?"

"Hmm . . ." Erik Schäfer tore himself away from his thoughts and looked at Connie, who was sitting on the other end of the dark-red velour sofa. "I'm sorry, honey, did you say something?"

She laughed. "This is the third time in ten minutes that you've spaced out. Where'd you go?"

"Oh, it's just a work thing that's bugging me." He took a slightly firmer hold of her foot, which was resting in his lap, and massaged it. "I'm working on a case right now that I can't figure out."

"Tell me about it," Connie said.

So, he did.

Most of the men Schäfer knew in his line of work didn't share the details of their work with their wives. They packed the workday's experiences away in a little mental box when they punched out and left it back at headquarters. Then they drove home to their typical Danish suburbs, where they ate typical Danish dinners like meatballs with stewed cabbage and talked about typical everyday things and watched Netflix series with their wives. The next day they went back to work and opened the box again.

Schäfer didn't work like that.

He didn't know how to separate himself from his work. And he couldn't and didn't want to separate himself from Connie, so she got him the way he was: the whole package, the skin, the hair, and everything else, including the occupational damage and the scars from his investigations.

He told her everything he could think of about the case, but he was still left with a nagging feeling that there was something he had overlooked.

"I've got this nasty little worm digging tunnels inside my brain, and I just can't get rid of it. It feels like I've forgotten to do something. Or like there's some angle I'm missing that I should be looking at the case from," he said, and scratched himself irritably behind the ear. "You know?"

"Maybe you just need a good night's sleep," Connie said. "You worked the whole weekend, and you've been tossing and turning for several nights now. Go to bed early tonight, and tomorrow you'll be able to look at the whole thing with fresh eyes."

Schäfer chuckled. "The apostle of health has spoken: Remember to get eight hours of sleep! Drink more water! No smoking! Eat less butter!"

"Yes, go ahead and make fun," Connie protested, "but it helps."

She looked down at her foot in his hands and sighed. "How can you love a woman with such ugly bunions and crooked toes?"

"That's the part of you I like best," Schäfer retorted.

He lifted her leg and held it in front of him like a guitar, while he turned the toes as if he were tuning the strings.

Connie giggled, and Schäfer felt happy deep in his bones. But when they went to bed that night, he slept an uneasy sleep, woke up several times, and lay there in the dark thinking. He followed the worm around through the corridors, reviewing every detail of the case, dozed off, woke up again, and started over again.

At 6:20, he got up to go take a shower.

"Where are you going?" Connie asked groggily, looking at her watch.

"Shh . . ." he whispered, and kissed her. "Just go back to sleep. I have to go to headquarters."

*   *   *

The morning traffic at the airport in Copenhagen was thick as fish scales. The check-in line at the Norwegian Air counter ran more than half the length of the departures hall, and Heloise was grateful that she had bought a premium ticket, which gave her access to faster check-in and the fast-track line through security. The last available ticket on the morning flight to Orly in Paris.

She was one of the first to board the plane, and she settled into seat 3A as the other passengers noisily made their way into the cabin with their carry-on luggage and toddlers.

Normally she wasn't a big fan of flying. She had covered too many plane crashes in her days at the news desk, seen too many ripped-out airplane seats strewn across mountainsides and Ukrainian beet fields with stocking-clad feet sticking out from underneath, too many black, mushroom-shaped smoke plumes rising from the crash sites like ominous smoke signals from the dead.

She had once read that most plane crashes happened during the first three minutes after takeoff, and since then she hadn't been able to relax until the plane had reached a certain cruising altitude and the seat belt signs had been turned off. And even then, even once the plane was well on its way toward its destination and the cabin crew had started handing out peanuts and beverages, she always felt a primal sense of worry.

Today she felt nothing.

Last night she had surrendered to her emotions and allowed herself to roll around without resistance in the sea foam from the wave that had broken. She had allowed the rage and the shame to recede into the background for a while and had opened the room inside herself that had been locked for years. She had told Martin about it and given herself permission to feel the grief as it was—sheer and brutal—and the emotions had nearly killed her.

But by the time Norwegian Flight DY3638 took off from Copenhagen Airport, her facade had been restored.

Numb on the outside, shattered on the inside.

When the plane broke through the cloud cover and the morning sky revealed itself, she took her computer out of her bag and started to write the first part of the story.

*   *   *

Erik Schäfer found a parking spot in front of Glyptotek Museum and walked from there over to police headquarters. He stuck a cigarette in his mouth and lit it.

He didn't smoke as much anymore as he once had. Up until just ten years ago, life as a smoker had been completely different. Back then he had started his day every morning with a cup of coffee and a smoke while he read the newspaper at the kitchen table at home, and Connie had only occasionally quibbled about the smell. At police headquarters he had always had an overfilled ashtray sitting on his desk, and the end of every meal was marked with the sizzling click of the lighter. But then the smoking bans had come and the health missionaries had made their move, and suddenly a smoker was reduced to a revolting subhuman who was sent outside into the rain like a disobedient dog. There you could stand under a roof overhang with your collar turned up around your ears, puffing fiendishly like any old addict, before you were once again allowed back in, and Schäfer had no time for that bullshit! No one was going to decide where and when he was going to smoke. So instead of smoking twenty cigarettes a day in the microscopic smoking booths with the jet engine exhaust hoods at police headquarters or obediently staying inside the lines in the specially designated smoking areas on the sidewalk in front of the building, he had scaled back his consumption significantly. Now he only smoked a couple of cigarettes a day, sometimes three or four, but never like a cowed animal, and never in the "designated smoking areas." Instead he lit up on his way from A to B in the spaces where—at least for the time being—smoking was still allowed: the street, parks and natural areas, and on his patio at home.

He tipped an imaginary hat when he passed the security guards in the lobby and took the elevator up to his office on the second floor.

"All right!" He clapped his hands decisively and talked to himself as he walked into the room. "What the hell have I been missing?"

He started at the beginning. He reread every single page of all the case files and was halfway through Christoffer Mossing's autopsy report when Augustin walked into the office.

"You're already here?"

"Hmm," Schäfer replied without looking up.

"What are you doing?"

He pulled off his reading glasses and tossed them onto the desk in front of him. "I'm going fucking nuts here."

Augustin smiled and walked around to her side of the desk.

"There's something," he said, rubbing his eyes.

"What kind of something?"

"Something I can't put my finger on. You know, like when you can't remember a name even though it's on the tip of your tongue? That's how I feel. What the hell is it that I'm trying to come up with?"

"That I don't know," Augustin said. "But you'll let me know when you figure it out, right?"

Her phone rang, and she answered it. After a brief conversation, she hung up and said to Schäfer, "That was Bertelsen. The got a hit on one of the palm prints that was lifted from the inside of the front door to Ulrich Andersson's apartment."

"Whose was it?" Schäfer asked, looking up.

"Guess!"

"Stefan Nielsen?"

"Bingo!"

Schäfer nodded in satisfaction. "Well, then that's settled."

"That also gives us something to put some pressure on him with."

"No, we can forget about all that. He's not gonna say a word about Mossing."

"Do you really think he'd rather go away for a long time than hand over Johannes Mossing?"

Schäfer nodded. "But I don't think it's a loyalty thing. It's not about his not wanting to be a snitch. I also don't get the sense that he's afraid of any potential repercussions."

"Then why?"

"I don't know. But there was something about the way he was looking at me, the look in his eyes, the smile. It was as if he was enjoying it."

"Enjoying what, being questioned?"

"The whole situation."

"Huh." Augustin walked over to the door. "You want anything?"

Schäfer glanced up. "What kind of anything?"

"Coffee. I'm going to pop down and get a coffee. Do you want me to bring you one?"

Schäfer shook his head, and Augustin left the room. He clasped his hands behind his head as he scanned the bulletin board on the wall over her seat.

There were photos from the crime scene in Taarbæk, of the bloody bed in Christoffer Mossing's bedroom and of the murder weapon: a filleting knife that had been jabbed down hard into a *Vanity Fair* magazine with George Clooney on the cover. There were pictures of the blood-splattered headboard and the wall, pictures of the juice carton Anna Kiel had drunk out of after the murder and left her DNA on.

In the middle of the bulletin board was a picture of her—the picture the newspapers had printed in the weeks following the murder. In the picture she was standing so far out on a ledge of Grand Canyon that she looked as if she were floating in midair. There was a drop-off behind her that looked like it was probably a thousand feet down, and anyone who felt even a trace of fear of death would look a little uncomfortable in that situation. Alternatively, the thought of the free fall would trigger some kind of adrenaline-induced reaction—a panicky laugh, bulging eyes, clenched fists, beads of sweat on the forehead.

But Anna Kiel's face mostly looked like a television test pattern: she had all the correct instruments to display emotion, but it was like her machinery had been set to standby. Her arms dangled limply at her sides; her smile was perfunctory, docile; and her eyes . . . they were just like the little lady with the purse had said.

Extinguished.

Schäfer walked over to the bulletin board and stared at the picture. Then he fiddled around, removing the staples from the copies of Anna Kiel's letters that were hanging there, and took them down.

What was he missing?

He got out a neon highlighter and highlighted some of the sentences.

Maybe I was born defective. Maybe I am that way because of her.

We are connected through him, I understand that now.

If I say *Amorphophallus titanum* . . .

Do you see? Do you see it now?

Schäfer stared at the lines as the worm dug its way deeper into his thoughts.

"What the hell am I missing?" he mumbled to himself.

He looked up at the bulletin board again and took a step back to get a better overview. He almost fell, tripping over the wastepaper basket, and swore to himself. Then he kicked it.

The basket flew through the office and knocked over a fern that was sitting on the windowsill. The pot hit the floor, shattering, and the dirt scattered over the light-gray linoleum.

A colleague passing in the hallway stopped and poked his head through the doorway.

"Everything okay in here?"

Schäfer grumbled, trying to shoo him away with a hand motion.

"That's quite a temper you've got there, old man. Be careful so you don't demolish the whole office. You'd better get that swept up again."

Old man.

Schäfer glared at the guy and for a brief instant considered sweeping up the potted plant with *him*. Instead he turned his back to the door as the man continued down the hallway, whistling.

Annoyed, Schäfer started looking for something he could sweep the dirt up with. He knew there was a broom in the kitchenette at the far end of the department, but he didn't feel like walking all the way down there. Instead he found two pieces of cardboard and used one as a dustpan while he pushed the dirt onto it with the other.

He looked up and scanned the office to see where the wastepaper basket had landed.

His eyes fell on Augustin's desk, and a tickling sensation suddenly spread through his chest.

He dropped the cardboard, and the topsoil landed on the floor again. A strangely liberating feeling spread through his arms and all the way to his fingertips.

He got up and walked over to the desk.

The pink Post-it note was still sticking out of the book on the desktop, but it was the book at the bottom of the stack that had caught Schäfer's attention. He pushed the stack of history books aside, and they fell to the floor with a bang. He grabbed the book and looked at the cover.

It was titled *Abélard et Héloïse: Lettre d'amour*. It was in French, and Schäfer didn't understand a word of what was in it. But the author's name on the spine of the book had sent a cascade of adrenaline coursing through his body.

Kaldan, it said.

Nick Kaldan.

35

THE BLACK UBER driver in the freshly pressed dark-blue suit opened the car door for Heloise, who climbed out onto the gravel path at the Place des Vosges. She thanked him and crossed the street, pulling her little silver-gray wheeled suitcase behind her.

The building lay hidden behind the arcade and wasn't visible from the square, but Heloise knew the place. She had stayed there before.

She opened the big glass door and stepped into the atrium, where the facade was revealed to her. It was over-grown with malachite-green ivy, which had been trimmed only around the small mullioned windows and the white shutters and towered up before her, beautiful and lush. The whole building oozed innocence and beauty and looked like a young girl waiting to be asked to dance.

"Welcome to Paris, mademoiselle," said a female recep-tion clerk wearing a striped tailcoat. She spoke English with a strong French accent, so the city's name sounded more like "Bari" than "Paris," and she gave Heloise a key card to a small room on the hotel's third floor.

Heloise took an elevator the size of a tin can up to the

floor and let herself into room 311, where she collapsed onto the bed's crisp, white rustling bedspread.

She lay there for a while, looking around the room. It was a small room, a small room in a lovely, expensive hotel. The mattress practically touched the gilded wallpaper on either side of the bed, and the bathroom, which opened right beside the nightstand, contained a tiny shower stall instead of a bathtub. From the open double window, there was a view of a courtyard and a large hazelnut tree, whose branches reached right up to the rooftop. You could pick the nuts right from your bed if you wanted to.

Heloise didn't.

Instead she stretched her leg over to the minibar next to the headboard and pushed open the door of the minifridge in a quick motion. It hit the doorframe behind it with a bang, and the liquor bottles clinked on the shelves. She sat up and reached for one at random and looked at it.

Black rum.

There was a crisp, metallic sound as the seal under the cap broke. Heloise brought the bottle to her lips and tilted her head back. The liquor burned her throat and warmed her stomach in a strangely comfortable way.

She grabbed the handset of the old, ivory-colored rotary phone that sat on the nightstand and slowly dialed Gerda's cell—one number at a time—as the antiquated phone dial spun and hummed.

"Hello?"

"Hi, it's me."

"Hi!" Gerda's voice sounded surprised, happy. "Where are you calling from? I didn't recognize the number. You're not still in the hospital, are you?"

"I'm in Paris."

Gerda didn't say anything for a moment. Then she asked, "In Paris?"

"Yes," Heloise said slowly. "I was thinking that it was about time to get it over with."

"But . . . why didn't you tell me anything? I would have gone with you if—"

"I know you would have. You're a good friend, Gerda—the best. But this is something I need to do alone."

"Okay. I hear you. But why now?"

"I think . . . I think that's what Anna Kiel wants me to do. She's trying to tell me something about him."

"Anna Kiel?" Gerda sounded skeptical.

"Yes."

Heloise told Gerda about Schäfer's call the day before. About the reference to the letters and what they meant.

"There can't be any other explanation. He's the one she wants me to get in touch with. Her letters to me are about him. The whole thing makes sense now: the private things she knows about me, her reference to a corpse flower, which pretends to be something it isn't—like a pedophile running around with a bag of sweets convincing kids that he's a nice cozy old uncle. My address, he knows it. And the picture on Instagram. He must have been the one who took it, before he went to prison. Don't you see?"

Gerda tried to sound calm when she replied, "Are you planning to visit him?"

"Yeah."

"When? Today?"

"I don't know yet. I'll call the prison as soon as I hang up here. Then we'll have to see how quickly I can get permission to get in there."

"Promise me one thing," Gerda said. "When you're sitting across from each other . . . try to see if you can forgive him. Not for his sake, but for yours. Try to see if you can see him as the human being he once was, as a person you loved."

Heloise didn't respond.

"For your own sake," Gerda repeated.

"I'll call you later."

"Heloise," Gerda hurried to say. "Take care of yourself, okay?"

Heloise promised her that she would be careful. They said good-bye, and she found the number for the prison in her notebook.

The call was answered, and she introduced herself politely in her student's French and asked the man who answered if he spoke English.

He did.

"I would like to visit one of your inmates," Heloise said.

"Which one?"

"Nick Kaldan, prisoner number eight-one-nine-eleven."

"What's the purpose of the visit?" The voice was professional, unmoved.

"It's for personal reasons."

"What is your relationship to the prisoner?"

Heloise swallowed.

"I'm his daughter."

36

"WELL, WHAT DO you know!" Schäfer slammed the book down hard on the table in front of Augustin and pointed to the cover.

She set down her coffee, looking puzzled. "What?"

"Look at the name of the author!"

Augustin looked from the book to Schäfer's open mouth.

"Heloise's dad wrote that," Schäfer said. "Author and historian Nick Kaldan."

"Shut up! Are you sure?"

"Positive."

Augustin put her hand over her mouth. "Well, then she darned well must have recognized the reference!"

"Yup."

"So, she lied to us."

"No shit."

"But . . ." Augustin sat down on the edge of the desk and then immediately stood up again. "Why?"

"I have no idea. I've barely had a moment to look into it while you were gone, but from what I can see, Nick Kaldan is in prison in Paris."

"In prison?"

"Yes, in Fresnes on the outskirts of Paris. It's one of those really grim places."

"Why? What's he convicted of?"

"Of being in possession of child pornography."

Augustin closed her eyes as if Schäfer had spit in her face. When she opened them again, she asked, "Kiddy porn?"

"Yes."

"Oh God . . . Tell me more."

Schäfer sat down at his computer and skimmed the newspaper article that had come up when he searched the name. "He apparently lived in Paris for a number of years while he was teaching medieval literature at the Sorbonne."

Without taking her eyes off Schäfer, Augustin reached for her coffee and took a sip of it as she listened.

"He and three other men were arrested when the local police raided an apartment that belonged to a local sex offender. There were two minors in the apartment when the police broke open the door, and several of the kids and the men were naked."

"Fucking psychos!" Augustin's voice sounded angry and filled with hate.

"One of the men was Nick Kaldan. His home was also raided. His computer was confiscated, and he was brought in for questioning."

"And then what happened?"

"The children in the apartment showed clear signs of sexual abuse, and the police found a large quantity of pornography on Kaldan's computer. Pictures, movies, a bunch of really messed-up stuff."

"And then he went to prison?"

Schäfer nodded. "Then he went to prison."

Augustin put her hand to her head and exhaled. "Okay, I totally get why Heloise doesn't exactly go around bragging about this."

"Yeah, it's not a feel-good story."

"When did all this happen?"

Schäfer looked at the screen in front of him.

"Four years ago." He hit the back button and returned to the page of Google search results. "There's more . . ."

He clicked on another newspaper article.

"This looks like courtroom printouts, but it's in French. See, there's a sketch of him."

Augustin walked over and stood behind Schäfer.

The charcoal sketch on the monitor depicted a burly man with bushy, close-set eyebrows, a prominent nose, and a dark, full beard that blended behind his ears into dark, curly hair.

"Is that him?" she asked. "Is that Nick Kaldan?"

"Yes."

"He doesn't look like Heloise. Or to be more precise, she doesn't look like him. Are you sure they're related?"

"Yes, I looked it up in the national CPR2 database. They're father and daughter."

"Okay." Augustin nodded at the screen. "What does it say there?"

"I don't know. I don't speak French."

"Hello? Just use Google Translate." Augustin reached across Schäfer, copied the text of the article, and pasted it into Google's translation site. "The translation is never that great, but at least you get the general gist."

She hit *translate*, and the French text on the left side of the screen appeared in a rough Danish translation on the right side.

Augustin read out loud. "It says, 'The atmosphere in the Paris courthouse today was solemn for the sentencing of Mr. Nick Kaldan, a Danish citizen. A painful man stood in front of the crowd throughout the procedure. He showed remorse. He even cried'—yeah, right. Cry me a fucking river!— Um . . . 'The judge in the case is presumed to be unaffected by the accused's state of mind and remorse. Mr. Kaldan was found guilty of charges one through three and was sentenced to eight years in jail.' Boom!"

"Eight years," Schäfer repeated. "Ouch!"

"But that's just a slap on the wrist for that kind of thing!"

"No, I bet eight years in jail at Fresnes will feel like a hundred. That place isn't like the Danish prisons; there's no DVD players in the cell or nice little field trips to attend Great Aunt Ketty's birthday party. That place is hard-core. Personally, I'd rather eat a bullet than spend eight years there."

"Well, he got what he deserved, that fucking pig."

"It's hard to disagree with you there," Schäfer said with a shrug.

Augustin set her coffee down and walked over to a whiteboard mounted on the wall across the room. She picked up a blue marker and started making a timeline.

"Okay, Anna Kiel killed Christoffer Mossing in April 2016. After that she disappeared into thin air."

The pen squeaked as she vigorously moved it over the board's glossy surface, and Schäfer couldn't make out a single word of her hurried handwriting.

"There hasn't been any trace of her for several years," Augustin continued. "Until we heard from a witness that she was in France, right?"

"Right."

"So, she started writing letters to our young journalist—"

"Heloise is almost eight years older than you are," Schäfer said.

"Yeah, but she's still a knockout and love has no age limits. As I said, Anna Kiel writes letters to our young journalist, and we can see from the postmarks that she's moving around in France: from Cannes north to Lyon, and where was the most recent letter sent from?"

"From Gare du Nord in Paris," Schäfer said with a nod. He knew where she was heading.

"And that's not far from where Heloise's father is locked up."

"Correct."

"And Anna ends all the letters with a reference to a pair of lovers from the Middle Ages—"

"—whom Nick Kaldan wrote a whole book about."

"Exactly!"

"In the second letter she sent . . ." Schäfer got up and pointed to the bulletin board, where it was hanging. "She writes, 'I know so much about you. You know a lot less about me. But we are connected through him, I understand that now' . . ."

"Yeah?"

"This whole time we've been assuming that she was referring to Mossing, but Heloise's father is the link. It's the father."

Augustin nodded. "It has to be. And Anna Kiel seems to know obscure, simple childish thing about Heloise, like her lucky number and her favorite flower."

"And her middle name, which she never uses otherwise."

"Right."

"So maybe Anna has this information from him," Schäfer said. "From Heloise's father."

"Maybe."

"But then how are they connected, as Anna Kiel puts it?"

Augustin shrugged. "You don't think that this guy, Nick Kaldan, abused her? Abused Anna, I mean?"

"Anna, Heloise—who knows? Maybe that's why Heloise lied when I told her about that medieval reference on the phone last night."

Augustin glanced over at the bulletin board and clasped her hands behind her head, thinking.

"But if that's true, then why not just write, 'Hey. Do you remember your dad, that bastard? He messed with me when I was a kid. Did he mess with you too? Why don't we meet and reminisce?' She doesn't write that. Instead she tiptoes around, plagiarizing cryptic sentences from ancient love letters. Why?"

Schäfer chewed on his lower lip, and the office was silent for a long time as they both contemplated this.

"Why does she write to Heloise about Christoffer Moss-ing? What does he have to do with Nick Kaldan?" Schäfer asked. "How does it all fit together? If we assume that the connection between Heloise and Anna Kiel is Heloise's dad, then how does Christoffer Mossing fit into the story?"

"Maybe that murder really was a coincidence, like we always thought," Augustin suggested.

"No." Schäfer shook his head. "If there's one thing I'm sure of by now, it's that nothing in this case is a coincidence."

"At any rate, Heloise knows more than she told us," Augustin said.

Schäfer got up and grabbed the car keys from the desk in front of him.

"Well, let's go pick her up."

37

Aɴɴᴀ's ᴘʜᴏɴᴇ ʙᴀʀᴇʟʏ had a chance to ring once before she answered it.

"Hello?"

"It's me."

"Nick? Did she call?"

"Yes."

Anna closed her eyes and exhaled heavily through her mouth. "Okay, good."

A couple of seconds' hesitation, and then, "I don't know . . ."

"What are you talking about? This is what you've been waiting for."

"I know, but . . . what if she changes her mind?" He sounded nervous, wavering.

"She won't."

"But what if she—"

"Nick, stop it, okay? She's coming!"

Anna interpreted his silence as agreement.

"Do you know what time she's coming?" she asked.

"Two o'clock, today."

"Good."

"What happens next?"

"Next?"

"Yeah."

"What do you mean?"

"Will you and I see each other again?"

Anna was on the verge of bursting into stunned laughter. She controlled herself instead and replied, "No, Nick. We won't see each other again."

She could almost sense his shoulders dropping over the phone.

"So, what are you going to do now?" he asked. "Where will you go?"

"Don't worry about that."

"But if he finds you. You need to be careful. You—"

"Don't worry about that," she repeated.

"Well then . . . So, then, I guess this is good-bye?"

"It is."

"Thank you for—"

"Don't do that," she snarled. She couldn't keep the disgust out of her voice.

"Do what?"

"Don't thank me. I didn't do this for you."

"Yeah, but you—"

"No, Nick. I needed some information. You had it. It cost me something to get it. End of story!"

Silence.

"I didn't do any of this for you," she continued coldly. "Don't kid yourself."

"No, well then . . . take care of yourself, Anna. Good-b—"

Nick didn't have a chance to say any more before Anna hung up.

She checked the time on her phone. It was 11:21 AM. That gave her plenty of time to get ready, to reach the right location, and then just wait for the right moment.

Only a few hours left to wait.

Then it would be over.

Almost.

CHAPTER

38

IT WAS ALMOST an hour's drive from the hotel to Fresnes.
Traffic was heavy and the cars were honking and accelerating aggressively, passing on the inside, their drivers gesturing with angry fists.

Heloise didn't pay attention to any of it. To her it felt like the trip had lasted only a split second as the driver pulled over in front of the big, gray concrete facade and turned around to look at her.

"Mademoiselle?"

"Hmm?" Heloise snapped out of her reverie and looked up at him.

"Voilà! We're here."

"Oh, already?"

She looked out the window but made no move to get out of the taxi. Her muscles suddenly felt paralyzed, every cell in her body resisting. She didn't want to go in there. She wanted to turn around. She didn't want to see him. She never wanted to see him again. She had said that. She had sworn it!

You're dead to me. You'll never see me again, never again . . .

The old, toothless cab driver looked from Heloise to the gate outside the car.

"This is the right place, *non*? La Prison de Fresnes?"

"Yes," Heloise said, and reluctantly put her hand on the door handle. "This is the right place."

She got out of the taxi and looked at the building in front of her as the taxi drove past her, heading back into Paris to pick up its next customer. It was an older building—not the kind of modern maximum-security prisons you always saw in American movies. It looked more like something out of a World War II documentary, with razor-wire fencing along the top of the wall, like a long, stretched-out Slinky with sharp blades on it. And there were guards standing in the white tower with automatic weapons, vigilant, ready to shoot down any escaping prisoners.

Heloise shuddered.

She had never visited the prison before. It had been almost four years since he had been arrested, four years since she had seen her father. Their last conversation had been over the phone. She hadn't believed the charges when she heard them. It must be some sort of terrible misunderstanding, she had said. Someone must have been using his computer, someone who had taken advantage of his kindness, his trusting personality. Her father was not a monster. He could never harm a child. He was a *good* man, a caring man. Someone who filled the world with words and poetry and beautiful literature. He was the embodiment of art and love, safety and warmth.

He was not a monster.

The whole thing was just a misunderstanding.

Her father had cried over the phone, and at first Heloise had thought that was because he was afraid, afraid that he would be wrongfully convicted, afraid of losing his freedom, his reputation, his life.

"I'm sorry," he had said. "I'm sorry, Heloise. Please don't leave me, sweetheart. I can't live without you."

"I'll never leave you, Dad. I promise I'll get you out. We'll clear your name!"

"I never touched those children."

"I know that, Dad. I'm going to—"

"But I'm not well."

". . . not well? What are you talking about?"

"I can't help it. I never asked for this."

He had sobbed so violently and begged for her forgiveness, and Heloise had hardly been able to understand what he was saying.

"What are you talking about, Dad?"

"It's true, what they're accusing me of. It's true."

Heloise had laughed, an angry, hysterical laugh. "No, there's no way it's true! What the hell are you talking about?"

"Yes, I'm sick. It's a sickness. I . . . Oh, God, help me!"

That was when it happened.

That was the instant when life as Heloise had known it changed. She had felt like an astronaut who had been tethered and was now floating free in space—rotating, groggy, doomed—as she drifted farther and farther away from Earth. *Wait, come back, help me!*

She hadn't said anything while he spoke. He had explained himself, made excuses, opened up a secret drawer from his life and shown her the vile, disgusting contents that she wished she had never seen.

"I never touched them. I promise you that, Heloise. But I wanted to—oh, I'm ashamed to say that—I wanted to, and I've looked at them. I've watched while other people . . . I've been there and I've watched while they . . . I didn't do anything to stop it, but I never touched them myself. I swear it."

She had woken up with a start in the middle of that phone call, with her pulse racing along with her thoughts, as if waking up from the middle of a dream in which she was falling.

"Stop," she had said. "Stop! I don't want to hear anymore."

"But, Heloise, you have to understand that—"

"No, I don't want to hear anymore. I don't want to talk to you."

He had cried even harder, and Heloise had never felt so alone. It was more than just loneliness. It was the feeling that she didn't belong anywhere. Her mother was dead, and her father—the man she had known and loved more than anyone else in her whole life—no longer existed.

She felt like an orphan.

Lost.

"You're dead to me," she had told him before hanging up. "You'll never see me again."

CHAPTER

39

SCHÄFER PRESSED THE apartment building's door inter-com button with his chapped thumb and held it in until the whole building vibrated as if someone were jackhammer-ing the sidewalk out in front of the building.

He didn't let go until a window up on the fourth floor was flung open and a man with curly bedhead stuck his head out and glared angrily down at the street below. When he spotted Schäfer and Augustin by the building's front door, he yelled in a hoarse voice, "What the hell are you doing?"

"Kaldan, fifth floor," Schäfer yelled back. "We need to speak to her. Have you seen her?"

"No, and unless she's deaf, I'm going to go out on a limb and conclude that she's not home, you idiot!" The man loudly slammed his window shut.

Schäfer was about to push the intercom button again out of childish spitefulness when Lisa Augustin grabbed his arm.

"Come on," she said. "She's not home."

"Let's stop by the paper and see if she's at work."

The car was parked farther down the street. Schäfer unlocked it remotely as they started walking toward it.

"Do you really think she's back at work already?" Augustin asked. "After such a violent attack?"

THE CORPSE FLOWER   239

Schäfer shrugged. "Why not?"

"Uh, maybe a person should take a little break after an experience like that? You know, take a week or two off to recover, maybe talk to a crisis counselor?"

"Yeah, maybe if you're a hair stylist or an English teacher at the University of Copenhagen, but someone like Kaldan? She's like us. Her job isn't just a necessary evil that she does to pay her bills—she *is* her job."

Augustin raised one eyebrow and nodded. "That explains why she's single."

"No, that doesn't have anything to do with it."

"Yeah, it does. You and Connie are just the exception that confirms the rule, that people who live and breathe their jobs aren't able to maintain healthy romantic relationships."

Augustin glanced over at Schäfer and discovered that he was no longer paying attention to her. His eyes were focused on something at the end of Olfert Fischers Gade.

"Aha," he said, pointing ahead of them. "And another exception is walking right over there. With a bakery bag in his hand and what looks like a postcoital smile on his lips. Wonder if he can maintain a healthy romantic relationship?"

Augustin looked to see where he was pointing, and her eyes landed on Martin Duvall, who was heading toward them. He was pulling a pastry out of the brown paper bag he was holding and hadn't noticed them yet.

Schäfer called out to him. "Duvall!"

Martin Duvall's head jerked up like a frightened horse's, and something undefinable—was it hesitation?—flicked over his face as he spotted Augustin and Schäfer. But he didn't break the rhythm of his gait. Instead he gave them a friendly nod and continued toward them.

When he reached them, he held out his hand. "Good morning!"

Schäfer took his hand and squeezed, not so the knuckles turned to dust between his fingers but far harder than he would have normally. It was a bad habit, a way of asserting himself when dealing with suits and suspects, a sort of mine-is-bigger-than-yours machismo.

"Good morning," he said. "Funny to run into you here. I thought you lived down by the harbor."

"Yeah, I do."

"Maybe you were on your way over to Heloise's?"

Duvall nodded. "I was."

"Great, then we'll join you. We just have a few questions for her."

"She, uh . . . she's not home," he said, slowing down.

Schäfer looked puzzled. "But you just said that you were going to her place."

"I'm on my way to her apartment, yes."

"But she's not there?"

"No."

"What, you have a key?"

Duvall smiled hesitantly, looking from Schäfer to Augustin, who both remained silent, before he answered.

"Yes. Is that a problem?"

Schäfer frowned and shook his head slightly as if to say it wasn't.

"Is she at work?"

"Yeah, she had a thing. She left early."

"Do you know where we can find her? Sergeant Augustin here and I just have a couple of question we need to ask her."

"I'm not really sure," Duvall said, and he started meticulously folding the top of his bakery bag. "Did you try to catch her at the newspaper?"

Schäfer scratched his neck as he peered questioningly at Duvall. "You're a communications director, aren't you?"

"I was. I quit."

"Were you any good at your job?"

"At least at one time I was, yes." Duvall shrugged modestly.

"Hmm," Schäfer said. He pulled a pack of cigarettes out of his inside pocket and then tapped one out of the package. "I also sometimes pound my chest about how good I am at my job, and do you know why I'm good at it?" he asked out of one corner of his mouth as he lit the cigarette hanging out of the other. He took a deep puff, scrunched up his eyes, and zeroed in on Duvall.

"No." Duvall smiled and shrugged. "But I presume you're about to tell me."

"I can tell when people are lying."

"Oh."

"Yeah," Schäfer said, and pulled a bit of tobacco out from the inside of his bottom lip without breaking eye contact with Duvall. "So how about you tell us where she is?"

"I'm sorry?"

"Heloise. Where is she? And don't bother saying she's at work. We both know that's a lie."

For a second Martin looked as if he were considering his options. Then he said, "She asked me not to tell you."

"Do you know what the penalty is for intentionally withholding information that could lead to solving a criminal investigation?"

Martin furrowed his brow. "I fail to see how information about Heloise's whereabouts could lead to solving a criminal investigation."

"That's why you do what you do, and I do what I do," Schäfer said, tapping ash off his cigarette.

"Are you kidding me?" Duvall asked, chuckling and turning to Augustin. "Is he joking, or is he always such a caricature?"

Sergeant August stared at him blankly.

"Listen up," Schäfer said. "I understand how Heloise thinks. She wants to put the story to bed. She wants to be the first to break it. I fully sympathize with that, and I think it's really admirable that she takes her work so seriously. But this story is bigger than Heloise, bigger than a newspaper article."

Duvall hesitated. "This isn't just about the story . . ." he began.

"Heloise is in danger," Augustin said. "Do you understand that?"

"Yes, thank you. I sort of figured that out." He held his battered knuckles up in front of her.

"Good. So if you care about her, then tell us where she is," she said.

"Sorry, I can't." Duvall shook his head.

Schäfer placed a heavy hand on his shoulder.

"Martin, we need to talk to her. It's important. Not just for the investigation, but there's some real lowlifes trying to take her out. Do you get that? We still don't know which way is up with this case, and if we're going to ensure Heloise's safety, then we need to know where she is."

"I'm sorry, but I can't help you." Martin Duvall started walking away down the street.

Schäfer raised his voice slightly as he appeared to study his nails. "What do you think Heloise would say if she knew that last winter you forced a coworker at the ministry to have sex with you?"

Martin Duvall stopped abruptly in his tracks and turned around slowly.

"The poor girl," Schäfer said, shaking his head.

Duvall's voice was guarded when he spoke. "I've never forced anyone to do anything. The woman you're talking about was angling for a promotion. That's all there is to that story."

"Sure. So, you offered her a better position if she screwed you?"

"I never touched her." Duvall shook his head insistently. "She also retracted her story when it turned out that I wasn't even in the country on the date in question."

"Yes, of course." Schäfer nodded in mock sympathy. "Be sure to mention that to your new girlfriend when Augustin and I tell her the story."

Martin Duvall looked back and forth between them. Then he let his hands fall limply at his sides and sighed. "What do you want to know?"

"Well, since you're asking so nicely, I would like to know where Heloise is."

Duvall stared at him blankly. "She went to Paris."

"To see her father?" Augustin asked.

"How did you know that—"

"Did she go there to see her father?" she repeated.

"Yes."

"When? When is she going to see him?"

"I don't know. I haven't talked to her since she left."

"Is there anything else we should know?" Augustin asked.

Duvall blinked a couple of times. Then he looked over at Schäfer and took a deep breath before he said, "Anna Kiel called her yesterday."

Schäfer eyed him for a long moment without responding. Then he took out his phone. When his call was answered on the other end, he said, "Hello? This is Sergeant Schäfer speaking. Contact Interpol right away and inform them that Anna Kiel may be staying in the proximity of Fresnes Prison south of Paris and it is highly likely that she visited an inmate of the prison sometime in the last week, a Danish citizen by the name of Nick Kaldan."

He held the phone away from his mouth and looked over at Duvall. "Where is Heloise? Where is she staying while she's there?"

Martin Duvall held out his hand, palms up, and shrugged. "Some hotel in the Quartier du Marais," he said. "I don't know the name."

Schäfer turned his back to him and spoke further. "We also need credit card information for a Heloise Eleanor Kaldan—that's Heloise with a silent H and then E, L, O, I, S, E . . . Yes. Kaldan. She flew to Paris this morning and is staying in a hotel somewhere in the city center. Find out where. It's urgent!"

He hung up the call and looked back over at Duvall.

"Is there anything else you're keeping from us?" he asked, then tossed his cigarette butt on the asphalt and stepped on it.

Duvall shook his head.

"All right. If you hear from Heloise, then tell her that she needs to ditch this moronic solo trip she's on. You got it?"

Duvall nodded reluctantly.

"Tell her to call me right away and to wait at her hotel until she hears from us. Do you understand?"

"Yes, got it. But I don't think it's going to make any difference."

Schäfer looked puzzled. "Why not?"

"Because . . . Listen, this thing between us is still pretty new. I don't know Heloise all that well. She's a very secretive person, and she has a hard time trusting people. It's hard for her to open up, so she can come off as extremely cynical and cold, but she really isn't. She's a sensitive person, and that father of hers? He's her Achilles' heel. The way I understand it, this is the first time in four years that she's wanted to see him. There has to be some reason for that, so I don't think I can convince her to stop now."

"Try," Schäfer said, his face unsentimental. He nodded to Augustin. "Let's go."

They got into the car.

In the rearview mirror, Schäfer could see Martin Duvall watching them.

"Where are we going?" Augustin asked.

Schäfer turned the key so the engine started humming. He buckled his seat belt with one hand as he pulled out onto the street with the other.

"To the airport."

CHAPTER

40

HELOISE SAW THE man from behind and wondered why the guard had sent her into the wrong room. It wasn't her father sitting there at the metal table under the fluorescent light that was flickering tremulously from the lamps above him.

It was a frail old man, whose hair—with the exception of a couple of dark tufts at his temples—had gone completely white. An old, emaciated man. He sat there with his shoulders slumped and his head stooped so his spine was clearly visible through his orange prison uniform, like the spikes on a stegosaurus's back.

But then the image changed before Heloise's eyes as she passed the man, like a work of art—an anamorphosis— that depicted one thing when viewed from one angle but appeared to dissolve and transform into something totally different when viewed from another. It didn't take more than a few seconds. The old man looked up when he heard her approaching. He looked into her eyes, and then she knew.

Heloise looked into his warm, dark-brown eyes, at the scar across his left cheekbone from the swings at the playground by Saint Paul's Church, at the mouth, which curved upward into a tentative smile as he exhaled in relief.

"Heloise," he said, getting up gingerly from his seat.

Stunned, she took a step back and remained there, about five feet from the table, as she looked at him without saying anything.

She almost couldn't believe her eyes. It was like finding a fossil of the man she had been raised by, deep inside a soulless block of cement. He looked so much older than she remembered him, modified, unfamiliar. He looked like a stranger. And yet . . .

It was really him.

"Heloise," he repeated. "Sweetheart?"

He reached out a hand toward her.

Heloise stared at it for several seconds. Then she looked him in the eye again, still without saying anything.

She wanted to hate him, to be cruel and nasty, to tell him that he meant nothing to her, that she no longer loved him. But something welled up inside her as she looked at him, a tenderness. And even though she tried with all her might to suppress the feeling, she knew it would never disappear completely. It would always be there inside her.

For him.

He slowly pulled his hand back. Then he nodded hesitantly to the empty chair across the table from him.

"Would you like to sit down?"

Heloise took a deep breath. She felt dizzy. Her chest quivered and trembled, and her vision seemed cloudy, as if she were wearing a pair of glasses with the wrong prescription.

She looked down at the floor and blinked a couple of times. Then she walked over to the table and pulled out the chair. She sat down across from him, and he lowered his frail body back onto the hard metal seat again.

It was quiet for a long moment. When Heloise finally spoke, the first thing she said was, "You look like shit."

"Yeah, I guess I do." He smiled meekly and nodded.

"Don't they feed you in here?"

"Well, I don't have much of an appetite these days."

It grew quiet again between them. Heloise looked down at her nails as she struggled to hold back her tears.

Her father cautiously leaned in over the table. He looked like he was considering reaching for her hand but didn't dare. Instead he said, "I've missed you, honey."

Heloise looked into his eyes. Her chin began to tremble, and tears flowed silently down her cheeks to land on the cold, metal table, where they formed a salty little puddle.

"You haven't answered my letters," he said. "Eventually they started being returned to me unopened, and when I called, you hung up. I've needed so badly to talk to you."

"I don't want to hear your excuses," Heloise said, wiping her eyes with the back of her hand. "That's not why I'm here."

She straightened up in the chair, composing herself.

Her father started coughing, and a lengthy, dry rattle could be heard from his throat. He pulled a tissue out of his pocket and wiped his mouth with it.

"I know," he said.

"Anna Kiel."

"Yes."

"You know her?"

He nodded.

Heloise pulled a voice recorder out of her purse. She hit the record button and set the recorder on the table in front of her father.

"What is that?" he asked.

"I'm recording our conversation, and that's a condition for my being willing to talk to you. It's not negotiable."

"Is this an interview?" He smiled briefly, almost bravely.

"Yes." The word fell like the crack of a whip, hard, stinging.

The pain of missing him that had so recently overwhelmed her tear ducts was now replaced with unprocessed bitterness, with indignation and blame. This was about the story now, about work, not about him.

"How do you know Anna Kiel?" she asked.

"She came to me four months ago."

Heloise shook her head, not understanding. "Came to you? What does that mean?"

"I found out that I had a visitor, and as I'm sure you can imagine, I was thrilled. I hadn't talked to anyone from outside the prison aside from my lawyer for several years. One day there was just a guard standing there. I was being summoned. At first I thought it was you . . ."

"And she just waltzed in here? Anna Kiel, who's wanted for murder in Denmark, who's wanted by Interpol, she just voluntarily strolled in here, behind these walls, into one of the biggest prisons in France?"

"Yes. But the police didn't know that."

"How is that possible? I had to show ID, and they did a full-body search before they even let me through security."

"Margaux, they said."

Heloise blinked a couple of times. "Margaux? What does that mean?"

"I was told that there was a Margaux Perrossier who wanted to visit me. I thought, okay, let's find out who that is and what she has to say to me. After all, a stranger is better than no one." He laughed a brief, joyless laugh. "She was better than no one." He nodded to himself.

Heloise ignored the implied accusation. "What happened next?"

"Next . . . well, then we sat here, where you and I are sitting now. She asked if I knew who she was. I said no. I couldn't remember having seen her before. She asked if I had really repented, if what I was convicted of was something that I regretted."

"And?"

"And I told her that I had, I did." He looked down at the table as he spoke. "That I had always struggled with the feelings I had inside me." He looked up. "And I really have, Heloise. I have always struggled against my—"

"I don't want to hear about that." Heloise held her trembling hand up in front of him. "I don't want to hear about your feelings, so put away your excuses. There must be a priest or someone here that you can talk to, but I don't want to hear a word about it, is that understood?"

"Yes."

"I mean it." She looked him up and down coolly. "If you start with your excuses again, I'm leaving."

He nodded.

"What happened next?"

"She asked if I could . . . if I remembered her."

Heloise closed her eyes and put her face in her hands. She knew that she could no longer escape hearing him talk about it. If she wanted the story to be over—both Anna's and her own—she was going to have to let her father share details from the parallel life that she had been trying for four years to forget he had lived.

She looked up again. "She asked if you *remembered* her?"

"Yes."

"And did you?"

"Not to begin with. But later, after we had talked a little more, then yes. Then I remembered."

"What did you remember?"

He looked up to his right and closed his eyes for a few seconds. When he opened them again, he said, "It was in the early nineties. There were a few of us who met occasionally and . . . exchanged stories."

"Stories?"

"Yes, anecdotes. And pictures and that sort of thing. That was before the internet, before all the fancy cameras that exist today, where everything is available in the blink of an eye. Everything was analog back then. We had actual film, negatives, processed photos that were swapped around."

"Who were the people you were meeting with?"

"There were a bunch of different people, depending on the event." He shrugged. "Just ordinary people."

Heloise snorted. "Ordinary?"

"No, you know what I mean, people who lived ordinary lives outwardly—schoolteachers, lawyers, people who worked in retail, doctors, those kinds of people. They weren't hoboes or mass murderers. They were people you would normally feel safe running into on the street."

"And where did you meet these people?"

"In a building in Nordhavnen Harbor, an empty warehouse somewhere not far from where the cruise ships dock today."

"How did you find out about that place?"

"I had an acquaintance who recommended that I become a member . . ."

"A member?" Heloise asked. "How did one become a member?"

"You had to be interviewed. It was a . . . a club. The Lullaby Club, we called it. A sort of a secret society. You couldn't just show up and knock on the door. You had to know someone who knew that you . . . shared their . . . weaknesses."

"Was there any sexual activity at this . . . club?"

"Sometimes, yes."

"With minors?"

He nodded.

"So the members of the club were all pedophiles?"

"To varying degrees."

"It's a yes-or-no question. Was it a club for pedophiles?"

"Yes."

"And where did the children come from?"

"I . . . uh, I don't know . . ." He shrugged vaguely.

"How old were they?"

"It varied." He shook his head uncomfortably.

"Ten, twelve—what?"

"Yes."

"Younger?"

"Sometimes."

Heloise stood up so quickly that her chair tipped over behind her and she spat in his face.

"You're disgusting!" she yelled. "I hate you! I fucking hate you, do you know that?"

The door at the far end of the room opened, and a guard stepped in.

Heloise composed herself.

She looked over at the guard and gestured that there wasn't any problem, that he could step out again.

Once the door was closed again, she picked up the chair and sat down again while her father wiped his face with his hands. He started sobbing, and they sat across from each other for a long time without talking, without looking at each other.

Then Heloise picked up where they had left off.

"Did you meet Anna Kiel at one of those events?"

"Couldn't we just not talk about—"

She raised her voice. "Did you meet Anna Kiel at one of those events?"

He nodded.

"Once? More than once? What?"

"I . . . I can't remember that. I was only there occasionally, but Anna says that she was there several times, that she saw me there more than once."

"Did you hurt her?"

"No."

"You didn't touch her?"

"No." He shook his head.

"Did other people?"

"Some did, yes." He nodded grimly.

"How old was she at the time?"

"I . . . don't know—"

"But she was raped?"

He nodded.

Heloise shook her head in disgust. "How do you know that?"

"I . . . I saw it happen."

"You watched?"

"Yes. But I only watched, though. I never touched her."

"Is that how you're rationalizing this to yourself? You didn't touch the children, you just watched, and so, somehow, it's all okay? Somehow that makes you less of a monster?"

"Heloise, honey, please stop . . ."

"What about me?"

He looked up. "What do you mean?"

"What about all the times we were at the beach when I was little? Or at the pool? Or when we slept together in your bed, you and me? What was going on inside your head when we were lying there?"

"What in the world are you talking about?"

"Were you thinking about it then? Did you look at me that way too?"

"What? No!" His face crumpled, and he looked repulsed at the thought. "Heloise, don't say such things. Of course I didn't. You're my child!"

"The others were someone's children too, Dad. They were someone's *children*! How could you have let this happen? How *could* you?"

"I wish I could take it all back, I do. And Anna could tell. She knew that I wasn't like the other men."

"You're *exactly* like the other men," Heloise said.

"No, I'm not. She knew that if I could, I would undo it. She came here because she could tell that I was different."

"What did she want from you?"

"She wanted my help."

"With what?"

"With documenting everything."

Heloise leaned back in her chair and watched him for several seconds.

"What specifically was she looking for?" she asked.

"Names, passwords, access to the club's files."

"And you were able to give her that?"

He nodded.

"What kind of files are we talking about?"

"When the internet came along, it became easier to share material. If attending the events wasn't possible for someone, they could still be part of the, well, the *club*. A confidential chat forum was set up, a secret portal where we swapped photos, short stories, that sort of thing."

"And you gave Anna Kiel access to that portal?"

He nodded again.

"What is she planning to do with it?"

"She didn't tell me that. That wasn't part of the agreement."

"The agreement?"

"Yes, she wanted some concrete evidence against her abusers—IP addresses, pictures and videos they appeared in—and I . . ." He looked up. "I just wanted you. That was the agreement. If she got you to come here, I would give her the information she needed."

"So, you were behind this the whole time?" Heloise nodded. "The letters she sent were to get me to show up here with you?"

"You didn't give me any other choice." He shrugged his shoulders.

"People are dead because of you. Do you know that?" Heloise felt the anger trembling all the way to her fingertips.

"Wait, what? No, I—"

"One of my colleagues was murdered because I talked to him about those letters." She yanked the collar of her shirt down so that he could see the marks around her neck. "Do you see these? I was attacked in my own home! I could have died, and for what? For you? Because of your guilty conscience? Because you're sitting here bawling while your psycho friends back home try to cover their tracks?"

He opened and closed his mouth a couple of times, stunned, but no sound came out.

"Who's behind the Lullaby Club?" she demanded to know. "Who? Is it Johannes Mossing?"

Her father's face suddenly drained of all color. "Heloise, you must stay away from that man."

"It's him, isn't it?" A wave of adrenaline surged through her body. "If you know something that can help catch him, Dad, then now is the time for you to speak up. If you really want to protect me from him, then say something now!"

"An . . . Anna has all the information," he said, disconcerted. "She has the evidence against him."

"Where is she?"

"I don't know . . . I—"

"How can I use this for anything if you don't have any idea where she is?"

"She'll contact you. That's the plan. She's somewhere nearby. She's here. I talked to her, and she—" He started coughing again.

This time he was gasping frantically for breath between exhalations. He spluttered and tried to clear his throat as if he had gotten something down the wrong pipe.

Heloise watched stony-faced and didn't offer any other assistance.

"Oh, Heloise, sweetie," he said, once he had recovered. "I'm sick."

"Stop it!" Heloise stood up, irritated. "I told you that I don't want to hear your excuses."

"No, it's not that. I . . . I have cancer."

Heloise stopped and looked down at him. It was quiet for a moment before she spoke.

"Cancer?"

"In my lungs." He nodded and cautiously touched his chest. "But it's metastasized to my liver and my bones and . . . it doesn't look good."

Heloise's hand was shaking as she pulled her chair back out and sat down.

"But you're . . . you're getting treatment?"

"Not anymore." He shook his head. "There's nothing else they can do."

Heloise looked up at the ceiling as she tried to hold back her tears.

"It's okay," he said. "I've made my peace with it. And now that I've seen you one last time, I'm ready to die. I'm not afraid."

"How long do you have left?"

"They say six months, nine if I'm lucky. But . . ." He shook his head slightly. "I'm not planning to hang around that long."

They looked into each other's eyes for a long moment.

He smiled.

Heloise took a deep, shaky breath. "You were my whole world. You know that, right?"

"And you were mine."

She nodded and was quiet for a moment. Then she quickly wiped her tears from her eyes.

"Okay, so I'll hear from Anna Kiel. Is that what you're saying? She has the rest of the story?"

"Yes."

"Good." Heloise got up and started for the door.

"Wait!" His voice choked up with desperation.

Heloise turned around and looked at him.

His eyes were big and wet.

"I love you."

The words fell, not like a statement of fact, but as a plea.

She smiled sadly at him.

"Good-bye, Dad."

CHAPTER

41

THERE WAS A thud as the landing gear was released and the woman in the seat next to Schäfer grabbed the armrest so hard that her knuckles turned white.

He looked at her for a moment. The wrinkles in her age-spotted forehead and the lines around her green eyes made him guess she was in her early seventies. She was pretty, feminine, and elegant, with graceful features in a face that made her look like she had lived a rich, peaceful life. But right now, she looked tense. She rested her head against the seat's royal-blue upholstery with her eyes closed, taking short, panting breaths.

"I'm assuming you don't fly very often?" Schäfer said, leaning over to her.

The woman opened her eyes to see who was talking to her. Her eyes roved from side to side until she identified Schäfer as the source of the voice. She looked briefly embarrassed. Then she shook her head.

"No, I don't like to fly."

"But you know what the statistics say, don't you?" He smiled soothingly. "It's the safest form of transportation there is."

The plane tilted sharply to the right, and the sky vanished from the little oval window by the woman's shoulder.

A low moan slipped from her lips, and she squeezed her eyes shut again.

Schäfer looked past her out the window, down at the ground, where he could see the highway beneath them. The cars looked like little ants dashing along the asphalt in a long column, and he followed the traffic's gradual rhythm with his eyes.

"Don't worry," he said. "We'll be landing in a minute."

The pilot straightened out again. The miniature buildings below them grew into high-rises, and a few minutes later the wheels touched down on the runway with a hissing rumble. The brake flaps on the wings flew up, and the plane screeched to a halt.

He patted the woman briefly on the shoulder with one hand as he pulled his phone out of his pocket with the other. "See! It all worked out."

The woman smiled in relief. "Yes, thank goodness. Thank you."

Schäfer turned on his phone, called Lisa Augustin, and waited for the call to go through.

"Hello?" she answered.

"It's me."

"Hey, are you in Paris?"

"Yup, just landed. Although it took me forever to get permission to come. My passport expired, and it's at the Municipal Services office. So I missed the first connection while I was waiting for a green light from the airport authorities, but now I'm here. Any news?"

"Yes, there's a summary of charges from Heloise's credit card from the last twenty-four hours. She took an Uber from Orly Airport this morning, and she checked into a hotel in the third arrondissement called . . ." There was a pause and then: "Le Pavillon de la Reine. It's downtown, close to the Seine, close to Notre Dame."

"Okay, anything else? Has she used her credit card anywhere else?"

"Yes, she withdrew some cash from an ATM at the airport. Two hundred fifty euros. Other than that? Nothing."

"Have you talked to the French police since I boarded?"

"Yes, I was just speaking with them. They'll grab Heloise if she shows up at the prison in Fresnes before you—wait! Just a second. Hang on for a minute . . ."

He could hear her talking to someone, but the connection was bad, and the voices flowed together. When she came back, her voice seemed accelerated. "Hello?"

"Yes?"

"She's already been there!"

"Where?"

"In the prison, with her father. They just called from the prison—she already left."

"When did she leave? How long ago?"

"Just a moment ago."

"Why the hell didn't they stop her?"

"The prison staff hadn't gotten the message that they were supposed to—"

"Damn it!" Schäfer exclaimed.

Augustin was quiet for a moment. Then she said, "So, now what?"

Schäfer chewed on his lips as he contemplated this. "Call them back. Explain to them that Heloise just left the prison and that Anna Kiel may be staying somewhere nearby."

"Okay. What about you?"

"I'm still going to go to Fresnes. I have to talk to Nick Kaldan. I need to know what the visit was about—what all of this is about."

"All right. Let me know once you've been there, okay?"

Schäfer promised that he would keep her updated and then hung up and exhaled loudly.

A *ding* could be heard as the seat belt sign turned off, followed by a symphony of metallic clicks. The whole cabin lumbered to their feet. Carry-on bags were hauled down from the overhead compartments and people started making their way slowly, pushing, down the central aisle.

"We seem to have swapped facial expressions. Have you noticed that?"

Schäfer looked back and saw that the woman who had been sitting next to him was behind him now.

"I'm sorry?"

"That worried look," she said, nodding toward his furrowed brow. "You're the one who looks burdened now, whereas I'm just happy to be alive." She smiled. "Is everything all right?"

"Everything's fine, thank you. It's just work."

"Oh, is that all?" The woman smiled encouragingly. "Well then, it's hardly a matter of life and death."

Uh, yeah, Schäfer thought. That's exactly what it is.

*   *   *

Heloise clicked on the Uber app on her phone, but nothing happened. She checked her network coverage. It was pretty much nonexistent where she was. She looked down the road, first in one direction, then the other. There were cars driving by and a few people who passed her, walking quickly down the monotonous stretch of road. But there were no taxis to be seen.

She started walking in the direction of traffic, away from the prison, back toward downtown, as she held her phone out in front of her in hopes of finding better cell coverage. She felt drained, completely sapped of energy. It felt like her heart had been transformed into a liquid substance that was flowing around inside her, like an indefinable, reddish puddle, a weightless fluid in a spaceship.

She had just seen her father for the last time ever, and now she felt . . .

Nothing!

She kept her eye on the bars at the top left corner of her phone as she walked. Hypnotized by the screen, she walked right into someone who stepped out from a bus stop just as she passed the gray concrete structure.

"Sorry," Heloise said mechanically without looking up.

She walked on in a sort of trance, raising her phone higher, searching for some invisible network cables, as if a couple of inches this way or that would make any difference.

"Heloise?"

She turned around toward the voice. She squinted and stared at the woman behind her as she contemplated whether she ought to stand still or run away.

Anna Kiel didn't look directly at Heloise.

Instead she took a couple of steps closer to her and then stopped by an overfilled poster pillar a few feet away.

"Heloise?" she repeated, as she appeared to study a poster advertising a theater.

She looked different than in the pictures Heloise had seen. Her long blond hair had been replaced with a nut-brown, boyish hairstyle. She looked pale and thin, almost emaciated, and she was shorter than Heloise had imagined. Shorter than the five foot six that had been listed in the police description of her. She almost looked like a little girl. Heloise had a hard time imagining that the woman in front of her had murdered a tall, burly man, that she could have overpowered someone with Christoffer Moss-ing's build.

Heloise nodded. "Yes, it's me."

"Follow me, but not too closely," Anna Kiel said, and started walking.

Heloise followed her, staying ten to twenty yards behind her. They walked for about fifteen minutes, down streets with little, dilapidated houses on either side, across a footbridge over a road with heavy traffic, and continued past ghetto-like apartment blocks where tiny balconies were crammed full of trash, withered plants, and satellite dishes.

When Anna Kiel finally turned off the road, she walked straight into something that looked like an Algerian restaurant, which was located between a nail salon and a business that sold pet food.

Heloise hesitated for a second, and then she followed her. She walked through the door and stopped. She furrowed her brow, looking around the small, dark space that smelled like cinnamon and cumin. One table in the restaurant was occupied by a young couple. A waiter stood behind the bar, an older, dark-haired man, who was pouring a drink into a purple glass. Aside from that, the restaurant was empty.

Heloise couldn't see Anna Kiel.

She was about to ask the waiter about her when he nodded toward an opening in the far back of the place.

The plastic beads in the ruby-colored curtain rattled together as Heloise walked through the doorway. She was in a back room with orange paper lanterns hanging from the ceiling. The room looked like it was used for parties and other events. There was a massive oak refectory table in the middle of the room with about eighteen to twenty chairs around it. Anna Kiel was seated at the end of the table.

Heloise stood there for a moment, waiting.

Anna Kiel pointed with her chin to the chair next to her. "Have a seat."

Heloise walked over to her. She stopped three chairs away from her, pulled one of them out, and sat down. Then she flung up her arms.

"You wanted to talk to me?"

Anna Kiel smiled fleetingly. "That actually wasn't the plan, not to begin with. *Nick* wanted to talk to you, and my job was to make that happen. I had no idea who you were until he told me about you. But now, since you're here anyway . . ." She shrugged. "Why not?"

"So, you weren't going to use me for anything at all?"

"Not in the beginning, no."

"So, all of this—the last several weeks where I've been running around back home in your footsteps and trying to make some sense out of the Mossing case—there was no point to that?"

"It brought you here."

"Why did you send those letters to me? You could have just called me up and told me what was going on."

"Would you have come if I had done that?"

"To get your story? Yes."

"Would you also have visited your father?"

Heloise was quiet for a moment. "No, maybe not."

"And then I wouldn't have had a story to share with you. I wouldn't have had any documentation."

Heloise eyed her without responding.

"I'm sorry that you've gotten mixed up in this," Anna Kiel said. "But you have the opportunity to make something good come out of this situation."

"Something good?"

"Yes, you can help me put away some very bad people."

"What about yourself?"

"What do you mean?"

"You murdered a man, so in my eyes, you're in the same category as the people you're after. Why should I help you throw other people in jail when you yourself are trying to avoid it?"

Anna Kiel nodded as she pensively chewed on her lower lip.

"Let's make a deal," she said. "Once these people have been revealed, so the whole world can see them for the monsters they are, then you're welcome to come after me."

"No thanks," Heloise said. "When this is over, I'm out, do you understand? I don't want to hear any more from you after today. Anything that happens from here on out is *your* problem. Agreed?"

"Agreed."

"But you can't run forever. You know that, right?"

Anna Kiel smiled. "I'm willing to take the chance."

"How are you getting by?" Heloise asked. "Is Kenneth sending you money?"

Anna Kiel's face softened for a second. "You don't need to worry about that."

"If you're really his friend, then doesn't it bother you that you're risking causing him serious problems with the law by letting him help you?"

Anna Kiel smiled briefly. "You don't need to worry about that," she repeated.

CHAPTER

42

THE TWO WOMEN looked at each other for a moment. Then Anna Kiel broke the silence. "Do you want to hear the story or not?"

Heloise nodded. She took her voice recorder out of her inside pocket and held it up in front of Anna.

"I'd like to record this. Is that okay?"

"Sure."

"You should know that I'll probably use whatever you tell me in my article. You will be quoted."

Anna leaned in over the table, put her hands together, and looked down at the top of the table for a moment, as if she were studying the knots and the grain of the wood. Then she said, "Do you have any idea what it feels like to grow up in an empty house without any real contact with grown-ups, totally alone?"

Heloise shook her head.

"No." Anna smiled. "Your father told me about your life together, about when you were little. It sounded like you had a good childhood."

"I did," Heloise agreed.

"Yeah." Anna nodded. "It sounds like it. He loves you. You know that, right? But it wasn't like that for me. There was no love in my home, no grown-ups present. My father was always at work or in town, and my mother"—she smiled sarcastically—"she was too busy to be a mother. She was always out spending all the money my dad earned."

"On gambling?"

"Yeah, on gambling, exactly." Anna nodded. "Anyway, there was rarely any food in the fridge, just beer, and no one came home and tucked me in at night. No one took care of me."

"Why didn't anyone intervene? No one at school reported what was going on at your house?"

"Reported what? I learned to get by. I took care of myself. I never complained to anyone. The teachers never found out what was going on at home. They just thought it was me, that I was difficult. Or maybe they didn't care. I don't know. Either way, no one said anything."

"So, what happened?"

"My father disappeared at some point. I think he got tired of life at home, tired of us. He moved to Greenland, got a job up there, and sent money home for a while."

Heloise considered for a moment telling her that she had met with Frank Kiel, that he had tried to use his own daughter's situation to bilk some money out of her. But she didn't have the heart to be the one who keyed yet another scratch into the paint job of Anna Kiel's existence.

So, she bit her tongue and listened.

"When the money stopped coming, my mom fell into a black hole. She started spending money we didn't have, a lot of money. She borrowed huge amounts that she gambled away, and when she lost, she couldn't pay what she owed." She paused for a moment, thinking back, trying to blink the memories away. "I remember the night they came to our house. My mom wasn't there. She was out somewhere. I don't know where. I never knew where. But it was late, and I had already gone to bed. And then they rang the doorbell. I thought it was her. She was always coming home drunk or high, always losing her keys or her purse. So I assumed it was her at the door."

"But it wasn't?"

"No. It was two men."

"Did you know them?"

"No, I had never seen them before."

"What did they want?"

"They asked for my mother, and I told them she'd be home soon. But of course I didn't know if she would come home at all. I was just standing there in my nightgown, scared shitless and hoping they would leave again. One of them was this real slimy guy. He smiled and told me I was pretty and asked me how old I was."

"How old were you?"

"Eight."

Heloise shook her head, dismayed.

"Then he leaned down and put his hand around the back of my head, and he kissed me—stuck his tongue in my mouth. I can still remember the taste, cigars and wine, and the feel of his sticky spit in my mouth."

"Did you push him away?"

"No, I was too scared. I just let him do it. As I stood there, I felt something warm running down my leg. I had peed my pants, I was that terrified. When they realized what had happened, they just laughed."

"How did you get rid of them?"

"Somehow I managed to get the door closed and I stood there in the dark, just inside the front door, listening while they waited for my mother out in the front yard. When she showed up, I heard them grab her and slap her around a little. I heard them threaten her. They said she owed them money. 'You have until Friday,' they said. She told them she couldn't get the amount she owed, that there had to be some other way out, a different way for her to repay the money."

"What did they say then?"

Anna shrugged and smiled cheerlessly. " 'Your daughter,' they said. 'What's her name?' "

"They wanted you instead?" Heloise's stomach turned.

"I still remember how eager to please my mother's voice was when she realized how easily she was going to be able to get rid of her problems. It didn't even take her a split second to offer me up."

"She paid off her debt with you?"

"Yes." Anna nodded. "She drove me to a place the next day, an abandoned factory building down in Nordhavnen Harbor, dropped me off, and said, 'Have fun!' Can you believe that? She actually fucking said that." Anna laughed, speechless for a second.

Heloise closed her eyes.

She didn't have enough imagination to comprehend the depth of betrayal in the life Anna had lived, and she could only guess what that kind of thing did to a kid, to a soul.

"I'm so sorry," was all Heloise could say.

Anna nodded without looking at her. "That first time, there were two of them. They smelled like sweat and cigarettes, and they just took turns, you know . . . and the next time there were three of them. It went on like that for a while. My mom would drop me off in front of the building and they would bring me inside."

"How many times did it happen? How many times were you in that building with these men?"

"Seven or eight times, I think, spread out over a period of about a year. At some point they got tired of me, I guess. They probably wanted something new. Either way, it just suddenly stopped. I never asked my mother why it stopped— we never discussed it."

"How many men participated in this?"

"Nine that I can remember."

"Nine men?"

"Yes. There was also a tenth, but he always just watched."

Heloise tried to swallow, but her mouth felt dry. "Was that . . . was that my dad?"

Anna Kiel nodded.

"How did you get in touch with him—now, so many years later? How did you know he was here in Paris?"

"I happened to stumble across an article one day. It was just a little note in a newspaper back home where it said that a Dane had been convicted for child pornography and that he was in jail in Paris. A Nick Kaldan, it said, and that just resonated with me: *Nick.* I could remember the voices around me in the room in that warehouse building: *Come on, Nick. Try her, Nick. Don't be shy, Nick.* I looked into the name and found an old author's photo of him in a book and recognized him from back then."

"And then—what? Then you came out here?"

"No, not until later. Not until after . . ." She held out her thumb and dragged it across her neck. "When I fled Denmark, I came here. To France. I remember your dad being . . ." She searched for the right word to describe it and then settled on, "Somewhat timid. He wasn't like the others. The articles about his trial also gave me the impression that he was distraught over what had happened. So, I went to see him, and we made a deal. And now we're sitting here . . ."

Heloise exhaled as she rubbed her temples. "All right. So, you can prove all of this?"

"No, I can't prove what they did to me. As far as I know, there's no documentation of that, no movies or photos, and even if I could document it, the statute of limitations has expired. There's nothing I can do about that—not legally, anyway." She paused as she took a manila folder out of her backpack. "But I can prove that they did the same thing to other children," she said, sliding the folder over in front of Heloise. "You father gave me access—"

"—to their internal communications. I know." Heloise nodded. "He told me."

"Yes, I have it all here. Information on the nine men I remember and on three new people who have joined in the meantime." She patted the cover of the folder. "But there was also a boy back then."

"A boy?"

"Yes. One day when I was in the warehouse, I saw him. He was hiding in this big tool closet, and the door was ajar. He was a young guy, must have been about fifteen. Our eyes met while one of the adults was standing behind me moaning away, and for a second I though he wanted to help me, because at first he looked so shocked. But he didn't say anything, and he didn't do anything. He just sat there, hiding and looking at me." Anna nodded to herself. "And I remember his eyes so clearly. They lit up like a cat's in the dark, but the expression in his eyes changed as we were looking at each other: it changed from empathetic into this cold, mocking look. He just observed me surreptitiously, captivated by what he was seeing, and then he winked at me. And it wasn't a wink like he was on my side. It was like a chilling wink, one that said, 'You're suffering, and I kinda like it.' "

"Who was he? How did he end up in that cabinet?" Heloise felt a tingling sensation at the back of her neck.

"At first, I figured he was just a guy who had snuck into the building to see what was in there. Later, after the grownups had left, I was lying on the bed alone. I wasn't crying, because I had shut down completely. I was dead on the inside and didn't show any emotions. But I was bleeding, and I was in pain."

Heloise sighed and shook her head, speechless.

"I had put some of my clothes back on, my underwear, my dress, as I waited for my mom to come pick me up, and then he walked into the room. I started talking to him, but he shushed me. Then he carefully closed the door behind him and pounced on me right away. He said that he would kill me, cut my throat, if I made a sound."

"Then what happened?"

"Then he ripped off my underwear and got down to business. It was violent, brutal—he hit me. He was sadistic and extremely domineering. I think he had something he needed to act out. He tried to imitate the adults, and he hurt me for the fun of it. Like, he thought it was *fun*. He enjoyed it."

The plastic bead curtain hanging in the doorway where they had entered rattled, and Anna looked up tensely. Heloise also turned toward the sound. The waiter stood at the far end of the room.

"Would you like to order anything to drink?" he asked in French.

"Tea, please. And water," Anna replied in French. She glanced over at Heloise, who nodded.

"Just water. Thanks."

The man went away again.

"You were telling me about the boy," Heloise said.

"Yes, that was the only time I saw him there. For some reason it felt like he took the humiliation to a new level. Maybe that was because for a split second, while we had that eye contact when he was in the closet, I thought he was going to . . . it sounds ridiculous when I say it now, but I thought he was going to save me." She smiled and shook her head, as if the thought was absurd. "But in reality, he was just waiting his turn."

"Didn't you ever tell anyone about this? Wasn't there anyone in your life aside from your mother who knew what you had been through?"

"Yeah, I told Kenneth."

"Do you think he would be willing to corroborate that? To me, I mean. For a quote?"

"Kenneth will do anything for me, as I would for him." She nodded.

"Then what happened? After a year, your mom's debt was paid off, or what?"

"I presume."

"And you never went back to that warehouse? You never saw any of them again?"

"I never went back there physically, no, but in my thoughts, I was there all the time. Every night when I closed my eyes, I was in that room again on that mattress. It destroyed me. I became hardened, warped. I had a short temper. I had so much hatred inside me, and I didn't trust anyone."

Heloise nodded. That matched Anna's school history and the psychologists' evaluations.

"The police profile on you says that you're suffering from psychopathy or antisocial personality disorder."

Anna raised her eyebrows. "Really, just like that? That sounds serious."

"It is." Heloise shrugged.

"Huh. Well, I had my reasons for acting the way I did. So, they can call me a psycho if they want. That's fine. Maybe that's what I am," she said. "Maybe that's what they made me into."

43

THE WAITER CAME back into the room and walked over to the table. He set two glasses of water in front of them, two cups, and a small, black ceramic teapot. He poured each of them a cup of tea and then quietly left the room again.

Heloise reached out to open the folder in front of her, but Anna calmly rested her hand on top of it.

"No," she said. "Everything you need is in there. When we're done here, you can write your story. You can pass all the documents along to the police, and together you can take these people down, one by one. But our time together today is limited—we have this one meeting, and then we'll never see each other again. So right now, I'm talking. You can read later."

Heloise gave up on the folder. She glanced at her iPhone on the table in front of her to make sure it was still recording their conversation. The red record button was lit and the line on the screen jumped every time it registered sound waves, like an irregular heartbeat on an electrocardiogram.

"All right," she said. "Please continue."

"I met Kenneth when I was in the seventh grade. He was a year older than me, and the main thing we had in common was that we were both lonely. We felt like outsiders, like we were different, wrong. We became very close friends. Unlike me, Kenneth comes from a good family. He has a loving home, a solid foundation. So, he taught me that there are people in this world who are willing to do anything you, people you can count on. We both had a hard time in school, but we had each other, and that helped. I slowly started doing better."

"So, you felt good again?"

"I started doing better, I said." Anna smiled. "I didn't say I felt good."

"Could you please elaborate on that?"

Anna took a sip and set her teacup down again. Then she said, "For years I tried to forget what had happened. I moved away from home as soon as I was old enough to get a job, and I never looked back."

"You mother also told me that she never saw you again."

"You talked to my mother?"

"Yes."

"So, are you surprised that I never went home again?"

Heloise shook her head.

"I got by on my own. I worked at a lot of different places: cafés, restaurants, nightclubs. You know, the kind of jobs college students get. None of my coworkers were serious about their jobs—they were just service jobs, almost demeaning for them to do while they were in school waiting for a better life. But I didn't know what else I should do. I didn't feel like there was any better life waiting for me."

"You didn't want an education?"

"Well." She shrugged. "I couldn't wrap my head around it. I felt lost, and time just passed. Suddenly it felt like it was simply too late. I didn't have the guts. I had settled into a kind of peace, a tolerable routine in my job, in my existence. It wasn't a happy life, but at least it wasn't running off the rails anymore. I was doing better."

"What happened then?"

"At some point several years ago I was working at a restaurant on Store Kongensgade. Madklubben, you know it?"

Heloise nodded. She knew the place well.

"It was a good job with nice coworkers, and the clientele was really varied. There were students, jet-setters, retirees, tourists, celebrities—all kinds of people. It was a nice place. I was really happy to be there."

"Then what happened?"

"One night when I got to work, the manager of the restaurant assigned me to work the banquet room. A group had booked the room for a bachelor party. A group of twenty-two people was coming for dinner, and I was to be their waiter. That was fine. I was good at the job, so I could easily handle an event like that on my own. The guys arrived at around eight thirty. They had already been drinking and were in a good mood. One of the hostesses seated them in the separate banquet room, away from the other diners, and I got to work placing bottles of wine on the table while they took their seats. I welcomed them and presented the evening's menu."

She paused for a moment, thinking back. Heloise was about to ask her to continue when she began again.

"They all looked up at me, and I started describing the menu: dry-cured scallops, rib eye steaks and mash, buttermilk pudding with cookies for dessert. I stood there with my hands folded over my apron and peered invitingly around at the group." She paused for a moment. "And then our eyes met."

"Who?" Heloise asked. "Whose eyes met?"

"The boy from the closet. It was him. He had grown up, as had I, and he looked a little different—or maybe he just looked older. He had broader shoulders, was taller, and he had a few wrinkles and dark stubble on his chin and cheeks. But it was him. It was definitely him. I practically threw up when I saw him. I started shaking. I was so scared that he would recognize me."

"Did he?"

"Not to begin with, no. I don't actually think he did. He ignored me while I gave my little talk. You know the way wealthy people treat waitstaff and housekeepers and serving people, like they don't *really* see them? You can serve a whole dinner to a party from Hellerup and do a tap dance on the table in front of them, but five minutes later they wouldn't be able to pick you out of a lineup. They simply don't see people like me."

Heloise nodded. Anna had a point.

"At some point later in the night, he came up to me. He wanted to find out if they could have a specific brand of cognac with their coffee. The one I had set out apparently wasn't good enough. But I told him that we only had the brands we had. Then he pulled out his wallet, took out his card, and tucked it into the pocket on my apron. 'Just pop over to the restaurant across the street,' he said. 'Get a couple bottles of Rémy Martin Louis XIII. Show them my card and say they're for Christoffer Mossing. They know me over there. Just have them send me the bill.' "

"It was Mossing?" Heloise blinked a couple of times, and her breathing sped up. "The boy in the closet that time was Christoffer Mossing?"

"Yes, and he seemed like he was doing just dandy when I saw him that night at the restaurant," Anna nodded. "Our little rendezvous way back when, him punching me repeatedly while he raped me?" She frowned and shrugged. "Apparently that didn't ruin *his* life. He didn't have any trouble completing his education or getting himself set up with a good life. His business card even said that he was a criminal defense lawyer for a law firm up north, so he had plenty of money too. He definitely seemed to be doing well."

"What did you say to him?"

She shrugged. "Nothing. I got the liquor he requested and set the bottles on the table in front of him." She got a faraway look in her eyes as she spoke. "Later that night I saw him again, out by the coat check. He was looking for some cigarettes in his jacket pocket, drunk and tense, and he grabbed my arm as I walked by. I tried to yank it back, but he held on harder, squeezed so that it hurt. I told him to let me go, but he held on tight and leaned in close to me. 'I forgot your name,' he said, 'but I remember you.' Then he winked at me. Motherfucker *winked* at me. I was this close to getting a knife from the kitchen and jabbing it into his throat right then and there."

"Was that when you decided to do it, to kill him?" Heloise tensely adjusted her position in her chair.

"No." Anna shook her head. "I just wanted to get the hell out of there. I told my manager that I wasn't feeling well, and she let me go. So I left."

"Did you ever see him again? I mean, before the night when you . . ."

"I tried for a while to forget having run into him, but I couldn't. The next few months, it just got worse, and my nightmares from when I was a kid came back. I wasn't doing well. It was really bad."

"Were you afraid of him?"

"No, I wasn't afraid. I was . . ." She paused for a moment and put her hands together behind her head. "I was infuriated. I was filled with a red-hot, consuming rage, which only grew and started overflowing inside me. He didn't see me as a person. I was worthless in his eyes; I was nothing! A toy he had played with one time a long time ago."

"Then what did you do?"

"I started looking into who he was and where he lived. I read articles online about his work, about the cases he was involved in, the sorts of people he defended. At some point, while I was searching his name, I happened to come across an interview in the business newspaper *Børsen* with his father, the powerful Johannes Mossing. And then . . ." She spread her hands out and smiled wanly. "Then all the pieces fell into place."

"What do you mean?"

"It was him," Anna said. "He was the one who came to my house when I was a kid that night and rang my doorbell. He was the one who selected me. He was the one who bought me from my mother."

"Johanne Mossing was the one who kissed you in the doorway? When you were eight years old?"

Anna nodded.

"Was he also involved in the Lullaby Club? Was he ever present in the warehouse by the harbor?"

"Present?" She laughed briefly. "He hosted the event. It was his building, his club, his idea. He's the reason my life ended that night the doorbell rang."

"Can you prove it?" Heloise was filled with adrenaline.

"It's all in there." She pointed to the folder. "There's pictures, conversations, links to audio files."

Heloise let the feeling blissfully sink in. This clinched it. She had her story. Before the week was up, she could break the news that Johannes Mossing wasn't just a criminal but that he had systematically abused young children with members of a secret club he had set up. That his own son had lost his life for the same reason. This was big. Huge!

"Why did you kill Christoffer Mossing?" Heloise asked. "Why didn't you let the police deal with it?"

"He deserved it." Anna leaned back in her chair.

"Did he see it coming? Or was he asleep when you attacked him?"

"He was asleep. But I woke him up with the first stab, right here." She pointed just above her left collarbone. "It wouldn't have been hardly as satisfying if he hadn't gotten to see me. If he had died without knowing who stole his life from him."

"And the security camera in the driveway? What was that about? Why didn't you just get out of there?"

"I knew Johannes Mossing would end up seeing that surveillance footage. Even if he couldn't recognize me, someone would be able to identify me, and my name would come out. And then it would hit him, who I was. He would realize what it was all about, and he would understand that his son was dead because of him. Because isn't that what people always say? That nothing is worse than losing a child?"

"So I hear." Heloise nodded.

"Yes, so I think it was a fitting punishment, considering what they did to me. It was a good start, at least."

"But you killed a person, Anna. How can you live with that?"

"Oh, I'm not going to lie to you. It felt good."

"But you can't just go around killing people! Not even if they're rapists and child molesters. I mean, don't get me wrong: it's outrageous what they did to you, inhuman! And the people that did that deserve to be punished to the fullest extent possible. But this isn't how things are done. The idea is for them to be prosecuted, convicted, and punished—not murdered in cold blood in their sleep."

Anna shook her head patronizingly. "But that doesn't work. The system doesn't work. Look at similar cases in Denmark. When have these kinds of men ever gotten what they deserved? Show me one rapist who has received an appropriate punishment."

Heloise searched for a response but found none. Instead she said, "You're going to end up going to jail yourself for what you did. You know that, right?"

"Maybe." Anna shrugged. "Maybe not. There are cases in which women in abusive marriages murdered their husbands and got away with it, situations in which even the judge was able to see that it was the women's only option. Maybe that will be the case for me too."

"But that wasn't your only option."

"To get peace of mind, justice? Yes, it really was."

"But your life wasn't in danger."

"I think most people will sympathize with me when they hear my story, when they understand my motives."

"If you really believe that, then come with me," Heloise said. "Let's go to the police together. I can call my contact back home. He's on your case. And you can tell him all about—"

"No."

"You're going to have to—"

"No." Anna held her hand up to stop Heloise. "Like I said before: we'll talk now, and then we're not going to see each other again."

"But I'd like to help you."

"You already are."

"What do you mean?"

"I started all of this my way. Now you can finish it your way." She pointed to the folder but happened to bump her cup, knocking it over. Lukewarm tea spread across the table-top, flowing to the edge and down over one of Anna's trouser legs. She leapt up and tried to brush the liquid off her pants with a rapid motion.

She looked around for something to clean the mess up with.

"Do you want me to get something?" Heloise asked.

"No, I'll just grab a cloth from the bar—one second."

Anna rustled out through the beaded curtain, and Heloise reached for the folder as soon as she was out of view. She couldn't wait any longer. She had to just take a peek at the contents.

She flipped open to a random location and skimmed the page. It was a chat between two people. Their names and IP addresses were listed next to each statement, each disgusting comment. Someone had gone over them with a bright-yellow highlighter, and Heloise read the names: Reinar Boysen, Poul Mark Iversen. She had never heard of either of them. She scanned their chat messages to each other.

The Harbor Pool opened today!
I know. I was there. Took pictures of a pretty little bathing beauty wearing sunny yellow bikini bottoms.
No top?
No.

Blond?
Of course.
How old?
Six, maybe seven. JonBenét Ramsey lookalike.
Mmm, I like! Upload!
Tonight.
Can't wait!!
Tonight.
OK, anything else? Other pictures?
Skydebanen Park in Vesterbro. I stopped by there this afternoon, after the harbor. There's water in the wading pool now. You can sit nearby, cell phone out, and snap away. The moms don't even notice.

Heloise flipped onward through the folder. The next page was a plastic sleeve with a matte finish. She couldn't see what was inside it, so she tipped the contents out onto the table, at a safe distance from the puddle of tea that was beginning to soak into the tabletop.

It was pictures, pictures of children. But they weren't taken on a warm summer's day in Copenhagen, and they weren't of children playing in a wading pool, nor were they pictures of a sunny-yellow bikini on a schoolgirl. They were naked children—a new face in each photo—lying on a blue-and-white-striped mattress on the floor of a junky room. Several adult men were standing around the mattress, some without shirts, saggy, hairy bellies, and others with their genitals exposed.

Heloise's eyes filled with tears.

She had never seen anything more repulsive. But the children in the pictures weren't crying. They didn't even look like they were afraid. Their expressions were just completely vacant, with no discernible emotion.

Heloise looked up, suddenly aware that several minutes had gone by and Anna hadn't returned yet. She got up and quickly strode through the doorway that led back into the front of the restaurant. She looked around. The couple who had been sitting over in the corner were gone now.

And so was Anna Kiel.

"Hey!" Heloise shouted to the waiter. "That woman I was with. Where is she?"

He looked up from his spot behind the bar and shook his head apologetically, holding his hands up in front of himself as if to say *calm down.*

"English, *non.*"

Heloise ran out the front door and looked down the street. There was no one to see. She chose a direction at random and started jogging, frantically looking around. Her voice cut through the air as she tried yelling.

"Anna!"

She scanned the buildings and noticed little paths leading back behind the buildings, vans that were parked on the street, an overweight woman in a burka walking down the street with a baby in her arms.

But no Anna Kiel. She was gone.

Heloise put her hands on the top of her head for a moment before she allowed them to drop limply to her sides again, frustrated, despairing.

Then she remembered the folder.

She ran back to the restaurant, past the man at the bar, through the beaded curtain, and exhaled in relief.

It was still there. So were the pictures, spread out over the table, and Anna's backpack hanging over the back of the chair, three seats away from Heloise.

She went over and picked it up. She looked in all the compartments and pockets, shook it, and turned it inside out. There was nothing in it. Not a crumpled receipt from a store, not a key to an apartment or a safe-deposit box. No cryptic note that the police might be able to work on further. The backpack was just empty.

She tossed it aside just as the waiter cleared his throat at the other end of the room. Heloise turned toward him.

"You . . . okay?" He pointed to her, seemingly concerned.
Heloise nodded.

She pulled a twenty-euro note out of her back pocket and
gestured to him that she would like to pay. He left the room
again, and Heloise pulled her chair out and sat down.

She looked at the pictures on the table again and shook
her head. Then she pressed her palms to her eyes until she
could see nothing but colored dots.

44

"WE COULD HAVE had her now. Do you understand that? Has that sunken into your head at all?"

Schäfer paced back and forth in front of Heloise, snorting. The color of his face matched the burgundy lounge sofa she was sitting on.

She said nothing, just let him rage. She waited until he was done.

"Damn it, Heloise. Why the hell didn't you tell me you were coming here? We could have picked up Anna Kiel in front of the prison. Don't you see that? It would have been so easy. Man, she could have been sitting there right now, in handcuffs!" He pointed animatedly to the empty sofa cushion beside Heloise.

She nodded.

"What did she say? Where did she go?"

"I don't know," Heloise said with a shrug. "She just disappeared."

"Disappeared? Into thin air? One second you were with her and the next, poof? Gone?"

"Yes." Heloise shrugged her shoulders again.

"You father wouldn't say a word to me when I was out there. So, we're going back to Fresnes now, together. And *you're* going to get him to talk!"

"He doesn't know where she is."

"How can you know that for sure? Maybe he lied to you. As I understand it, that wouldn't be the first time."

"Knock it off," Heloise said, looking up.

"Knock what off?"

"Don't talk to me about my dad. I know I should have involved you in what was going on. I should have told you about him when you called last night. But what happened between him and me—our personal relationship—that's *my* business. It's none of your business, not yours or anyone else's. So, you can just drop it. I'm not going back out there."

They stared into each other's eyes for a long time. Neither of them blinked.

"He doesn't know where she is," Heloise repeated. "Besides, you must be able to track her down. There must be cameras outside the prison along the route we took. You must be able to follow her from the restaurant with the surveillance cameras. Don't they have them all over the place here in France?"

"They're already looking into that."

"Who's *they*?"

"My contacts here, the French police," Schäfer said, and then sat down in the armchair facing Heloise.

Through the window behind him, she could see the blue flashing lights from the police cars on the street outside, lighting up all the glass around the hotel entrance. They had been there when she returned to the hotel—the local police, Interpol, and Schäfer. They had been waiting for Heloise, and when she finally turned up, they had descended on her like a flock of gypsy children, aggressive, clamoring, hungry for information.

Out in the lobby, people were gathering to peer curiously into the lounge area, where she and Schäfer were sitting. The open double doors that led into the lounge were being blocked by two uniformed officers, and the hotel manager was shuffling around nervously next to them. It wasn't good advertising for the place to have such a visible police presence here. In a city that had been dramatically affected by terrorist attacks, the blue lights felt particularly alarming.

Schäfer leaned forward in his chair and rested his elbows on his knees.

"Okay," he said, and then gestured with one hand. "Tell me what happened. What did she say to you?"

"Are you done chewing me out?" Heloise placed a hand on Anna Kiel's backpack next to her.

Schäfer raised an eyebrow and shrugged ever so slightly in consent.

"Good, because I think your mood will improve once you hear what she had to say."

"What did she say?" he asked, straightening up.

Heloise pulled her iPhone out of her pocket. She found the sound file and set the phone on the dark-green marble tabletop in front of Schäfer.

For the next forty-seven minutes they listened to Anna Kiel's hoarse voice.

When it was over, Schäfer said, "Please tell me that you have the documents she talked about."

He had stood up halfway through the recording, too tense to stay seated. Now he had his hands on his cheeks, like a game show contestant waiting to find out if he had won the jackpot or not.

"I do." Heloise nodded.

Schäfer squeezed his eyes shut and did a fist pump with his right hand.

Heloise pulled out the folder and handed it to him.

"This is it?" he asked. "These are the documents?"

"Yes. I only had a chance to skim through them, but what I saw was completely insane. There are DVDs of pornography, pictures of assaults, chat conversations, and all sorts of other dreadful stuff. There are a bunch of names of people who participated, their IP addresses, pictures of them. We can nail those assholes, Schäfer, all of them."

"We?" Schäfer asked, looking up.

"Yeah."

"No, Heloise. You can't write about this. Not yet."

"I'm sorry. What did you say?" She jumped to her feet. "I'm the one who landed this story. It's mine!"

"Not yet." He shook his head. "You have to wait until I give you the go-ahead."

"One of the richest men in Denmark abused children. If I don't write that story, someone else will—believe me. It's *my* story, Schäfer. *I'm* going to be the one to break it."

"Yes, of course you will, but not yet. Not until our investigation is squared away. If you write anything before these assholes are locked up, then you'll just warn them off, and I am not going to let Mossing get away from me again."

"Well then, what are you suggesting that we do?" Heloise asked, crossing her arms.

Schäfer walked past her, over to the big double doors, and spoke quietly with the officers blocking the entrance to the lounge. Then he closed the doors and locked them so that he and Heloise were alone in the room.

"I suggest that we prepare properly before we proceed with this," he said, allowing himself to sink back into the armchair. He opened the folder. "Come, have a seat," he said, nodding to the sofa. "We'll start at the beginning."

CHAPTER

45

"**Y**OU'VE GOT TO be fucking kidding me."

Schäfer flipped through the documents again for a third time as pictures and newspaper clippings skittered across the coffee table and fell onto the long-haired area rug.

"I don't believe this!"

"I . . . I don't understand," Heloise said.

"There's nothing here! It doesn't say anything about Johannes Mossing here."

"But Anna said it was him. She said there was evidence in the folder that he—"

"Goddammit!" Schäfer yelled, and hit the folder, sending it flying across the room. "Where the hell is it, then? Where's the evidence that implicates Mossing? Where are the pictures of *him* with his dick out?"

Heloise shook her head in confusion. "This doesn't make any sense. Why would she lie about that?"

"She didn't," Schäfer seethed. "Mossing is behind all of this. I *know* he is. He's the one Anna is gunning for. That's what she said. This whole thing is about him. If only we could get her to testify against him . . ."

"I tried to make her understand that too," Heloise said. "I told her that she should report him to the police. But she said it was too late, that the statute of limitations had expired."

"That's not true," Schäfer said, shaking his head.

"Yes, she said that. You heard it yourself."

"Yeah, she *said* that, but it's not correct. The statute of limitations for aggravated rape cases, which this case would qualify as, is fifteen years. And when it involves the rape of a person under the age of fifteen, the statute of limitations isn't until fifteen years after the victim's twenty-first birthday. So, Anna Kiel has a year or two to go before it's too late to do anything about the matter legally."

"Okay, but then she doesn't know that."

Schäfer narrowed his eyes and peered skeptically at Heloise. "Oh, she knows."

Heloise stood up and started gathering the things up off the floor, while Schäfer took a couple of deep breaths and looked down at the notes he had taken as they reviewed the contents of the folder.

"We have twelve names," he said. "Twelve people we can build a case around."

"Yes, but not Mossing."

"Anna said it took place in his warehouse," he said, scratching the back of his head. "She said that Johannes Mossing owned the place. So, if I can get one of those other guys to testify against him . . . Someone must know something that can bring him down. At least one of the twelve must be willing to negotiate once they're caught."

Heloise nodded.

"I've always known that this asshole was up to something illegal, but I wasn't expecting him to be this . . . this cruel. Children, man . . ." Schäfer flipped through the pictures, and Heloise could tell from his jaw movements that he was clenching his teeth. "For the love of God, they're just *children.*"

"What do we do now?" Heloise passed him the documents she'd gathered up from the floor.

"You just get to work writing your story so that it's ready to go. But you need to sit on it until I give you the go-ahead. Got it?"

Heloise nodded reluctantly.

Schäfer turned to look at the hotel's courtyard, which was now lit up by strings of incandescent lights, draped so they zigzagged through the air between two buildings.

He looked at his watch. It was almost midnight.

"Are you done here? In Paris, I mean."

Heloise took a deep breath and then exhaled slowly. Then she nodded.

"Good," Schäfer said. "Then we'll fly home first thing tomorrow."

*　*　*

The day's newspapers sat fresh and crisp in a rack at the gate. Heloise grabbed a copy of *Demokratisk Dagblad* and unfolded the paper as she stood in line on the jet bridge on her way into the plane.

The front page was Bøttger's follow-up story on the Skriver case. It revealed how sources inside the Ministry of Commerce had deliberately misinformed one of the newspaper's journalists a few weeks ago about the production facilities in Bangalore for a well-known fashion brand. It described how the journalist in question had been fed forged documents to discredit Skriver.

Heloise wasn't mentioned by name in the story.

The article was accompanied by a sketch drawing of the secretary of commerce and his spray-tanned spin doctor, Carsten Holm. In the drawing, both men had fangs and tridents and Holm appeared to be whispering conspiratorially into the ear of the secretary, who in turn was responding with a resounding Dracula laugh: *Muaaahaha.*

Heloise skimmed the front page and then flipped through to the spread on pages four and five, where a more detailed examination of the case was printed.

Martin was named as the source.

A warm, bubbly sensation flowed through Heloise's body as she saw his name in print. She had hardly thought of him in the twenty-four hours she had been away. Her thoughts had only revolved around her father, Anna, the story. But now she felt the urge to go home, a desire to start with a clean slate, to start over.

She pulled her phone out of the inside pocket of her black leather jacket and wrote a text.

Hi. On my way home. See you tonight?

He replied in less than a minute.

Tonight? What's wrong with this afternoon?

Heloise smiled.

I'm boarding in a second and I'm reading the paper. Is your phone lighting up yet with calls from TV news show like Deadline?

Yup. It has been ringing off the hook. I'm on my way to the Danish Broadcasting Company studio right now. How about you? Are you okay?

Long story, but yes. I'm okay.

I miss you.

"What's with the goofy smile?"

Heloise looked up at Schäfer, who had turned around in the line ahead of her and was eyeing her with an eyebrow raised.

"Nothing."

"Is it the guy with the cuff links?"

"Shut up," she said, and smiled.

Schäfer nodded in agreement. "You look lovestruck, Kaldan. Like maybe Cupid has started shooting hollow-points, the kind that do maximum damage."

Heloise rolled her eyes. Then she looked down at her phone again and sent one last message off to Copenhagen before switching her phone to airplane mode.

Me too.

CHAPTER

46

"COMPLETELY OUT OF the question." Editor in chief Mikkelsen drove his point home by repeatedly hammering his chubby forefinger on the mahogany tabletop. "If that's all you've got, then we're not going to run it."

"Why the hell not?" Heloise sat up straighter.

Mikkelsen looked from her to Karen Aagaard with a look that said he couldn't believe his own ears.

"You're asking *why*? Tell me, didn't you learn anything from the Skriver case? Do you have any idea how many lunches at Café Victor I've had to pay for to sooth the egos of those goddamned fashion people? How much damage control I've had had to do to save your ass?"

"*My* ass or the newspaper's?"

"Don't get cute with me, Kaldan. If you had done your job to begin with, we wouldn't have been in this mess with Skriver. And now you're expecting me to publish a story that portrays Johannes Mossing as a predatory pedophile—like some kind of Danish Jimmy Savile—without having so much as a shred of evidence for the allegations?"

"I agree that, initially, the Skriver story was a disaster. I fucked up." Heloise nodded as if she were negotiating. "But it did in fact turn out quite well for the newspaper, right? The revelation of the secretary of commerce's role in the matter has been the top story in all the media outlets since the story broke last week. I mean, the man resigned, for crying out loud!"

"Yes," Mikkelsen snorted. "Thanks to Bøttger."

"Heloise was actually the one who handed him the story," Karen Aagaard interjected.

"The point is that the real story came out in the end," Heloise said. "Imagine where we'd be if we had been too scared to speak up. Then we would have a secretary of commerce who'd gotten away with trying to sabotage one of the biggest companies in the country."

"That is a completely different scenario."

"It's Martin Duvall's word against the secretary's. What's the difference?"

"Duvall turned out to be a reliable source," Mikkelsen said. "That's the difference."

"And Anna Kiel isn't? Is that what you're telling me?"

"The woman is wanted for murder, Kaldan. She murdered one of the partners at one of the country's most highly respected law firms. She is declared mentally unstable—psychotic, even—and now you want to smear an old man's reputation because a mentally disturbed murderer has made undocumented accusations against him."

"You're not serious!"

"I'm sorry, what?"

"You don't really believe Mossing is innocent, do you?"

"There is something that you don't seem to get, missy." Mikkelsen shook his head in annoyance. "What each of us believes is irrelevant. The only thing I'm interested in is what you can *prove*. Find the evidence against Mossing! Document that he had something to do with this sickening Lullaby Club, and then we'll go to town. Then we'll clear the front page and lynch the bastard. But I'm not printing an article that will destroy a person's life just based on this." He pointed at the draft article Heloise had brought to the meeting. "Not a chance!"

"Say something!" Heloise said, glancing over at Karen Aagaard in frustration.

"I'm sorry, Heloise, but he's right," Aagaard said.

Heloise closed her eyes and sighed.

"What do the police say? What's the status of the case?" Aagaard asked.

Heloise shook her head slightly as she looked resignedly down at the table. "They have arrested eleven men in the case, raided their homes, confiscated their computers. There is a twelfth person on the arrest warrant—a high school teacher from the Aarhus area—but he's disappeared."

"Skipped town?" Aagaard asked.

"No one knows," Heloise said with a shrug. "He disappeared a little over a month ago, and up until recently the police were treating it as a criminal case. In the beginning they thought the man had been the victim of a crime. But now they think maybe he ran off instead."

"Then I simply can't understand why you're sulking," Mikkelsen said grumpily, and stood up. "There's plenty of material for you to dig into. Eleven men have been accused of taking part in this filth, and a twelfth might've managed to flee the sinking ship. I mean, good grief, woman, that's huge! Go home and write *that* story!"

Mikkelsen left the room, and Heloise and Aagaard could hear him cursing as his heavy footsteps echoed down the hallway of the editorial department.

* * *

Detective Sergeant Erik Schäfer had had a busy week full of raids and interrogations. The chief superintendent had assembled an investigative team of eighteen men, who had been working on the case around the clock since Schäfer and Heloise had returned from Paris. Schäfer was in charge of the team, and this case was the highest priority of the Violent Crimes Unit.

He had sat in the interrogation rooms across from every single one of the assholes who had been charged in the case in recent weeks. He had looked them all dead in the eye and seen several of them sweat and tremble and blubber as the realities had hit them like a sledgehammer. A couple of them had seemed arrogant and overly self-confident, completely calm about the charges and the future imprisonment they appeared destined to face. The rest had been downright panic-stricken and more than willing to negotiate. Three of them had even sobbed during their interrogations. But none of them—not a single one of the eleven charged—had implicated Mossing in the case, no matter how much pressure Schäfer had applied. And he had definitely tightened the damn screws on those three crybabies. He'd threatened to release footage to the media and to send the video recordings to their children.

I guess you could call the movie Daddy's Greatest Hits. I bet your daughter will cross you off her Christmas shopping list when she sees it! What's her name again—Vivian? And I see here that she works for Save the Children. Ironic, isn't it? No doubt she'll be pretty peeved when she sees how you have been treating kids.

Several of the men charged had been more than willing to accept the maximum sentence in order to avoid causing their families any more pain. They had also volunteered the names of other sex offenders and been willing to testify against their buddies who were sitting in the other interrogation rooms.

But when the topic turned to Johannes Mossing, they closed up like clams.

Every single one of them.

Schäfer hadn't been able to find anything that connected him to the case. There were no warehouses in Nordhavnen Harbor that belonged to Mossing, not now, not ever.

Schäfer had dragged Jonna Kiel in for questioning, but she had stubbornly insisted that she couldn't remember anything from the late eighties until the midnineties. Sure, there had been a gambling problem, she conceded, but she had been drinking so heavily and smoking so much pot back then that her memory was as full of holes as Swiss cheese. She claimed she had never heard of Johannes Mossing and that she had no clue as to whether or not her daughter had been sexually abused.

Word of the arrests, which the press hadn't yet gotten wind of, had obviously made its way to Vedbæk, and Johannes Mossing had gone underground. Schäfer had pounded on his front door several times this week with an angry fist. The first three times, Marcus Plessner, that dwarf of a lawyer who catered only to the rich, had opened the door and denied any knowledge of the old man's whereabouts.

This morning, Schäfer had caught Ellen Mossing in the driveway with a yoga mat under her arm. She'd broken down sobbing when he told her that her son had been murdered because of her husband's predilection for minors. But she hadn't said a word.

Schäfer felt like he'd been through the ringer as he sat in his black Opel Astra now, heading for his little brick house in Copenhagen's Valby district. He was so exhausted that he wanted to hop on the first plane to Saint Lucia, to hell with Mossing and the whole case. He wanted to just collapse into a hammock between two palm trees, drink one ice-cold beer after another, and enjoy the view of Connie's curvy body in the crystal-blue waters of the Caribbean.

Only three weeks to go, he told himself, taking his foot off the gas. Only three weeks to go.

He rolled to a stop in front of his house and parked in his usual spot next to the rusty mailbox that hung crooked from the white picket fence around his yard.

The plastic slats over the ventilator from the kitchen were rattling their familiar mealtime melody on the outside wall of the house, and it had the same effect on Schäfer as the bells had had on Pavlov's dogs. The scent of Connie's chili con carne reached his nostrils as he neared the front door, and his stomach rumbled in anticipation.

He unlocked the door and tossed his suede jacket on a chair in the entryway.

"Hi, honey, I'm home."

"Perfect timing!" Connie's voice replied from the kitchen at the far end of the house. "Dinner will be ready in ten minutes."

Schäfer undid the top two buttons of his shirt as he lumbered into the living room, drawn toward the aroma of the food cooking on the stove in the kitchen.

He heard Connie laughing and smiled in surprise.

He saw her through the kitchen doorway. She was wearing a yellow dress. She stood there laughing as she peeled avocados on a wooden cutting board on the island in the middle of the kitchen. Her curly, black hair was unbraided and surrounded her face like a lion's mane. She looked happy, pretty, always so pretty . . .

Schäfer smiled as he stepped into the kitchen to greet her.

"What's so fun . . ."

The smile vanished from his lips, and he instinctively reached for the Heckler & Koch 9mm pistol in his shoulder holster.

"Hi, babe." Connie glanced over at him as she started slicing the avocado into the salad. Her white teeth shone, lighting up her whole face.

"Hey," Schäfer replied, but he wasn't looking at her. His eyes were fixed on the battered leather armchair in the corner of the kitchen.

Johannes Mossing was sitting in the chair.

Sprawling, his legs crossed, a beer in his hand, relaxed.

"Ah, there you are," he said. "I was starting to think you'd forgotten about our appointment."

"You should have told me we were having company," Connie said. She came over and planted a kiss on Schäfer's lips as she wiped her hands on a dishcloth. "I would have tidied up a little."

"Oh, don't worry about that, Connie. Your place is charming," Mossing said, giving her a flirtatious look, which made Schäfer want to yank his gun out of its holster and empty the clip into Mossing's chest.

"Our appointment?" he asked instead. His voice was neutral, but every muscle in his body was tense. "Could you just jog my memory—which appointment was that again?"

"You said you had something you wanted to talk to me about."

"Johannes tells me that you've recently started working together," Connie said. "That he's helping you with the cases you're working on at the moment." She turned to Mossing. "Actually, I didn't catch your last name?"

"Madsen." He smiled warmly. "I'm normally with the police in North Zealand, but I've been temporarily assigned to the investigation in Copenhagen. Your husband is just so busy—dashing around, breaking down doors, and asking a lot of questions—and, I mean, we can't have that, have him getting burned out. So, one of the head honchos thought he could use a little help."

"You see? Now that's what I like to hear," Connie said, bending down to take plates out of the cupboard in front her.

Mossing looked over at Schäfer. He wasn't smiling anymore.

"Did you say dinner would be ready in ten?" Schäfer asked, without taking his eyes off Mossing.

"Well, now it's more like . . . eight," Connie said, looking at the timer on the stove.

"Okay. I just have some paperwork I'd like you to take a look at," Schäfer told Mossing, and stepped aside so the path was clear to the doorway leading to the living room.

"Oh?" Mossing folded his hands in his lap, expectant, defiant.

Schäfer looked at what he was wearing, the dark-blue blazer that hung down over his loose khakis. Could Mossing be hiding a weapon in there? he wondered. A gun? A knife?

"Yeah," Schäfer said. "The papers are out in my car. Why don't you come on out for a sec and I'll show you?"

Mossing stood up. He walked over to Schäfer and pointed to the door. "After you."

Schäfer grabbed the grip of his gun. "No, after you."

* * *

They had only just reached the front door when Schäfer drew his weapon and aimed it at Johannes Mossing.

"You motherfucker! What are you playing at? You show up in my house?! You talk to my *wife*? I ought to put a bullet between your eyes right now, you son of a bitch!"

Mossing looked nonchalantly down the barrel of the firearm, which was aimed right at his nose.

"Here is the deal," he said. "You stay away from me and my wife, then I'll stop bothering you and yours." Mossing's voice was calm, almost friendly. "But if you *don't* stop knocking on my door, then both you and your plantation wife in there will end up on the bottom of the ocean. Got it?"

Schäfer grabbed the collar of Mossing's blazer with one hand while he pushed the gun's muzzle hard against the underside of his chin with the other.

"Oh, yeah? I think I'd rather just shoot you right here and now."

"Well, you could." Mossing smiled. "But you won't. We both know that."

"I know what you did, and I'm going to make sure you get put away for it. It's only a matter of time. Then you're going down for this."

"It's not about what you *know*, Schäfer. It's about what you can *prove*."

"You won't get away with what you did to those children."

Mossing yanked himself free from Schäfer's hold and started walking toward the gate at the end of the gravel path.

"Do you hear what I'm saying, asshole?" Schäfer yelled after him. "You won't get away with what you did to those children."

Mossing turned and looked at Schäfer with a smug expression.

"That's what you don't seem to get, Schäfer," he said as he opened the gate. "I've already gotten away with it."

CHAPTER

47

HELOISE SAT AT the coffee table and stared at the screen in front of her. The cursor sat there on the blank page, blinking.

She had asked Karen Aagaard for a day off when she had caught her on her cell phone that morning. A little alone time. Just today, and then she would be back at work tomorrow.

Her story about the Lullaby Club had broken three weeks ago. The public prosecutor's office had indicted the eleven men in the case, and the other media had jumped on the story like slavering wolfhounds. The tabloids were still running daily extras about the men, attracting readers with special supplements and feature stories including gruesome pictures and details from the evidence that were way, way too explicit. Things that *Demokratisk Dagblad*—and any other media outlet with any self-respect—would never dream of reproducing in such graphic horror.

By now, more victims had come forward: seven women between the ages of fifteen and twenty-seven. They had recognized several of the accused men, but there still wasn't anything new on Mossing. No one had pointed an accusatory finger in his direction. No evidence or witness statements had connected him to the case.

Heloise looked at the clock. It was 1:27 p.m. She got up and fetched a bottle of white wine and a glass from the kitchen. She was just about to take the first sip when her phone rang. She pulled it out and looked at the caller ID.

Erik Schäfer.

They hadn't talked to each other since they'd returned from Paris, and she was surprised at how happy she felt to see his name light up on her display.

"Hi."

"Hey, Kaldan. What's up?" His voice was deep and raspy but delightfully cheerful. "Are you writing any revealing articles? Bringing down any assholes?"

"Well, a couple here and there."

"That's the spirit," he said. "And other than that? Everything all right?"

"Yes." Heloise caught herself nodding. "I'm okay. How about you?"

"I'm great. I've been busy, but you know all about that. I can see from the paper that you've been following along from the sidelines. That's actually one of the reasons I'm calling," Schäfer said. "I have a follow-up story for you, if you want it."

"Uh, yes please!" Heloise set down her wineglass and grabbed a pen. She clicked the top and was ready. "What've you got?"

"I just received a call from the police in East Jutland. That high school teacher, you know—our twelfth man?"

"Yeah, what about him?"

"A herring boat just hauled him up somewhere off of Aarhus this morning."

"Is he dead?"

"Yes, otherwise this would be a new world record for free diving. The pathologist thinks he's been in the water for almost two months."

"So, since he disappeared?"

"Yup."

"Could it have been an accidental drowning, do you think?"

"The body was tangled up in an iron chain."

"Oh . . ." Heloise raised an eyebrow.

"Right. Oh!" Schäfer said. "The family has already been notified, and I thought it would be better if you ran with the story before the tabloids got wind of it."

"Thank you."

"Oh, you're welcome."

"Anything else? Any news about Anna?"

"No, nothing."

"And Mossing?"

Schäfer sighed so heavily that Heloise could almost smell his tobacco breath over the phone. "Nothing."

They were both quiet for a moment, and then Heloise said, "My father's dead. He hung himself in his cell."

"Yeah," Schäfer said. "I know."

Heloise blinked a couple of times, surprised. "How do you know that?"

"The police in Fresnes contacted me this morning."

"Is that why you're calling?"

Schäfer cleared his throat. "I, uh . . . I just wanted to make sure you were all right."

Heloise mulled that over for a moment. "I am," she said then, and she meant it.

"Good," he said. "Is there anyone who can be with you today?"

"Martin's coming over tonight."

"Okay, good . . . Good."

Heloise could hear some kind of announcement echoing in the background, a woman's voice over a staticky loudspeaker sound. "Where are you?"

"At the airport."

"Where are you going?"

"The Caribbean."

"For real?"

"For real."

Heloise looked out the window. The sky over the Marble Church was a dazzling white from the fall clouds, and the leaves of the little fig tree on her patio were wrinkled and brown.

"That sounds amazing. Have a great trip," she said.

"You bet I will."

"And hey, give me a call when you get back, okay? We could grab a bite or something."

"On one condition," Schäfer said. "None of that vegetarian crap for me, okay?"

"It's a deal." Heloise smiled.

* * *

She took a single sip of her wine after she hung up. Then she found a number in her phone's contact list.

She leaned forward in her seat as she waited for the call to be answered.

"Yes, hello. This is Heloise Kaldan with *Demokratisk Dagblad*," she said. "I understand that you fished a body out of the water off of Aarhus this morning."

CHAPTER

48

I T WAS ONLY nine o'clock, but the asphalt in front of the hotel was already on the verge of melting in the summer heat. Anna studied every single pedestrian who crossed the street from the balcony of her suite. On the Grand Hyatt Martinez's private beach across the street, the cabana boys in their white polos and lavender shorts were setting up sun umbrellas, putting out towels, and serving morning mojitos for aging rich men and women in dental-floss bikinis.

Car after car materialized in the hotel's driveway. The luxurious ones—the Bentleys, the Ferraris—were lined up near the entrance, exclusive and sparkling, with license plates in Arabic or Russian. The less ostentatious vehicles were hidden away in the underground parking garage below the hotel.

Anna had been staying at the hotel since the middle of May. That had given her two weeks to get to know the place, to get her bearings and learn the various escape routes, the layouts of the suites, the employees' daily routines, and the colors of the uniforms.

She was ready now.

He had shown up on June first, just like Nick had said he would. The sight had sent a curious tingling sensation through her, right to the tips of her fingers. She tasted acid in her mouth, and her temples throbbed. For the first six days, she had observed him from a distance. She had waited, recording his movements, his eating habits, his routines.

She had gotten a running start.

Now, as the climax seemed to be imminent—now, when what she had been waiting for for so long was finally a possibility—she somehow felt like drawing it out just a little more. She wanted to savor the lead-up to what was going to happen just a bit longer.

She jumped when she saw him come out the revolving door two floors below her.

He crossed the street in front of the hotel and walked down the stairs to the waterfront promenade. She followed him with her eyes as he strolled out onto the pier, and she watched for the next two hours as he sunbathed on one of the blue chaise longues.

He went into the water only once, a quick dip—down and up again—and then back to his chaise longue.

At lunchtime, Anna took a seat three tables away from him in the restaurant at the base of the pier, just as she had done on the other days. He didn't notice her today either.

He ordered oysters and Sancerre. *Again.* Followed by crème brûlée. *Again.*

His food was served at the very same second that a little Asian girl wearing floaties and a bikini approached his table and poked the waiter's arm.

The girl's lips moved.

Anna couldn't hear what she said. She turned in her chair, looking for the child's parents. She spotted a woman sitting on a beach chair close to the water's edge. The woman was smiling as she watched her daughter venturing out into the world on her own.

The waiter handed the girl a soft drink. She paid with a handful of coins and ran back to her mother, flung her arms around her mom's neck, and proudly showed her what she'd bought.

Anna smiled briefly.

Then she attentively turned back to him. She could see his jaw muscles working as he ate. She could also see that he had noticed the girl. It was like a membrane had come down over his eyeballs. The look in his eyes was at once drowsy and intent, clinging to the little girl's body.

Anna recognized that look.

He watched for the next hour as the girl waded and squealed joyfully every time a wave broke on the beach, and the quivering sensation in Anna's chest told her she was done procrastinating.

She knew that he stayed in his suite between five and seven every evening. After that he would go to the hotel bar, order a pisco sour, and take a seat at the grand piano in the middle of the lounge, where he would play Billie Holiday songs until his table on the patio was set.

That was what he had done every night since he'd arrived.

He wouldn't get that far today.

*   *   *

There were two quick knocks as she rapped on the door of the suite with her knuckles. He opened it, and she held the folded white towels up in front of her and bowed her head.

"Fresh towels."

He barely registered that she was there. He invited her in without saying a word. Just left the door open and turned away from her.

Anna's heart pounded as she stepped into his room.

She found the bathroom, set the towels down on the counter, and listened for a second. She could hear that he had the TV on. It was playing the BBC, and a news anchor was talking about a large terror attack in Amsterdam—80 dead, 142 injured. Parts of the city lay in ruins.

She came out of the bathroom and looked around the corner into the living room.

He was standing with his back to her, listening to the speaker's urgent, horror-struck voice. He had his arms crossed, his attention focused on the pictures on the screen, pictures of pulverized buildings, blood, and panic.

Anna was about to take a step toward him when she spotted it.

The suitcase.

The red, wheeled suitcase lay open on top of the bed and hadn't been unpacked yet. She scanned the contents.

White lace was peeking out. A dress with some sort of animal print.

A woman's swimsuit.

A wave of panic flooded through her, and she felt trapped, cornered. She was about to turn around and leave the room when she heard the sound of a key card in the door behind her and knew it was too late.

The woman was in the room before Anna had a chance to react.

Anna recognized her from old pictures taken from a time when she must have been happy. And from pictures taken outside Holmen Church, where she had stood beside the hearse that would carry her son away. Her face had been crumpled up back then, tormented.

Now she just looked broken, old and joyless, like a person who felt trapped in a life she didn't have the strength to escape.

Anna stood still as the woman approached. She reached her hand around behind her and grabbed the knife handle, waiting, ready.

When the woman looked up, her face stiffened midmotion. Then she stopped in the middle of the entry hall.

Anna held the woman's gaze.

Neither of them said anything. The two women stared at each other while the sound from the TV in the living room filled the hotel room and surrounded them.

Questions filled Anna's head.

How much did the woman know about her husband? Did she know what he was capable of—what he had done? Did she know who had ultimately caused her son's death?

"Ellen," he called from the living room. "Come see what happened in Amsterdam. There was a terrorist attack."

The woman looked over toward the opening to the adjoining room. Then she turned her eyes to Anna again, and she nodded very slightly in acknowledgment. Like a blessing.

"I'll be right there," the woman said, without breaking eye contact with Anna.

Then she turned around and exited the hotel room.

*   *   *

Anna didn't wait for the door to close behind the woman before she walked into the suite's living room. She moved in on him—silently, quickly—and didn't stop until her chest was a few inches from his back.

"Look," he said, hypnotized by the screen. "There has been an explosion of some kind."

She could sense his body heat through the bathrobe. She recognized his smell.

"Mossing," she whispered quietly, almost exhaling his name.

The sound of her voice caused his shoulders to rise with a start, and he started to turn his head toward her.

CHAPTER

49

THE EVENING TRAFFIC slowly crawled along the palm-tree-lined Boulevard de la Croisette, where the beach-front promenade was lined with stalls selling knock-off sunglasses and neon-colored plastic jewelry.

A young African man wearing at least twelve hats on his head stepped out in front of Anna. He flung out his arms and flashed her a radiant, toothy grin.

"Ten euros, miss," he said, and removed the stack of hats from his head. "Pick one, pick one!"

Anna laughed in consent. She got out her money and pointed to a sand-colored straw hat with a black band.

She continued on toward the casino and the carousel, which gleamed golden at the end of the promenade, and enjoyed the sensation of the evening breeze on her bare shoulders and legs.

She had reached the marina by the time sirens sliced through the air.

With great difficulty, the cars on the road pulled off onto the shoulder to make room, and people along the road stopped to rubberneck. A convoy of police cars and ambulances lit up the evening twilight as they raced by.

Anna proceeded down the dock. Her footsteps felt light now, bouncy.

She stopped at the end of the dock and looked back over her shoulder. She looked for the hotel's white facade at the far end of the bay. The EMTs were hurrying in vain, she thought. The noise of the sirens would soon fall silent.

There was nothing they could do.

She took the hand that was offered her and stepped onto the narrow gangway. The yacht had been in the marina for several weeks, waiting, and was now ready to sail on.

"Ready for Mallorca, miss?"

Anna nodded. "Let's go."

The man in white pulled up the gangway and nodded at the terrace on the upper deck. "He's waiting for you up there."

Anna jogged up the stairs as the big ship rocked very gently.

She stepped out onto the deck just as the foam overflowed, spilling over the edge of one of the champagne glasses.

Kenneth hastily took a sip as he looked up from his wheelchair. He grabbed the stem of the other glass and held it up to her.

"Is a toast in order?" he asked inquisitively, raising his shoulders ever so slightly.

Anna smiled and reached for the glass.

ACKNOWLEDGMENTS

Writing a first novel sometimes feels like arbitrarily creating a plot in a vacuum. That's why it's crucial to have a private fan base to cheer the book along and a direct line to oracles you can pepper with research questions. I have been blessed with both in my work on *The Corpse Flower*.

My biggest thanks go to my parents, Jette Aagaard and Per Anders Jensen, for cheering me along and for just basically being the best parents in the world. To my brother, Anders Aagaard Jensen, for introducing me to the thriller and mystery genre way back at the dawn of time and for helping with the final touches on the first draft.

To my friend and partner in crime, author Katrine Engberg: thank you—for everything!

My heartfelt thanks to police sergeant Jesper Arff Rimmen, and to medical examiner and professor of forensic medicine Hans Petter Hougen. Thank you to army psychologist Mette Arff Rimmen and to resident doctor Liv Andrés-Jensen. Thanks to a "murder mystery heroine's aging uncle," journalist Jon Kaldan, for generously loaning me the family name.

A huge thank-you to my brilliant publisher in the U.S., Crooked Lane Books, and to my superstar agent at Nordin Agency, Anna Frankl.

Last but most importantly: thank you to my children, Vega and Castor. The sun rises and sets with you.

Read an excerpt from

THE COLLECTOR

the next

NOVEL

by ANNE METTE HANCOCK

available soon in hardcover from
Crooked Lane Books

CROOKED
LANE

NEW YORK

1

THE MAN MOVED quickly, sliding past the bushes and the bare trees. The February wind seemed to come from all sides at once, feeling like thousands of little needles hitting his cheeks. He pulled at the strings on his hood so that it tightened around his face and he looked around.

There were no joggers or dog walkers out today on the grounds of Kastellet, the old seventeenth-century Citadel. The temperature had been like a buoy in the water for days, bobbing steadily up and down around the freezing point, and the strong wind made it feel like the harshest winter in decades. Copenhagen seemed deserted in the cold, like a ghost town.

The man stopped and listened.

Nothing.

No sirens to break the controlled rumble of the city, no flashing blue lights out there in the twilight.

He walked up to the top of the fortress's old earthwork rampart and looked over at the entrance to the grounds by the parking lot at Café Toldboden and Maersk's headquarters. He wrinkled his brows when he saw that the parking lot was empty, then looked at his watch.

Where the hell are they?

The man pulled a cigarette out of a pack in his inside pocket and squatted down in the lee of one of the cannons. He tried to light his lighter, but his hands were yellow from the cold and felt dead. He extended and bent his fingers a couple of times to get the circulation going and noticed the blood spot, a small, coagulated half-moon of purplish black substance under the tip of the fingernail on his index finger.

He made a half-hearted attempt to scrape out the congealed substance, then gave up and got his lighter lit. As soon as the fire caught, he thrust his hands back into his pockets and held the cigarette squeezed tightly between his lips as he paced back and forth on the rampart, impatiently eyeing the parking lot.

Come on, damn it!

He didn't like waiting. It always made him feel restless and gave him a twitchy feeling in his gut. He preferred to keep busy, constantly in motion. Silence meant time for reflection and made his thoughts wander back to a smoke so thick that he had to feel his way past the dead, mangled bodies, back to the blood running out of his eyes, down his cheeks, and to the silence, the deafening silence that followed the blast, when those who were able crawled out of the dusty darkness and gathered in front of the destroyed building.

Paralyzed. In shock.

If only he could shake those images, release them like a bouquet of helium balloons and watch them float away, dancing in the sky until they were out of sight.

The man looked down at the café again and spotted the silvery gray Audi pull up in front of the building and stop. The engine was on, its exhaust warm and steamy in the cold. A single blink of the high beams told him that the coast was clear.

Finally!

He started walking down toward the car, but halfway down the earthwork, he spotted something that made him slow his pace. He scrunched up his eyes and focused on the pedestrian bridge over the moat that surrounded the Citadel.

Then he came to a complete stop.

There was a figure standing in the middle of the bridge, almost camouflaged by the twilight, a hooded person wearing an orange backpack.

It was the strange, bent-over posture of the figure that had made him slow down. But it was the child the person was holding that had made him stop.

A boy he estimated to be eight or nine years old hung limply over the side of the bridge while the person with the backpack held the fabric on the shoulders of the boy's down jacket. The person was yelling, but the wind snatched up the words, punching holes in them, so he couldn't hear what was being said.

He looked over at the car again and saw yet another insistent blink of the headlights. He needed to hurry now, but . . .

He looked down at the bridge again.

Then the figure let go of the boy.

CHAPTER

2

THE CLINIC ENTRANCE was through the back side of
an ivy-covered building that leaned curiously against
the wall around Frederik VIII's palace. From the window
of the waiting room, Heloise Kaldan could see the top of
the Marble Church's frost-stained dome and the guards in
the palace square, who were parading back and forth in
front of Amalienborg Palace like loose-limbed sleepwalkers
in a snow globe.

She reached for a fashion magazine and swung one foot
back and forth nervously as she browsed through it.
Adrenaline tingled at the ends of her nerves, and her eyes
roved absentmindedly over the fashion reports and articles
about skin care regimens. Shallowness and the glorification
of teenage anorexia, wrapped up in pastel colors.

Who the hell reads this garbage?

She tossed the magazine aside and looked around the
waiting room.

The whole room looked like something right out of some
Californian interior design magazine. It was decorated in
white and cognac-colored hues, punctuated only by succu-
lents in oversized clay pots. The walls were adorned with
posters and lithographs of all shapes and sizes, hung so closely

together that you could just barely glimpse the asphalt-colored wall behind them. The floor was covered with a cream-colored Berber rug, which tied the room together in one final stylish touch. The whole thing was so delightful that you'd almost be able to forget why you were there.

Almost . . .

There were two other patients in the waiting room: a gaunt, elderly man and a young girl with milk-white skin and big silvery gray eyes. Heloise estimated her age to be no more than eighteen and hoped that the girl had come to the clinic for some purpose other than her own.

A tall, blond man in white canvas pants and a mint-green T-shirt stuck his head into the room and the girl across from Heloise immediately sat up straighter in her chair. She inhaled oddly through her nose, moistened her lips, and tried to make them seem fuller by half-opening her mouth into a pout. The expression left her looking like she had just detected some objectionable odor in the room.

Selfie face, Heloise thought. One of the era's oddest inventions.

The man in the doorway swept a lock of hair out of his eyes with a toss of his head and then nodded to Heloise.

"Heloise?"

She stood up.

She just had to get it over with now.

*   *   *

The doctor showed her into the exam room with a motion of his arm. He read her records on the computer screen and then looked at Heloise.

"So, Heloise . . . You're pregnant?"

He mispronounced her name. The hard "H" made her name sound harsh, like an effort. Heloise had corrected him at every appointment for the last four years. This time she let it go. Instead she said, "Yes, so it would appear."

"Have you ever been pregnant before?"

She shook her head and showed him the test, which she had brought in her purse. There were two red lines inside the plastic window in the middle of the stick. One was very clear, the other a misty watercolor, weak like the beginning of a rainbow that you could see best by not looking at it directly.

The doctor looked at the test and nodded.

"Yes, it looks positive. And am I to understand that this doesn't suit you well?"

"It wasn't part of my plan, no."

He nodded and sat down behind his white-lacquered desk.

"No, well, that happens, I guess."

Heloise sat down on the other side of the desk and set her purse on the old parquet flooring. The floor was like the rest of the building, strangely bowed and crackled like an old soup tureen, and made the chair rock under her.

The doctor smiled warmly to emphasize that she could speak openly. Dimples bored into his cheeks, like fingers in soft clay, and his blue eyes looked boldly into Heloise's. It had taken her a couple of years to discover that his magnetic charisma and forward eye contact were not reserved only for her. He was not flirting. He was just genuinely interested in her health. Plus, the gleam of his blue-green eyes was competing with the wreath of polished white gold that ran around his left ring finger.

"According to the information you provided when you called this morning, you're about five weeks along. Is that correct?"

Heloise looked down and nodded. That was what the calculator said on the due date website she had found online.

"That's good," he said. "The thing is, a medical abortion is only possible during the first seven weeks of a pregnancy. From eight to twelve weeks, the only option is a clinical termination of the pregnancy."

Heloise glanced up again. "Which would involve hospitalization?"

"Yes. It's a quick procedure, but nonetheless it's always preferable to avoid anesthesia. So instead you'll get this . . ."

He handed Heloise a single pill from a package that said Mifegyne in green letters.

"You'll take this once we've confirmed your due date, and that will effectively terminate your pregnancy."

He turned his chair halfway around and typed a few lines into the computer in front of him.

"I'll also write you a prescription for fifty milligrams of Diclon, which is a muscle relaxant, and a medication called Cytotec."

Heloise's heart began beating in a strangely irregular rhythm as he spoke.

That will effectively terminate your pregnancy . . .

What the hell was she doing? How had she ended up here?

"It shouldn't take more than a few hours, and for the most part it's pretty undramatic," the doctor continued. "But it's still best if you set aside a whole day for it and have someone around while it's going on. Are you seeing someone right now who can look after you?"

Heloise shook her head. "Yes and no. It's . . . complicated."

The doctor pursed his lips and nodded in understanding.

"This kind of thing generally is. It's a tough situation for most people."

Heloise looked down at the pill in her hand and thought about Martin.

She knew he would be excited about the idea of a baby, happy and far too hopeful, and it would force their relationship into the next phase. He would insist on taking a Neil Armstrong–sized step forward, whereas she would want to take three steps back.

Heloise preferred things the way they were. Or to be more precise, the way they had been. Their relationship was fun and comfortable and—most of all—still fairly casual.

ANNE METTE HANCOCK

But now, from one day to the next, it felt as if there was a ticking time bomb between them. The countdown had begun with those two lines on the pregnancy test, and Heloise could see red digital numbers blinking like a doomsday clock in her mind's eye. It was going to explode whether she cut the red or the blue wire, she knew that.

She might as well get it over with.

The doctor studied Heloise intently, as if he were trying to decode her inexpressive body language.

"If you're having any doubts, it's no problem to wait—"

"I'm not having any doubts."

"Okay, well then why don't we just see how far along you are?"

He pointed toward the exam table with his chin and put on a pair of steel-colored acetate glasses. The lenses looked curiously small on his square face.

"A home pregnancy test like that can be a little off, so we'll just confirm that you're on the right side of the eight-week mark."

Heloise took a deep breath and took off her leather jacket.

* * *

The silence in the room was broken only by the ticking of the clock above the table and by the doctor's calm breathing.

Heloise was holding her breath.

She lay with her face turned away from the monitor, away from the scanning images she was afraid she would never be able to erase from her mind again if she caught so much as a glimpse of them. She had tried all week to avoid imagining what was in there, but she had slept fitfully at night, tossing and turning, her sheets wet from sweat, seeing little arms and legs in her dreams. Fingers and toes. A head covered in brown curls.

But no face.

Each time there had been only a featureless circle at the top of the neck. A concave surface, without any further form or color, like a baby with a dinner plate where the face should have been.

What did that mean?

That she didn't want to pass on Martin's genes? That she was terrified by the thought of passing on her own?

She couldn't stop speculating about whether there were hereditary variants of evil, whether a rottenness could hide in a person's blood, like a sleeping cell, that could skip a generation or two. In any case, that was not an experiment she wanted to conduct.

"All right, Heloise," the doctor said. "As it turns out, the test was accurate."

Heloise reluctantly looked up.

"Here's your bladder and your stomach." The doctor pointed at the screen in front of him, where a vague black and white shape filled the screen. "And there, that's your uterus. Do you see?"

Heloise tilted her head and stared blankly at the splotch in front of her. It could have been an ultrasound scan of anything: a human brain, a cow's stomach, Jupiter! She wouldn't have been able to tell the difference.

He drew a circle on the screen with his finger around a little peanut-shaped spot.

"There. You see? It looks like you're right around five weeks—give or take a day or two."

Heloise nodded and looked away.

"Are you okay?" he asked, turning off the monitor. "Your mind is made up?"

"Yes." She raised herself up a little on her elbows. "But there's actually something else I'd like to ask you about. I've been having this uncomfortable trembly feeling for a while now."

The doctor pulled off his latex glove with a talcum-powdery snap and nodded for her to continue.

"Can you try to describe it in a little more detail?"

"I don't know how to explain it. It's just something that feels . . . *off*. A weird fog around me, as I'm looking at the world through a glass dome, and my head is teeming with thoughts. It's gone on for a long time now, I think. Several months, long before this." She nodded at her belly.

The doctor removed his glasses from his nose with a pincer grip and cleaned them on his T-shirt as he studied Heloise.

"You said a trembly feeling? Do you mean a type of uneasiness?"

"Yes."

"Pressure in your chest? Palpitations?"

She nodded.

"What are you doing professionally these days, Heloise?" Still that harsh H sound. "You're a journalist, aren't you?"

"Yes."

"So, does your job keep you fairly busy?"

"Well, I suppose so."

"Do you bring work home with you?"

"Doesn't everyone these days?" Heloise said with a shrug.

He crossed his arms and bit his lower lip as he regarded her. "It sounds like you might be under some pressure. Have you been through a particularly stressful period recently?"

Heloise noticed a tingling in her temples as the memories bubbled up inside her like foul-smelling methane gas in a swamp: Hands tightening around her throat. Children with closed eyes. The engraving on her father's headstone . . .

Memories that had left Heloise's heart blue-black with cold.

A particularly stressful period?

"You could say that," she said, sitting up.

"They sound stress-related, your symptoms," the doctor said. "But I'd like to get you tested for hypothyroidism, so why don't we just take a blood test to be on the safe side—"

They were interrupted by two quick knocks on the door. Without waiting, the elderly receptionist stuck her made-up face into the room.

"I'm sorry to bother you, Jens, but there's a call for you."
She pointed to the phone on a light Wegner table at the other
end of the room. "It's from the school's office. They say it's
important."

The doctor furrowed his brow, and a vertical line
appeared above the bridge of his nose.

"I'm sorry," he said, turning to Heloise and smiling,
mildly embarrassed. "Do you mind if I just . . ."

"No, of course not," Heloise said, waving his question
away.

He closed the frosted glass sliding door that divided the
room, and Heloise could hear him walking rapidly over to
the phone.

She looked down at the pill she was still holding in her
hand. It had grown damp from her sweat and some of the
color had come off onto the palm of her hand, filling her
lifeline with a white powdery mass. She set the pill down on
a small stainless-steel tray and half listened as the doctor
answered the call behind the sliding glass door.

"Hello? Yes, it's me. Why, yes, he should be. What time
is it, did you say? Well then, he got out twenty minutes ago
and he's probably on his way downstairs. He has certainly
been known to take his own sweet time at that kind of thing
. . . Well, maybe he went straight to the playground with
Patrick from the rec center. I know that they were going to
get together today. Have you checked there?"

Heloise got up and put on her pants and her leather
jacket.

"No, he's not," the doctor continued. "No, he wasn't
picked up. I'm positive about that because my wife is supposed to pick him up today and she's still at work and . . . Yes,
but I can't . . . Okay. Yes, okay. I'm on my way now!"

Heloise heard him hang up and dial a number on the
phone.

"Hi, it's Dad. Where are you? Give me a call when you
get this message!"

And then another call.

"It's me. Did you pick up Lukas? . . . They just called from the rec center, and he hasn't shown up there after school."

Heloise could hear the increasing panic take hold of his voice and squeeze. She turned to look at the framed photo on the windowsill. The doctor looked younger in the picture than he did now, but Heloise could recognize his kind eyes and pronounced jaw line. He had his arm around a pretty woman with dirty blond hair, who was wearing a yellow sun dress with spaghetti straps over tan skin, and standing between them was a child who looked to be about three or four years old, excitedly waving an Italian flag.

"I'm heading over there now," came the voice from behind the sliding door. "Yes, but let's just take it easy. He's gotta be there somewhere."

The fear churning in his voice emphasized to Heloise that she never wanted to live like that, in fear. The responsibility a child would entail. The vulnerability that would impinge on her life.

Better to feel nothing.

She picked up the pill from the metal tray, folded it into a paper towel and stuck it into her pocket.

Then she slung her purse over her shoulder and left the clinic.